Foggy Fairy Tale

by Denise Baer

Baer Books Press
Chicago   Hattingen

About the Author

 Denise Baer is the author of *Sipping a Mix of Verse* and *Net Switch*. Her poems have appeared in *Danse Macabre*. She is a native of the South Side of Chicago, Illinois, who now resides in a small town in Germany with her husband and four-legged baby, Shakespeare, working on her next adventure.

http://www.authordenisebaer.com/

ALSO BY DENISE BAER

Net Switch
Sipping a Mix of Verse

Baer Books Press
Published by Baer Books Press

Chicago | Hattingen
baerbookspress.com

Published in the United States of America
by Baer Books Press

This edition published 2014

Copyright @ 2014 by Denise Baer
www.authordenisebaer.com

Library of Congress Control Number: 2014909753

Fogged Up Fairy Tale / Denise Baer

ISBN-10: 0991326830
ISBN-13: 978-0-9913268-3-9

http://www.baerbookspress.com/

Designed by Denise Baer • Cover Art by Ana Cruz

To Martin
mein Partner der Phantasie,
Abenteuer und Romantik

"Memories are our personal narrative,
a work in progress.
They are wishes sprung from a wishing well,
and horrors from nightmares.
Our memories are strung together to
create our lifeline.
When they are taken away from us, our hearts
and minds are stolen."

Erased

~~~~~~

My name is Brand Rye and last year I lost my life—not literally, but mentally. I had amnesia, which erased my past memories. It was an awakening for me to recreate my life and regain my memory. With the help of my husband and friends, I learned about myself. This is an interwoven story of the days I struggled with amnesia and the past that I had lost and recovered.

Life is an ongoing battle of truth and happiness. This is about my battle. A second chance to see myself from the outside looking in and to mend the fractured parts. Over time, all my recollections returned.

Prologue

~~~~~~

Ablast of light and a deafening sound, intrusive and obscene like the buzzing of cicadas, were the last things I remembered. The sting of glass followed. My chest and face felt as if someone swung a baseball bat into them. Time stretched on, especially when the light and sound subsided. Something warm dripped down my face. My arms and legs were too heavy to lift. Or were they even there? A sound broke the silence, a sound that came from me, raw and infested with fear. Afraid of the worst, I kept my eyes closed to avoid seeing parts of me laying elsewhere. Smoke covered me as the car got hotter. I tried to scream, but coughed instead.

In the distance, I heard a siren, its volume increased as it got closer. Someone was talking and holding my hand when the ambulance arrived. I couldn't quite grasp what they meant—*horrible—get her out of there—the car's about to blow*.

Hands dragged my dead weight from the car as if I were a wet blanket. At times, my eyes fluttered open to the abuse of light and blurred images. I closed them to stop the dizziness. Moved to the ambulance bed, someone placed an oxygen mask on me, and darkness wiped out the moment. The back of my eyelids burned an image of a man who I had continuous visions of for whatever reason.

The next thing I remembered was waking in a hospital room with that man, who I had seen in the darkness, sitting next to me. He rose from the chair when he heard me and took my hand. I didn't know him, which intensified my existing fear. Why was a stranger in my hospital room? What happened? I wiggled my hand free and pulled myself upright. I touched my face and found patches of cloth. My eyes narrowed at the man with more confusion and fear.

A short, stocky nurse came into the room with a friendly smile. "Well, hello. It's so nice to see you awake."

I touched my head again. "What day is it?"

"It's Thursday, Sweetie."

"How long have I been here?"

She let out a hearty laugh. "Five days. I guess you needed your sleep."

I squinted down at my legs trying to remember. "A week? What happened?"

"You were in a car accident." I turned toward the man who was speaking to me.

"An accident?" I shook my head to jiggle everything back into place. It didn't work. "What accident?"

In silence, the nurse took my blood pressure.

He placed his hands on the bed rail. "You hit another car, your car spun around and smashed into a tree. You have been in a coma for several days."

"Did anyone else get hurt?"

"No. The other driver had only minor cuts and bruises."

Tears fell. Maybe the white light and noise erased the tragedy or masked it for a while. The nurse gave me a box of tissues as she continued to fiddle around with IVs and vitals. Similar to walking through a muddy stream, my murky thoughts kept getting stuck. When one thought came into mind, it sunk away as I pulled at another. The nurse finished, patted my hand, informed me that the doctor would be in soon, and left.

The room got colder.

The man cleared his throat before he asked, "How are you feeling?"

"Fine."

"You'll feel better once you get home."

I balled up the covers in my hands, pulling a little at a time, and stared at my feet. What was happening? I couldn't make sense of anything. To calm myself, I pressed a hand against my chest to ease my breathing, in hopes the air would cool down the heat inside my lungs. He put his hand on my arm. I slid it away and leaned toward the opposite side of the bed.

"Fine. I won't touch you." He threw his arms in the air signifying defeat, walked over to the foot of the bed, the ashen sky a backdrop for the mood in the room. Then he turned to me and said, "You know I should be the one pissed. You caused the accident because you were texting." He turned to me irritated by my lack of response. "Say the word and I'm out of here."

I pulled the sheet to my chin. "Who are you?"

His mouth dropped open, and then, as if in slow motion, he whispered, "Your husband."

(One) Petri Dish

~~~~~~

Home—to me it was a foreign place with zero memories. When we arrived my first day back, there were a few people waiting outside the door with arms full of food. Introduced as neighbors, they came inside, and watched for signs of ... What? I felt like a substance in a petri dish. These people stared at me, searching for a clue that I might remember. Or maybe curiosity got the best of them, and they wanted to witness a memory wipe. They watched every move I made as if all my memories would come flooding back with a simple wave of the hand.

I redirected my attention to my lap to avoid their stares. My hand stretched open so I could trace the dark red lines that created an M in the middle of my palm. Lines that trailed to my wrist. Did the M stand for marriage? I couldn't remember along with everything else. I bit my lower lip, scrunched my eyebrows, and raised my head to find nothing had changed. No one shifted or lost focus from me. I gave each strained constipated face a heavy sigh. A puff of air escaped my mouth with a tiny laugh.

He came to sit next to me, Easton, the one from the hospital who claimed to be my husband, and placed his hand on my upper back. "Is there something you remember?"

I shook my head and everyone released a loud breath of air, letting me know I deflated their hope. He rubbed my back, gave a reassuring smile and said, "That's fine. It will come to you over time." He addressed the few people there. "I'm sure Brand is tired after all that has happened. Maybe it's time we let her rest and reacquaint herself with her home. I, I mean we, appreciate all of your support."

The neighbors nodded in agreement. One by one, they pressed my hand between theirs, wishing me well and filed out the door. While they were escaping the uncomfortable situation, talking in hushed voices to Easton, I glanced around the living room. It looked like a picture from a Pottery Barn magazine. The couch and chairs resembled something found in a house by the sea. They were a light yellow, fluffy and comfy, balanced with the faux-painting aged effect of the distressed yellow walls. A rustic off-white coffee table with three wicker baskets underneath divided the couch and chair. On the large wall to the left of the bay window was a stone fireplace with pictures loaded on the mantel. At the time, I thought what great taste I had if I really was Brand.

I turned my head to find Easton watching me. He was handsome. I was awkward. For not knowing him, he made me feel safe, which was probably because of the days following the accident. We spent every day together as he sat in my hospital room telling me about our life. When he arrived, he introduced himself and told me about the different things we had done. Easton said we had been married for five years. The car accident had cut out the memories of our marriage—my life. I had to rely on a man I didn't know to spoon-feed me with glimpses of my past, which had vanished overnight.

Soon the stillness of the room started to itch, and our eyes glanced everywhere else but at each other, not knowing what to do next. Finally, I moved to the living room window to watch the cruel weather. Sheets of water came down, flooding the front yard and putting a strain on the tree branches. I wrapped my arms around the front of me, while I tried to figure out how I got here, in this living room, with a man I didn't know. I turned to see if Easton was still there. He was gone, but I heard noises coming from the kitchen so I walked over there. I leaned against the doorjamb to find Easton making sandwiches. He piled them high with turkey, lettuce, and tomato. A side of potato salad took up the rest of the plate.

He turned and said, "I'm sure you're hungry. You love turkey sandwiches, and I bought a nice supply of your favorite potato salad."

I slipped into the room to see, but he signaled toward the table, and sat across from me. I nudged a few potatoes with my fork before puncturing one and putting it in my mouth. The tangy mustard teased my taste buds, and I couldn't help but suck in the sides of my cheeks to tame the sourness. I liked it. The potato salad had sprinkles of chives, and it wasn't too creamy. I scooped more on my fork.

When I finished chewing, I readjusted in my seat before I spoke. "I can't remember this being my favorite potato salad, but it's really good."

He put his fork down when he spoke. "I'm glad. The doctor said that your memory will come back to you in pieces, little by little, so I thought I'd help by giving you things you like."

My hands pressed down on the sandwich to flatten it, then I picked it up. He smiled as I took a bite, which left globs of mayonnaise in the corners of my mouth. I didn't waste too much time circling my tongue around to scoop the rest of the leftovers.

"You always did that when eating a sandwich," he said. I gave him a questioning look. "Pressing down on it."

I swallowed and then asked, "Do I like cheese on my sandwiches?"

"Uh, yeah, I forgot the cheese."

He was about to get it when I said, "Don't worry about it. This is fine. I can have cheese another time, right?"

He hesitated and then nodded in agreement.

We ate the rest of lunch in silence. Sometimes I caught him glancing at me. I'm sure this was hard for him too. A wife not knowing her husband. We cleared the table, and I started washing the dishes under his protest. When he saw that I wasn't going to stop, he grabbed a towel and took care of the rest.

We wandered back into the living room, and he asked, "Would you like to take a nap? I can show you to your room?"

"No thanks. I feel like I've slept long enough."

I folded my arms and he slid his hands into his jeans' pockets. The uneasiness started drifting back. "If you have something to do, please, don't let me stop you. You don't have to babysit me. With all the time you spent at the hospital, I'm sure you probably have plenty to do here or at work."

The tension lifted and he flopped onto the couch. "I've got nothing to do today. I took off work because I wanted to make sure you were okay."

I imitated him by flopping down on the chair. My arms ran along the armrests while I hesitated before talking. "Do you mind if I ask you some questions?"

"Nope."

"I know we talked a lot in the hospital, but there was so much for me to take in that I can't remember everything. Again, what is it you do for a living?"

"I'm an investigator. I do undercover work.

Sometimes it takes me away from home for long periods of time."

"Sounds interesting. Do I have a job?"

"No. You worked with me on a case, which was how we fell in love and married."

I could only imagine how red my face got, but I skimmed over that fact and continued with the questions. "If I didn't work, what did I do all day?"

He didn't respond right away. Instead, he shifted on the couch until the words came. When that happened, he said, "There's a lot for us to talk about, and I don't think it's a good idea to bombard you with all the details right now. We should take it slow."

"What kind of details?"

"Brand! The details of your life."

I shifted forward, placed my hands on my knees to give them a slight squeeze, and said, "I don't remember anything other than a little bit of the accident and being in the hospital. I need something that will help me understand who I am and what our life is like. I don't want a nap, so please, *please* tell me about my life."

Easton put his right ankle over his left knee and fiddled with his shoelaces. He finally nodded. "Well, your mom kept you in-line before we met. You were close to her, and until your accident, you talked about her all the time. I have heard countless repeated stories and memories of your relationship."

My mother had laid the groundwork in my life. She pampered me with kindness, and guided me with a heavy hand. Easton teased my memory with stories of my mother, and in return, over time, the frozen memories melted and came flooding back.

(Two) God Wasn't With Me

~~~~~~

2000 - Peterborough, New Hampshire

Prior to fate bringing Easton and me together, I had been dealing with the loss of my mother, who during her life, aggravated, inspired, and saved me. There are endless memories of my life with her, but there are certain moments, turning points that I will never forget that signified the growth of our relationship.

My mother, Kalie, and I were small-town women with the typical strained mother-daughter relationship, different in many ways. It didn't help living in Peterborough, New Hampshire with a population of approximately 3,200. I struggled to create my own individuality while my mother tried to mold me into a lady, an upstanding, religious woman.

Our home had a cross in every room to ward off the evils of the world and scripture dripped from my mother's tongue whenever I did wrong, as if she was born into sainthood. Of course, she wasn't. I guess a prettier woman was better at stroking my father's ego, who left my young, pregnant mother. She was alone in this world, much like me before meeting Easton. Her parents disowned her for marrying my father. He didn't come from the same mold, a devout Catholic. Another one of life's slaps in the face to remind her of the mistake she made. I never saw my grandparents. The few times I asked about them, my mother simply said they were busy enjoying life. As much as my mother had it in her to forgive, I had it in me to hold onto anger and let it boil.

My mom raised me with one hand on the Bible, and the other to keep me on the straight and narrow. Like most teens, I rebelled. I used the anger I had of my father and grandparents' abandonment and fought for my own individuality. I didn't know who I was at the time, but I wanted to find out without any interference.

One time, my mother came home and noticed a strong whiff of smoke and alcohol. She didn't have to think twice about where it came from as she marched down the hallway and swung open my bedroom door. She found me sprawled out on the bed, vomit dripping from my mouth, and an ashtray with some embers still burning. I think God's power went through her, because she pulled me out of bed by the hair, threw me into the shower and turned on the cold water. With every 'fuck' I uttered, she slapped my mouth and pushed me back under the showerhead. After that, she dragged me back into the bedroom by my hair and told me to clean it up. I definitely didn't defy her. She brought God with her that day.

As my attitude diminished, and I started to grow up, I watched my mother with curiosity while remembrances of wonderful smells from the kitchen occupied my childhood and adolescence. My mother was a wonderful cook and baker. Every year she baked a cake for my birthday, and during the holidays, cookies covered our kitchen countertops. I asked her once why she baked so much, and she told me it calmed her. Baking was therapeutic, and she could pour her sadness or love into the batter and shape it into whatever she wanted. She shaped those cookies into happiness. My mother told me how we see the world, how we wake every day, is our choice.

At twenty-three years old, I decided to take my mother's advice and bake a cake. I wanted something to calm me since I had lost my job and I needed to start paying back my college loan even though I had never finished. I put the ingredients into a bowl, looked out the window, and began mixing.

My mom strolled into the kitchen and asked, "What are you doing?"

"I'm mixing the ingredients."

"With your hands?"

I sighed, shaking my head as if she was the stupid one and said, "Yeah with my hands. The directions say 'mix by hand.'"

She bent over laughing. Tears soon poured down her face. I mixed harder as my anger grew with her laughter.

"What is so damn funny?"

She tried to control herself so she could respond. "Mix by hand ..." My mom waved a hand in front of her face to cool off and finally stopped. With a grin as large as The Joker's, she said, "Mix by hand means not with a mixer, honey. Use a spoon."

I turned to the window, my hands still inside the bowl, squeezing the ingredients through my fingers like I wanted to do to my mother's neck.

Eventually I realized how much my mother meant to me. She saved me when my heart broke from the continuous assholes I dated. I had many loser boyfriends come and go out of my life, but the one constant in all the heartbreaks and good riddances was my mother. Without even noticing, I traded in dinners with boyfriends for dinners with my mom. We laughed at my baking disasters, and all my geographically challenged moments in life.

Baking wasn't the only time my IQ dropped a notch.

To me, the science of geography got me from place A to B. How I got there didn't matter. When I was nineteen and full of attitude and low on self-esteem, a friend and I drove to a college to hang out with the jerk I was dating at the time. By the end of the weekend, we were hungover and tired. On the way home, my friend nonchalantly commented on how nothing looked familiar. I assured her that everything was different from the other side of the road. Three hours later, coming home from Bennington, Vermont, we stopped at a rest area to stretch and find out how far away we were from Peterborough. The response was frightening. We were in Albany, New York. When I arrived home, many hours later, my mother didn't believe a word I said about getting lost. My guess is she didn't want to think that her daughter could be so asinine.

With age came closeness. Our mother-daughter relationship transformed into a friendship. I talked to her daily, and when life got a bit overwhelming, I'd receive simple text messages from her, such as 'I love you' and 'Thinking about you.' These gestures didn't get rid of the pain I was dealing with at the time, but it softened it like a bandage.

When I was thirty years old, there was a knock at my door. I hadn't even gotten out of bed that morning, so I cursed, threw off the covers, and shuffled over to the door, ready to yell at whoever was on the other side. My eyelashes tickled the peephole. In an instant, my body slumped down, but my mind flirted with sickening thoughts. It was the police. I straightened my pajama shirt, patted down my hair, and gripped the doorknob. Something wasn't right. I knew they had not come for me since I didn't go out much anymore. But my mother. My mother would be the only other reason the police were at my door. When this thought sprung into my head, I turned the doorknob and pulled it open. A male and female police officer stood with their hats in their hands, introduced themselves, and asked if I was Brand Rye. I nodded. They asked if my mom's name was Kalie Rye. I nodded. Then they asked if they could come inside.

No. No! They couldn't come inside. If I let them inside, then I'd have to hear about what happened to my mom. Because I knew it was bad. They asked again. Without a response, I turned and went into the living room leaving the door open. The officers came inside, closed the door and stood by the couch. On the other side of the room, I began to pace back and forth, pulling on my pajama sleeves, and mumbling.

The female officer cleared her throat and said, "Hi Brand. Again, I'm Officer Kelly," and she pointed to the other officer, "And this is Officer O'Shea." For a moment, I stopped to inspect them, but then started pacing again. "We're here because we need to talk to you about your mother." Officer Kelly took a few steps forward, swept her arm toward the couch and softly said, "Why don't you sit down?"

I ignored her, just continued to mumble that this couldn't be happening. I picked at my lips the salty tears moistened them.

Officer Kelly sighed and continued. "Early this morning, your mother was involved in a car accident. She was—"

I put my hands over my ears and said, "No. No. Stop."

She came over to me and in a low voice said, "Brand. We need to talk to you."

I stopped all movement as if she smacked me in the face. "I don't know you. We don't need to talk. My mother's fine. There's been a mistake. You have the wrong person."

Officer Kelly put her arm around my shoulders and asked, "Is there someone we could call for you?"

I moved away from her. "Why? I don't need anyone. You have the wrong person."

"Brand. I found your number on your mother's cell phone."

My screams spray-painted the walls. I fell to my knees and cupped my face. My body shook out of control. Officer Kelly came to my side, put an arm around me, and whispered the details. My mother was involved in a head-on collision with a drunk driver. She died upon impact. The room, the officers, and I began to disintegrate into darkness. The whispers died out. My breathing reminded me that I was still alive. Alone. God wasn't with me that day—He was tending to my mother.

(Three) I'm a Lush

~~~~~~

Easton waited for me to digest the stories and my loss. I wiped a tear from my cheek, feeling silly about crying over the death of my mother. A death I wasn't aware of in the first place.

"My mom's gone then. And I can't even remember her or her death. How sad is that?"

"I'm sorry, Brand. I wish I could tell you more about her. I never met her. All I can do is talk about the stories you told me."

I seemed to find comfort in my lap. When there was a lull in conversation, I focused on it, hoping time would fast forward or I'd find a memory. My heart quickened and slowed to an ache having to hear about my mother and her death from a husband I couldn't remember. At that moment, I felt empty and lost. I couldn't return to my childhood home to search for my childhood memories.

Easton got up and said, "I think we should take a break. I can show you to your—"

"How about a walk?"

"A walk?"

"Yes. I'm really not tired and we could probably both use some fresh air."

He pointed and said, "I'm sure we can, but it's still pouring outside."

I turned my head toward the window and sighed, realizing I had forgotten about the bad weather. As saddened as I was to learn about my mother, it only made me want to find out more. Sleep wouldn't give me any answers. Besides, I wasn't quite ready to sleep alone in the house with Easton.

He must have felt the thinness of air as much as I did. "We could maybe take a drive somewhere. I'm sure we can outdrive the rain."

I smiled.

Easton signaled with his head as he said, "Come on, let's get out of here."

The rain attacked the car, but the windshield wipers squeaked and kept up with the pellets. I looked out of my window, loneliness seeped in, pinching my nerves. I closed my eyes while I tried to picture my mother. Why didn't I ask to see a picture of her? I felt my eyes fill with tears, so I pressed them tighter to drain the accumulation. When I opened them again, we were stuck at a traffic light and Easton was staring at me.

Embarrassed, I turned and glanced out the windshield, swiping my eyes with the back of my hand and asking, "Do I have a picture of my mom?"

"Yeah. There are some at home."

"I'd like to see them."

"You have several photo albums at the house."

I shook my head to rid the uneasiness I was feeling along with the self-pity. "Where are we going?"

"I thought I'd take you to the place where we first saw each other."

My head swung his way as I asked, "Really? Where?"

The corner of Easton's mouth curled as he said, "You were never good at surprises."

I gave him a soft smile and sat back. He wasn't hard on the eyes. I remember thinking the same in the hospital. Even though I was scared of not knowing who I was, I listened to his stories, and couldn't help but sneak a few once-overs when he would rise for some reason. Easton's strong and captivating appearance made me sigh inside, enjoying what I saw. Every once in a while, I got a glimpse of muscle protruding from his shirt or pants. His dark hair accentuated a perfect angular face, strong bone structure, and a slight dimple on the chin. Brown eyes with specks of yellow burned bright against his tan skin tone, and his straight white teeth sedated me when he smiled. I tried to be discreet about checking him out, and if he happened to catch me, my eyes ventured in another direction.

Easton entered the front parking lot to a bar called Truth Serum. I laughed at the name. He grabbed the umbrella from the backseat. I was about to get out, but he stopped me when he held up a finger indicating to wait. He came around and held the umbrella above the door to protect me from the rain. When we entered the bar, the smell of stale alcohol and smoke smacked me in the face, but it was better than the nasty weather outside. It made me feel alive. The bar had a sourness of lingering perspiration left by drifters. I assumed the chipped and broken tables, chairs, and stools were the result of alcohol-induced brawls. A smog hovered around the bar as if the nicotine yellow walls continued to exhale.

We shook off the excess water at the door, and found several eyes on us. Easton walked over to some empty stools by the bar and laid our coats on one of them. The clock above the bar showed 4:00 pm.

Easton called the bartender over and asked for two Sam Adams. We didn't say anything until we had our drinks. Easton tipped his beer in my direction and said, "To your memory."

I grinned, clinked my bottle to his, and said, "May it come back very soon." We took a sip, appreciating the cold fizzle of beer sliding down our throats. I put my bottle on the bar and said, "So this is where we met. I wouldn't have thought of me as someone who came to this kind of place." I signaled an apology. "No offense."

Easton gulped his beer and said, "This is one of the busier bars around the area. It's a place to get lost in. A place to meet with old flames. Or a place to drink your troubles away."

"Was I here to get lost?"

He started tearing off the label on the beer bottle and shrugged. "In a sense. Let's just say, you weren't here to be found."

I rested my arm on the bar, and my hand held my head. "What do you mean?"

"I mean, you weren't here for anyone. You were on a mission."

"To drink?"

Easton's head angled to the side. "Yes. We met here, but you never remembered seeing or meeting me."

My head slipped off my hand and I jerked to stop myself from falling. "Was I that drunk?"

"Well." He laughed and continued saying, "Yeah, you were definitely drunk."

I closed my eyes and said, "Oh great, I'm a lush."

"No you're not, and you weren't then. You had a lot of things happening in your life."

I sat straight. "Did my mom die then?"

He nodded.

"What else?"

"I should probably start with the night I saw you in this bar."

I turned my stool toward him, ready to hear about my life as a lush.

"You weren't your usual beautiful self. The weight of the world was on your shoulders and the pain of loss heavy in the air. You came here for the sole purpose of getting numb."

As the saying goes, when it rains it pours. I made friends with alcohol during difficult times.

(Four) Truth Serum

~~~~~~

2001 - Peterborough, New Hampshire

I stomped into a bar called Truth Serum expecting to find comfort at the bottom of lots of beer bottles. My hair hung like wet pasta, and my jeans and T-shirt could stand on their own since I had worn them for the past five days. There were several empty stools at the end of the bar near the pool tables. I took the last one, nestled by the wall, and ordered my first beer with a chaser. That's right, I was on the road to getting good and plastered. I wanted to stop feeling, even if it was for one night. In a short period, I had lost everything and the tears had dried up days ago. I was at the anger stage. I seemed to have skipped denial and went straight to pain and anger.

My boyfriend, Mason, had left me for a skinny blonde, who struggled with walking in high heels and keeping her breasts concealed. The bastard had some nerve cheating on me four months after my mom died. I had nothing and he knew it! What was I supposed to do? Where was I supposed to go? The world and humanity left me depleted of hope, yet full of revenge. The drinks started to work and enhanced my payback plans. I wanted Mason to feel the same pain as I did. I wanted his dumb girlfriend to pay for taking him away from me.

A guy approached, offering to buy me a drink. I accepted, assuming not all of humanity was bad, except his ass found the stool next to mine. I wanted the drink, not the company. He wasn't that bad, and even if I was wearing beer goggles, I wouldn't see him again anyways. I started to caress his thigh, moving up to his crotch.

"Whoa! You are a horny one tonight."

I stood and let my hand rub his crotch in a more aggressive way while licking my lips. The thought of what I looked like never dawned on me. The loss of my mother drilled grief into my bones. My sorrow too deep to care.

He turned his stool toward me, spread his legs wider, and said, "I'm totally getting hard."

I wanted him to stop talking. To stop running his mouth off. It wasn't turning me on. My other hand smacked the side of his face while I still rubbed his crotch, my breathing increased. He looked at me stunned. "What the fuck was that for?"

Shut up! Shut up! I unbuttoned and unzipped his pants and slid my hand in and then pressed my mouth hard against his. My tongue flopped and slid around his mouth like a fish out of water, darting in and out. I could feel he wanted to move away, so I placed my hand on the back of his head, rubbing him and kissing him harder. The guy tried to get some air, but I wouldn't let him. Moans and grunts were all that escaped until I got so caught up with keeping his mouth shut to take my mind off everything that I bit his lip. He pushed me, and I fell back onto my stool.

The guy put his fingers to his lip and said, "You bit me, you bitch!"

I rubbed my hand across my mouth and started laughing when a trickle of blood appeared on his lip. I think my anger transferred to him because when he saw the blood on his fingers, he brought his hand high ready to smack me, but someone grabbed his wrist and pulled him away. My head fell back as I giggled about what happened. Once I recovered, I turned my attention to my beer and shot.

Time seemed to stand still. I didn't know how long I sat there with my eyes closed, thinking about life. I had put a twenty on the bar when I first came in. By the time I woke from my daze, only fifty cents sat in front of me. There were a few more gulps left in my beer bottle, and the shot glass was gone. I couldn't remember if I had drunk twenty dollars' worth, or if someone had taken it. I stood, checked my jeans for more greenery, but there was nothing left. My body plopped back down on the stool, pockets still inside out. The alcohol wasn't providing the effect I set out for, yet I was drunk enough to not remember the guy who sat next to me.

I turned toward the guy on the stool, rested my head on my palm, and asked, "What's your story?"

He grinned and said, "Not much of a story. Just enjoying a few beers."

My body felt loose and uncoordinated as it swayed a bit with my request. "Would ya mind buying me one? I seem to have lost all my money."

He put his beer down and said, "Maybe it's a sign to go home."

I pulled my body upright and pointed my finger at him. "Fuck you. I didn't ask you what it meant. I asked for a beer. Forget it." I waved a dismissal.

"Tell you what. I'll buy you a cup of coffee and take you wherever you want to go."

My eyebrows caved in over my narrowed eyes, as I said, "To hell with your coffee. To hell with you."

He smiled, shrugged, and took another swig of his beer. From a distance, I thought I saw the top of Mason's head and his dumb blonde girlfriend's lipstick. I got up to stand at the end of the bar. They were coming toward me. My eyes locked on him and the bimbo, but there was no recollection in his eyes. Mason stared past me to the pool table room. Without thinking, I stuck my foot out when Blondie approached and watched her fall. Time was sluggish as I jumped on top of her. My fingers entwined in her hair and the other hand formed into a fist. I punched her in the face while the other hand pulled her hair. She scratched at my face and I felt the burning. It didn't stop me, but Mason did. He grabbed me around the waist, tugged at me while Blondie untangled my fingers and distanced herself. Mason threw me to the side toward the guy sitting next to me, and I fell to the floor laughing as strands of hair and blood were on my hands. The guy whose crotch I rubbed, muttered, "This chick's a psycho."

The one who had been sitting next to me lifted me from the ground right before the cops came and handcuffed me. I spat at Mason and his bimbo before the police escorted me out of the bar. I didn't resist arrest and the cops took it easy on me. I remember the blurred lights of the city rushing by as I sat in the back of a squad car, smelling the dankness of coffee and grease. At least I had a place to sleep for the night.

(Five) The Bennets

~~~~~

Easton finished telling me about what happened at the bar, and I felt my face warm from embarrassment. The guy I had physically assaulted wasn't too far from the truth. I was a psycho. Easton took a sip of his beer and asked if I was all right.

"More like embarrassed. So you were the guy next to me."

He had watched me most of the night and had seen what I had done to the guy who bought me a drink. Easton prevented him from hitting me. He had been working all day before he had come to the bar to knock down a few. When he saw that I was out of cash, he took the opportunity to sit next to me to keep the creeps away.

He smiled, and his smile got rid of my nerves, like a blanket gets rid of a chill. "We've all been there, Brand." He threw a few bucks on the bar and signaled toward the front door.

I put on my coat. "Where are we going?"

"Home."

That word again. So distant of a word—internally and geographically speaking. Home brings you comfort. It's a safe haven. For me, it was more of a motel aloofness. Granted, I had only been home for a few hours, but because I felt so isolated, I didn't expect to find comfort. The loneliness had imbedded into my nerves, and sometimes, when I heard Easton talk about my life, it felt like a story about someone else. Much like losing all sensory input. This paralysis only made me want to know more about life, yet each story pushed me further away from the Brand I didn't know existed.

The rain had moved elsewhere as we drove in silence. I could only assume Easton was tired of feeding me bits and pieces of my life. So far, I lacked appeal, so I wasn't sure I would want to remember.

Houses, businesses, and schools moved across my window like an unfamiliar slideshow. Nothing triggered a memory. Even Easton talking about the past had a creepiness to it. I wanted to cry. Was I really a psycho lush? Did I love Mason or did the timing of my mother's death put me over the edge? I didn't know who I was or how I was supposed to act.

We arrived, and I remained in the car, facing *our* house. Easton stood outside the passenger's door and then opened it. I unbuckled the seatbelt and got out. Our house was a two-story stone brick home. A thick, green lawn enhanced the outside of the house. Bushes lined the brick-framed bay window and flowerpots colored the walkway. I shut the car door and followed behind Easton until I stopped in front of the little wooden sign above the doorbell that said "The Bennets." Bennet. Brand Bennet. My name sounded like a high-end clothing store, but what I had learned about myself was the complete opposite. It seemed my actions represented more of a Goodwill Store.

Easton held the door open for me. I ventured over to the fireplace with its large mantel crammed with pictures. For the first time, I approached the numerous pictures. Easton sat on the couch. All the pictures were of us, except for one of an older woman. I pointed to it and asked if it was a picture of my mother. He nodded and I held it. My finger traced along her face, but it didn't link me to the woman. My mother and the background remained alien to me. I placed it back on the mantel.

From left to right, I stopped and searched each picture for some recollection, but I came up empty.

Before even turning around, I felt Easton's heat near me, and I shifted toward him. He was gazing at the pictures as if he hadn't seen them before. Easton picked up our wedding picture and slid his finger along the side of the frame. Melancholy made his features droop. I moved next to him to get a better look. My hair was short with highlights. Easton cuddled my waist as I stood in front of him. My head tilted to the left, and his cheek rested against it while we gave the camera exploding smiles.

I asked, "Were we happy? I mean, are we happy?"

He put the picture on the mantel as he responded, "Yeah. We were happy. I mean, we had our problems like all other married couples do, but for the most part we were happy."

"What kind of problems?"

Easton went toward the stairs. I didn't pursue the line of questioning because exhaustion made his body slump forward. I followed him upstairs into a bedroom. He opened the closet and drawers to show me he had moved my things in there. The room had its own washroom. Easton had figured it would be too uncomfortable for us to share a room at that time. I thanked him for it, and he left closing the door behind him. I took it as a sign that he wanted a break from me.

The room was a decent size filled with more Pottery Barn décor and a queen-size bed with fluffy pillows and a feather comforter. A window faced onto the front of the house with a large Oak tree, which provided some shade and privacy. I sat on the side of the bed until my eyes gave in to sleep.

My body eased back onto the bed, and I flipped the comforter over me. I fell into a deep sleep of fitful dreams.

(Six) Punch-Drunk Bitch

~~~~~

My eyes opened to a face just inches from mine. The nicotine and coffee killed the air. Her face was a plantation for acne, which made me turn away.

She rolled me off the bed and said, "Hey! Punch-drunk bitch. Git up!"

This was what some of them called me. The unstable personalities I had the pleasure of meeting inside the lovely walls of a rehab center. To abide by the privacy rules, I will leave out names. I assumed all rehabs resembled the same grayish walls of despair, except Plantation Face might not have been my roommate.

When I hit the tile floor, my elbow wacked against it and I yelped. I laid on my back rubbing my elbow and stared at the dotted ceiling I had grown to know over the past few weeks

Punch-drunk bitch. Like she should talk. Plantation Face didn't become a resident at rehab because the Yacht Club closed.

All of a sudden, the bed creaked and she leaned over laughing down at me. "Quit actin' like it hurt. Git yer ass up. I'm not gettin' in trouble 'cuz yer dramatic."

Oh yeah, I forgot to mention she had a limited vocabulary and kept losing word endings. I wasn't sure if it was from the alcohol and drugs she consumed, or because she was from Alabama. Oops! Privacy. Plantation Inbred Bitch (PIB) didn't understand boundaries. Or hygiene.

As PIB stared down, I had to swallow back the bile when I saw the puss hills up close and personal. I thought, if puss was in high demand, she'd be facing a lot of money.

She left the room but I remained where I was, thinking about my situation. Punch-drunk indeed. My liver might not have appreciated the term, but my mind had enjoyed the ride. I didn't have to think about the horrible things in my life. But there wasn't enough alcohol in the world to act as acid burn to smolder the heartbreaking memories. In a short period, I lost my mother to a drunk, my home to an unemployment sabbatical, and my boyfriend to a tall, skinny blond with long legs. Well, the latter turned out to be a blessing. I should have known since he claimed whiskey dick every time I made a sexual advance toward him. Someone forgot to send me the memo that he lost interest months ago.

"Brand! You in here? It's group time and they're waiting for you," said one of the many facilitators, whose name was forgotten as quickly as my last bowel movement.

I took my time and said, "Yeah, I'm here," rubbing my elbow that still tingled from pain.

Funny bone my ass.

I went into the washroom, turned the faucet on, and threw cold water on my face. The cold made me flinch, but I appreciated the wakeup slap. It took my mind off rehab, PIB, and my elbow. I placed my hands under the water, added soap, and rubbed them together while transfixed with the soap booger on the dispenser. That's how I felt. Like a soap booger. Leftover and hanging.

With my face still wet, I turned the faucet off, and headed to group time. I dressed in my pajamas for the occasion, shorts and a T-shirt. I wanted to be comfortable while I had my weaknesses and emotional pain extracted from me for an hour.

Everyone sat in a circle in stackable molded green chairs with Celinda Everett, the group leader, luring everyone in, like a fisherman. Celinda, sober for twenty-five years, had acquired a motherly approach that pissed me off. She wasn't my mother, and her sweet concern accentuated with a face that resembled someone who sucked on a lemon, only irritated me more. I'm sure it was her way of dealing with those she had hurt, an emotional obligation, but she needed to give it a rest.

Next to Celinda was an empty chair. A plastic chair that swooped into a curved L with thin metal legs. Uncomfortable as a wedgie. Since the rest filled the chairs, I came around the circle of heartache and collapsed there. Celinda's hand grabbed hold of mine, gave it a slight squeeze and released it when she said, "Good morning, Brand! It's good to see you."

I was tempted to say, "Oh thanks, Celinda. I tried to hurry so I could sit around with people who I'll never see again, but who make my life seem so much better with their miseries." Of course I didn't say that. Instead, I responded with an obligatory smile and a nod of the head.

"Could I start? I tossed and turned all night because I wanted to tell someone how I feel."

Felicity. The woman should had been committed to the closest psych ward. Her entire life was tragic.

Celinda asked, "How do you feel, Felicity?"

"Awful. I can't stop thinking about how I failed Carl. I know he cheated on me. I know he gave me gonorrhea, but it doesn't mean he doesn't love me. It was my fault. My drinking took a toll on our relationship. I kissed more bottles than him. He was jealous, that's all. Now I have to figure out how to get him back."

Celinda pulled herself forward and asked, "Don't you

think you should take care of *yourself* before worrying about how to get him back? You're the important one here. We all want you to embrace yourself. When you can do that, you'll be on the road to recovery."

She twirled her hair. "But I need Carl. He's all I have."

"No he's not, you have us. We're here for you, and we will help you through it."

My attention flat-lined.

I never agreed that I had a drinking problem. The courts ordered me to embrace rehab in place of jail after I attacked the skinny blond with long legs, who happened to be wrapping them around my boyfriend. It was Mason and Blondie's fault for not recognizing my new look of a rabies-stricken wolf—crazed eyes and tangled hair. If they had noticed me in the bar, the pandemonium would not have occurred. I had sunk too deep into misery, oblivious of my actions. The judge, lawyers, they all filed me as a 'lost cause' without knowing what caused my heart to fill with grief and my veins with alcohol. I had become another alcohol statistic.

Once I was overflowing with drinks and made a move on Blondie, her shrills caught the attention of everyone in the bar. After they saw it was two women, the men chanted "Cat Fight" but it didn't get far before I felt the handcuffs on my wrists. Prison was not pretty. Not pretty at all. Steam came out of the cell toilet, a stench comparable to vomit-covered roadkill on a hot summer day. My cellmates' second-hand clothes, pimped up for a night on the town, faces lined from hard years, had me assume that they visited often. They were a tired bunch of women, ridden hard and hung up wet, their horizontal working days far from over. I don't know who paid my bond. The police said it was anonymous. It surprised me, because I didn't know anyone who had the money or the kindness to get me out.

For a fleeting moment, I thought about my mom and if she intervened, but my gut knew the truth that she hadn't sent anyone or any money. Alcohol had put me in jail, and a drunk driver had killed my mom. Irony knows how to taunt.

Celinda placed her hand on my arm to get my attention, at the same time she said, "Brand?"

My turn already?

"Brand, would you like to share? The last time you spoke, you told us about the fight. We'd like to know what made you turn to the bottle."

There were only two more weeks of this ... this trade of secrets and lies. I decided I might as well have some fun at the sessions. It spiced things up in comparison to the mundane sorrows that strode the halls and filled the rooms.

I adjusted myself deeper into the chair, placed my hands in my lap, sighed and then lifted my head to Celinda and the others.

"Okay. Well." I dramatically sucked in air then released it. "After the bar fight, I had to decide whether or not I wanted treatment or jail—"

"Brand, Sweetie. We know why you're here. We'd like to know when and why you started drinking. When was the first time you turned to alcohol?"

At sixteen. The night I lost my virginity.

I gave Celinda a bashful smile and said, "Oh. Um. It was in my early 20s after I lost my first love. I found out my boyfriend, the bouncer where I bartended, fell in love with someone else." A pause came as I pretended to wipe at my eyes. "I found him in the men's washroom in a stall with Roberto." I stopped to catch my breath.

"Girl, why you in the men's washroom?"

Leave it to Dorris to question that part of the story. Dorris was a strong, voluptuous black woman. Who am I kidding, she was huge with a mouth to match. The woman shook more than a small-scale earthquake. Lord only knew what was festering between her squashed flesh.

I said to Dorris, "Because it was my job to clean the toilets."

"You bartended an' cleaned toilets? You bettah be tellin' me you washed yo' hands bfoe you bartended?"

"Fo' shizzle my nizzle."

Dorris tried to get out of her chair at the same time saying, "What you say, punch-drunk bitch?"

With each attempt, she fell back into the chair. Celinda spoke and said, "Ladies, please. Dorris, stay in your chair, and Brand, please don't talk that way. We're here to help each other. Dorris was simply asking you questions."

The tilt of my head and Grinch smile made Dorris growl, but her fat ass found its way back into the chair. Poor chair, the metal legs bent with the strain of her weight.

I told Celinda I didn't want to talk anymore. She let me sit as the rest of the participants shared their woes. I lost interest in their problems and started to think about life outside of rehab. What would I do? Where would I go? My mother was gone. There had been no good-byes, and there wouldn't be any tomorrows. Some asshole had taken her from me. He had received three-years in jail for killing the one person in my life who I truly loved. Three years! I had lost my mother, which is a life sentence, and the asshole had received only three years. Where was the justice in that? After my mom had died,

I sold her house, stayed in a motel, and lived off the funds—the dwindling savings were all I had left.

Again, Celinda touched my arm and said, "Brand. Are you okay?"

My eyes focused on a circle of empty chairs. I turned my head toward Celinda and said, "I'm fine. I guess I'm a little tired."

With one hand on each side of me, I got up from the chair and left without pause. I wasn't in the mood for a psychoanalysis. When I arrived at my room, PIB's bed was made and her belongings gone. I stuck my head outside the door and saw, Juan, the custodian. His mop moved with his head as they both swept from side to side when a female passed by. Juan's black greasy hair with its specks of dandruff around the scalp and a puffed gut that protruded outside his shirt enhanced his creepy image. I waved him over. He came close displaying a gapped-tooth mouth with a remaining few teeth stained yellow. I wondered if he had tried eating a can opener.

He spoke, which released a whiff of shit as he said, "Yeah?"

My face crumpled, and I waved my hand in front of me and said, "Damn, Juan! What was your lunch, a double-shit burger?"

Juan let out the rest of the smell when he laughed, letting it drift into my room. I stepped outside the door, pointed back into my room, and asked, "What happened to psycho?"

He shrugged. "Me don't know. She gone though."

I patted him on the back, pushed him forward and said, "Good to know. Carry on then." In my room, I grabbed the air freshener and sprayed around the room before I fell face down onto the bed.

(Seven) Restraining Order

~~~~~~

2013 - Dover, New Hampshire

I woke to darkness with my face and pillow damp from tears. Punch-drunk bitch? If being in rehab had not been a dream, it sure sounded like me. The dream had been so vivid that it brought on more questions. Had I really been in rehab, and was I really that much of a smartass?

The moon lit the room, and I used it as a nightlight to make my way to the washroom where I splashed cool water on my face. I placed my hands on the sides of the sink and leaned into the mirror. My skin was pale with red splotches around my cheeks, eyes red and puffy, and shoulder-length hair in desperate need of a haircut, preferably like the one in the wedding picture. Fortunately, there were no signs of gray hair, only wisps of hair in all different directions. I washed my hands and found myself gazing at the soap booger. Maybe dreams are actually stories of our past, present, and future.

I headed downstairs to find Easton in the kitchen on the phone. Before he could see me, I pressed against the wall by the stairs so I could listen in on his conversation. It was difficult to hear because he whispered into the receiver. I strained my head as far as possible. I jumped and screamed when he came around the corner. Easton stared at me while he told whoever was on the phone that he'd call them back.

Busted. I felt guilty for wanting to know his business. "I'm sorry."

"For what?"

I hesitated with an answer. "For listening in on your

conversation."

"Oh. Is that what you were doing?"

I traced the floorboards with my toe.

He sighed and said, "It's okay. I'd probably do the same thing if I was in your shoes."

With desperate eyes, I asked, "So you're not mad?"

He shook his head and replaced the receiver. "Are you hungry?"

I looked for a clock, and then asked, "What time is it?"

"Eight. You slept for two hours."

I fluffed my hair and then smoothed it down in the back and on the sides. "Are you? Hungry, I mean."

"I'm always hungry."

We both gave awkward smiles.

"Well, maybe I can find something to make?"

"Nah. It's your first day home. We can go out to eat. Your pick." He stood with his hands in his pockets waiting for a response.

I shifted my weight from one leg to the next and shrugged. My heart pounded a little faster. "Um, well, I'm not quite sure what's around here."

"What do you want to eat?"

"I'll eat whatever—"

"Brand. What are *you* hungry for?"

His words spit out with aggravation, so I said Chinese food. We changed and left for a restaurant. Neither one of us attempted to talk even though I had so many questions about my dream. Had I been in rehab? Was that one of the choices I had received for attacking Mason's girlfriend? If I had spent time in jail then who bailed me out?

Punch-drunk bitch. I must have really left an impression.

We found a corner booth. I faced the outer window, and Easton faced the rest of the room. He ordered for us without asking what I wanted. Our drinks arrived and I chugged the water. The spring roll appetizers came first. I cut into it to see what was inside. Easton watched me and finally spoke. "You love these. They're stuffed with bean sprouts, tofu, and cucumbers."

I put a piece in my mouth, and my eyes widened with delight. Easton grinned, pleased with himself.

"Do I like all the food you ordered?"

My question took him off guard and he sat back in thought. "Yeah. I guess I should have asked what you wanted. Every time we come here, we order the same thing so I took it upon myself to order. Sorry about that."

"It's okay. I was just curious. I'm sure I'll love it."

Easton put his fork and knife down, wiped his mouth with his napkin and said, "This is hard for both of us. I'm not trying to take away from what you're dealing with, but I want you to know that this is new to me too. I've never had someone forget who I was let alone it being my wife. If I do—"

I cut in and said, "You didn't do anything wrong. I appreciate it all. The lunch, the bar, a separate room for me, it's all been great." I put my hands in my lap and continued. "I can't help asking questions, but they're not meant to question your motives. My life is strange to me. Other than you, your visits to the hospital helped diminish my nervousness. It's tough to go home with someone you don't remember, but I didn't fear you, so it helped."

He readjusted in his seat. Every muscle in my face felt tight and he noticed. His voice was weak when he spoke. "Your memory will come. I guess these things take time. It hasn't even been a day since you've come home, and there were too many people there when you arrived. I guess I should have told them to leave us alone for at least a day."

I twisted the napkin in my lap, and started to bounce my right leg under the table. The restaurant filled around us. I took the napkin by two corners, let it unroll, and then patted my forehead.

Easton leaned forward. "Are you okay?"

I jerked my shoulders, took a deep breath, and then blurted out, "I had a dream about being in rehab. It was so real."

Easton sat back, sighed, and nodded.

My eyes popped opened along with my jaw. "So I was in rehab?" He nodded again. I leaned forward, lowered my voice and asked, "Was that a court decision for what I had done to my ex's girlfriend?"

"Yeah. From what you told me, your attorney had said you could have possibly gone to jail. The judge might be lenient if you'd enter voluntarily. It had been the better option. In addition to treatment, your ex-boyfriend and his girlfriend had filed a restraining order against you. You had to stay a hundred yards away from them."

The rest of the food arrived, but my appetite had already left. I couldn't believe I assaulted someone and had gone into recovery. It was probably on my permanent record. How could I have let myself get out of control?

I put my napkin on the table and excused myself. In the washroom, I went into a stall, covered my mouth and cried to release some shame and loss. At the sink, I wet a paper towel to remove the smeared mascara. When I returned to the table I found Easton hadn't touched the food.

I slid into the booth and said, "You should have

started with the meal. It's going to get cold."

He noticed my red face and said, "Brand. This is all in the past, eleven years ago. You shouldn't let it get to you."

I folded my napkin back on my lap and responded with an unsteady voice, "I know. It's just a shock to hear. It's pathetic. I want to know about my life, but so far, it looks like I'm a loser."

"This is why we need to take things slow. Not force your memory. And you're not a loser. I wouldn't marry a loser. The blond deserved it." I frowned at him. "She did deserve it. The restraining order disappeared when she left your ex-boyfriend. And rehab was actually good for you then. You had nowhere to live. It bought you some time until you got out, which was when you met me." He popped a piece of chicken in his mouth.

"The blond left my ex-boyfriend?"

"Yeah, but I don't know why. It doesn't matter though because you moved on. Let's eat."

I started to pile my plate with rice and spooned on several dishes I couldn't recall or pronounce. We ate, but I couldn't let go of what I had already learned. I wanted to know more.

"How did we meet? Obviously after I got out."

Easton put is fork down and sat back. "This is too much for you. It's overload." He gestured toward me. "Look at how it's affecting you. You're upset."

I folded my hands in front of me, and asked, "Please."

He surveyed the restaurant then me. "I already told you how we met."

"No. How? Where? What did I do afterwards that brought us together?"

Easton took a few more bites of food. I saw the exhaustion in his eyes and heard it in his voice. Between bites, he talked about the day I got out of rehab. I listened and ate, taking it all in.

(Eight) Dee-lish

~~~~~

No one replaced my roommate, PIB, during the last two weeks of rehab. My last day arrived. I had played the cracked egg game long enough. Celinda kept on me about how my first drink led to the next drink. At first, I did a great Juan walk, a hard slide as I made my way to single and group meetings. With heavy sighs and eyes pinched with pain, I went from one made up story to the next, describing my struggles with alcohol. Every day I played the part of an alcoholic. After listening to a few lost souls, it was easy to follow along and understand their torments.

When I arrived at my last group session, big Dorris gave me a nudge and smiled. Everyone clapped when I plopped into the empty chair, again, next to Celinda. She grabbed my hand, pulled me closer and patted the top of my hand with her other one.

Celinda addressed the group. "Brand is leaving us today. She has found the source of her pain that has triggered her desire to drink." She then turned her focus to me. "We wish you the best in your pursuit of a new beginning." She leaned over to hug me while everyone clapped and hooted.

Not wanting it to continue, I waved my hands like a fan in front of me and said, "Thanks. Thanks. I appreciate it. I know I won't be alone fighting my demons." I swept my arm from left to right and continued. "You will all leave here and do the same." This prompted more hooting and clapping.

The group session ended with some cake and coffee.

They wrote "Brand" in whip cream on top of the cake. I felt a sting of guilt for some of the lies. It hadn't been my intent. Anger was the driving force behind the things I had done, and alcohol just so happened to have been involved when I attacked Blondie. In my attempt to smother the guilt, I went around to hug everyone and let them know how much they changed my life. Really, they did. Every person we meet somehow alters our lives forever. Our lives will never be the same as they were before meeting that person.

After I had returned to my room, I gathered my belongings in a duffel bag and a picture of my mother. Her picture next to my bed helped me survive all the emotions that plagued me. Irritated by anger, like a piece of hair in my eye, I blamed Whiskey Dick and Blondie for ending up in rehab.

I glanced around the room for the last time before leaving. Workers and other patients patted me on the back, congratulated and wished me well. The sun was hot that day. A June surprise after days of rain and below normal temperatures. No one came to pick me up. The center was miles from Peterborough. Besides, there was no one to call. The couple of friends I had were dealing with their own troubles, and so they had scattered throughout the country. It was why I had been alone at the bar, staring at the bottom of many beer bottles. It was why, after all I had lost and the troubles I had to make amends for, the numbness still remained. Outside the walls of rehab existed a world that had forgotten about me. There was no place to call home, and nobody to call—period.

Out the door, my legs raced each other until I reached the street sidewalk and turned right. I had no reason to turn right. I guess right is never a bad direction to follow.

The rehab was near a residential area buried in trees and bushes. Overhung (can't say that about Whiskey Dick) trees swiped the top of my head as I walked down the street. I'd change hands to carry the duffel bag with an occasional swat at the trees when one would smack me in the face. My jeans, white creases in the front seat area and a hole at the knee, struggled to stay on my hips. The food hadn't been too good at rehab. The Chris Daughtry T-shirt I had lived in that past month revealed sweat between my breasts and underarms. I could feel my face coloring from the sun, and knew I must look pathetic with my weeping willow hair.

With each step, I felt a pang of seclusion. Even though in treatment, solitude was a good listener, there were people around as reminders that I wasn't alone. I carried the weight of sorrow and desperation when I walked down the street that day. The thought that I had no one, that I was a loser constricted every nerve. I wanted to cry. I wanted to scream. I wanted my mom back. My loneliness shifted to anger.

When I approached a corner, free of greenery, I saw a car out of the peripheral of my eye idle next to me. I didn't turn my head to find out whose car crept along with me. I wondered what direction I should take. Because the driver remained quiet as they followed, I finally stopped a few blocks down to see who and what they wanted. My eyes drifted from the front of the car to the back, my mouth partly opened. In front of me was a 1969 Convertible Corvette with the top down, black interior and red exterior, and a *dee-lish* man in the driver's seat.

I wiped my face, put my hands on my hips, and squinted to focus on the man of my dreams ... I mean the man in the car. "Is there something I can help you with?"

Because I let my nerves get the best of me, my words came out as if they were assaulted—not much strength and confidence behind them.

He didn't seem to notice. "Not really. I thought you could use the help."

Damn! He could have helped me out of my clothes.

I put my right hand over my eyes as a visor, as if uninterested in his offer, and gauged the area. Desolate. I turned back to him, asking, "Do I look like I need help?"

A crooked grin tickled the right side of his mouth before he said, "Kind of. You look tired, hot, and not to be rude, confused."

"That bad, huh?"

His grin spread. "It's not that bad. Thought you could use a ride." He put the car in park, his hands high in surrender, and added, "I'm sure your mom told you never to take rides from strangers, but I promise I'm not crazy. I only wanted to offer you a ride, that's all.

Inside, I cringed at the mom comment, but I recovered when I thought, "That's it?" That confirmed it. I finally lost my touch. Gone were the sexy eye days that got me a phone number or better yet, a smack on the ass with some bedroom acrobatics.

He seemed harmless and too good to be true. I approached the car, bent down, and put my arms on the passenger's side window. Our eyes connected and I watched his reaction, which remained steady.

"Only a ride? Why? Why do you want to go out of your way to give me a ride? You don't even know where I want to go?"

"I'm guessing you don't either. I thought I'd give you a couple of choices." My right brow cramped up. Interesting. There was nothing wrong with hearing the man's choices.

I stood straight, tapped my finger on my chin and said, "Choices, choices, choices. I like choices. Whatcha got for me?"

He turned his head toward the windshield, and said, "One: You can continue to nowhere. Two: You can get in the car, let me drive you to get something to eat, and drop you off at a hotel. Or three ..." He shook his head and said, "Forget three."

"Forget three? But I don't like number one, which doesn't leave me with another choice."

"Or stay at my place if you don't have anywhere else to go or any money."

I stepped back with my hand on my chest. "Your place? WOW! How did we jump from just a ride to your place?"

He browsed the area and shook his head. "I was offering if you really didn't have anywhere else to go."

"Are you some kind of superhero without the power?" I moved closer, placed my hands on the passenger window, and said, "Or do you have super powers?"

"Oh, nice, a smartass."

I bent down to eye level, and asked, "Do you offer candy to children?"

He put the car in drive and said, "Sorry for bothering you," and took off, waving his arm.

I yelled, "Wait," and the car skidded to a halt as I jogged over to him.

I argued with myself. One: He was hot. I was too, but not in a good way. I could continue going nowhere in particular. Two: I could get in the car with him, eat and then have him drop me off at a place that doesn't want money. Or Three: I could go to his house, think about my next move, and if he didn't kill me by morning, I could have him drive me to wherever.

He cleared his throat. "Gas prices are on the rise."

I threw my bag in the backseat, opened the door and said, "Sure." We let the air settle before conversation. The wind cooled me off, gluing my shirt to my body. Then it dawned on me. I turned and asked, "What's your name?"

He took one hand at a time off the steering wheel, flexed and relaxed them, before gripping the wheel again. "Easton. Easton Bennet."

Easton, the dark, muscular, dee-lish man. I could roll that name around my tongue and suck on it for hours.

"And your name?"

I leaned back in the seat and smiled. "Brand Rye. But for some odd reason I think you already know that."

Easton had no response. I watched part of the world pass by.

(Nine) An Addiction

~~~~~~

Easton pushed his plate of food away. "You got in the car. No questions asked. And that's how we met."

"Wa ... What? You're going to end there? Come on. I'm sure I had lots of questions, like now."

Easton smiled. I leaned back, pushed my hands against my chest when I asked, "Oh god, did I go home with you that night?"

He responded with a "Yep. Don't act so appalled. I'm a great catch."

My arms and head fell. "I'm a slutty psychotic lush. What next?"

The waiter cleared some dishes and left the check. Easton took a last sip of water, threw some money on the table, and I followed behind. I bumped into him when he stopped to open the door. Once we were outside, the unseasonably chilly temperatures made me wrap my coat tighter as I said, "Did we ... you know ... have sex that night?"

In the car, Easton blasted the heat to get rid of the chill still laughing at my comment. I stood by the door before climbing in.

Easton said, "I apologize. I know this is tough for you. I really shouldn't make light of it, but your face is priceless. To answer your question," he lifted the collar of his coat, "no, we didn't have sex that night or the next night."

I relaxed and rested against the headrest. "How did you know when I was leaving rehab?"

Easton rubbed the stubble on his chin. Conflict

creased the lines on his face. He decided to answer. "Because I was the one who paid your bail. I followed the case and knew how long you would be there. I found out about your mother, who the guy and woman were at the bar, and your financial situation."

Offended by his intrusion, I said. "How the hell did you get the information?"

"I'm an investigator. I have access to many files."

I hugged myself. It was creepy of him to research me and then show up at the treatment center. But he was far from creepy, so the main question that kept swirling around my head was why? Why did he research my life and want to help? So I asked him.

He blew into his hand at a stop light. The emptiness of his response reverberated how I felt. At that moment, I felt icky that he had probed into my life to follow me. Then I wondered what made me marry him. Didn't I find it weird that he had bailed me out? Or did he never tell me until now? Or maybe I found out that there was more to him and us. I readjusted myself to face him for an answer.

Easton craned his neck to each side cracking it. "Because I saw you at the bar, and you didn't come off like just another drunk slut. My investigative intuition surmised that there was more to you."

"So because you felt there was more to me, you felt compelled to bail me out. No way. There's more."

He pulled the car over to the curb, got out, and slammed the door. Easton went to the trunk and leaned against it. I hesitated before joining him. He focused ahead while I inspected him.

"I know I'm asking so many questions. I'm sure you hadn't planned to relive our past, but the questions and story are addicting. Once I find out about a morsel of my life, I have more questions and need more answers. The story of our life is an addiction. Instead of becoming tired or satisfied with what I have learned, I want more, so I can piece things together."

"Have you pieced it all together yet?"

I responded with a defeated, "No."

Easton shoved his hands into his pockets. Our breaths heated the air in front of us, and for a moment, we listened to each other breathe. My nose burned, and the cold night wind poked at my eyes. The absence of traffic and people made me even colder. I pushed off the back of the car, about to tell him we should go, when he turned to me. We glanced at each other before he wrapped his left arm around me, and placed his right hand behind my head. Without another word, his lips touched mine, cautious at first, and then with more of a need. My mouth opened with his and he slid his tongue inside. I expected to stiffen out of fear, except I didn't. I found my hands on his waist, my mouth wanted more of him. We finally separated, the wind nipped at the wetness around our mouths. Arms fell to our sides. Easton got in the car first. Before I did, I took a deep breath to fight the urge to cry.

He started the car, but didn't drive away. We sat in the murkiness of our own thoughts. I was confused. Where did that come from? Maybe he missed me more than he had let on. It was the first time I felt like we connected. And I wasn't afraid. Here's a man who just told me he investigated my life, yet I didn't fear him.

Easton pointed to the sidewalk right next to my door, and said, "That's where you stopped to talk to me."

My hands pressed against the door for a better view as if a celebrity had been there. I strained my neck from left to right, and asked, "So rehab is nearby?"

"Yes."

I realized how ridiculous I probably looked, so I turned back to him and gave a slight nod of thanks. The car idled with the heat on as Easton continued regarding me getting into his car.

(Ten) The Exchange

~~~~~~

My stomach was growling, so Easton stopped for us to eat soon after we started to drive. It was a typical diner with booths around the perimeter, tables in the middle, and barstools at the counter. The booth we sat in faced his car. I loved his car. I stretched my legs under the table to check for cash. The whites of my pockets stuck out, lint clung to the seams but no money. A broke trend began. First, I ran out of drinking money, and then, I would waste away from lack of nutrition. Easton handed me a menu as I tucked my pockets back in. I pretended to study it.

He put his menu down and said, "I could eat everything here. What are you getting?"

I sighed as if the food didn't appeal to me. "Lots to choose from but I don't—"

"You don't know which one to pick yet, right?"

The menu moved down into my lap. I shrugged and said, "Um. I'm actually not that—"

"Good at acting? This is on me."

I whispered to him, "Easton. I can't have you pay for me. I don't even know you."

He leaned forward on the table and whispered to me, "Yet you got in my car."

I thought at the time if he kept talking like that, he wasn't going to get into my pants.

How could I let him pay for my food? He had already given me a ride. The list of favors had started to grow.

Easton gestured to me and said, "How much money you got?"

I ignored him before saying, "Right now, none."

"Then it's settled. I buy."

I moved the menu to avoid his stare and picked a cheeseburger.

We ordered our food and then I really took him in. His eyes—brown with yellow specks—warm like the color of a sunset. Golden orbs set into strong, prominent features, the central focus of his symmetrical face with a prominent chin. The bridge of his nose stretched down and merged perfectly into his high cheekbones, ending with a small flare. His hair, a little shorter than shoulder length, fell carefree to the sides. A few top strands dipped across his forehead, tucked behind his left ear. He was an unexpected mystery, the kind that never got resolved. Easton's secrets remained hidden and the pursuer became enchanted.

He turned to me and asked, "Do you like?"

I shook my head and said, "Not a shy one, are you?"

He didn't respond, just glanced out the window strumming the table with his rather large hands and untidy cuticles. They weren't calloused, which told me he wasn't into manual labor. I wished I had my jacket with me to hide the pink color from the sun, layering my pale skin, in comparison to his nutmeg color. Instead, I took my arms off the table and stuck them under it.

Our food arrived. The only sound that came from the table was chewing. From time to time, Easton watched me eat my half-pound cheeseburger and fries. My hands pressed down and then wrapped around the piled-high burger of lettuce, tomato, and ketchup. I picked it up and stretched my mouth to the height and width of it. He smiled when I took a bite. My tongue swiped away the globs of ketchup left in the corner of my mouth.

Unlike me, Easton didn't inhale his meal. Instead, he

observed me as if trying to figure out my secrets. He ate one fry at a time, either to savor the grease or buy time to come up with a plan. It didn't bother me at all. I had bigger things to worry about, such as where I would sleep, to care about whether the dee-lish man found me repulsive. But he remained at the table, obviously not put off at my food frenzy.

We finished our meal. Remnants of mine still stuck on my face and hands. Easton went to the cash register to pay the bill. I dipped my napkin into my water glass, wiped off my hands the best I could and joined him. I didn't know what was next, but noticed there was a run-down motel nearby.

I grabbed my bag out of the backseat, and said, "Well thanks for the ride and lunch." I rubbed my stomach. "It will keep me until tomorrow."

He shifted his weight and said, "Where are you going?"

Aside from a sundry store and a motel, the area was barren near the highway. I pointed to the motel. "I'll get a room there."

"With what money? You didn't have any for lunch. Or maybe you conned me. Either way, you don't have much left."

My head fell back to hide my embarrassment. He was right. I had nothing left. I rubbed my chin with my shoulder and said, "I'll find a way."

He got in his car. "Get in."

"Wait, what? You don't even know me. I don't even know you."

"So get in. We have time to get to know each other." Why not? I didn't know what he had to offer, but I didn't have any other option. If he wanted sex in exchange, I think I could do that for—his sake.

I threw my bag into the backseat. Still uneasy with my situation, I looked at my side of the street. Life sped by without me. Within ten minutes, we arrived at a ranch-style house. Easton got out, grabbed my bag, and held the house door open. It had been a long time since I could recall being shy, so it made the situation all the more awkward. I took timid steps into a small foyer, stopped as he shut the door behind us.

"I'll show you around." I trailed him around the house, admiring the décor and all of a sudden, I became self-conscious. To the right of the front door was an office, and to the left, a fireplace in a large living room that stretched the length of the house, and merged into the dining area. The kitchen was next to the dining area with oak French doors that led out onto a huge patio. Near the kitchen was the master bedroom and then another bedroom between the master and office. He put my bag in the room that had a few brown boxes piled in the corner. An old printer sat on top of a dresser.

"You can sleep here. Sorry about the mess, I'll clean it tomorrow."

My left arm crossed over my body and I ran my hand up and down my right arm. I couldn't figure out what to say. Why was he being nice to me?

I surveyed the room and let out a simple "Thank you."

He signaled for me to follow to the washroom across from the bedroom. "I have my own so you can have the privacy of this one." Easton bent down and opened the cabinet below the sink to show where I could put my things. Then another cabinet to show the towels. "You can shower or take a nap if you want. I'll have dinner ready around five or six."

I couldn't move or talk. His generosity muted me. Easton didn't wait for a response. He left me standing there like a scarecrow. Finally, I found the courage to retrieve some clothes from my bag so I could take a shower. The heat and power of the showerhead massaged my entire body as I let out a few moans of enjoyment. So I was taking a shower in some guy's house that I didn't know. What next, offer myself into the world of human trafficking? I couldn't figure out how I got myself into this situation. Fear influenced my decisions. A fear of finding myself face down in a gutter, gurgling obscenities at some homeless person for taking my blanket while the swirl of alcohol swished around my brain. There wasn't a home for me to go to, so the decision to get in the car with Easton was easy. It was the now and later I hadn't thought about. I shut the water off, but stood there for a bit to let the droplets run down the drain. I took a towel from the cabinet, wrapped it around my body, and wiped my hand across the mirror to get rid of the condensation.

It was still foggy in the bathroom. On tiptoes, I got closer to the mirror to see my reflection, not a good image. Attraction wasn't Easton's motivation to bring me here. The mockery of lines, along with reddened skin, were signs that youth had checked out. I ran my hand down the side of my face, smiled, stuck out my tongue, and lifted the right side of my upper lip, anything to hide the panic I had about my looks. They were fading. I had counted on my appearance to get through tough times. I opened my towel. The small breasts I had always hated didn't seem as bad as my thin, powdery white skin that hugged my bones, and the small creases that garnished parts of my body.

I peeked out and took long strides back to the bedroom.

The water woke me enough to discourage a nap so I slipped on the best pair of jeans I could find, a blue V-neck shirt with three-quarter length sleeves and gym shoes, and wandered to the kitchen where I saw him through the French doors on the patio.

I slid the door open and Easton said, "Have a seat. What do you want to drink? I have water, orange juice, coffee—" Easton was halfway in the house.

"Whatever you're having is fine." I sat and smoothed out my shirt.

"Cold coffee? I have some sugar and cream in it. Is that all right?"

"Sounds great."

The table umbrella protected me from the sun, not that I should have hidden from it. He returned and we drank to the sound of lawnmowers and children's giggles. I admired the patio's flagstones. There was a built-in fire pit to the right of me, not far from the grill, and the Jacuzzi was on the opposite side.

I made a mental note to keep my ass out of there, especially if alcohol was involved. It had happened once, in a Jacuzzi, the first time I met the guy. An unflattering moment in my life, and I couldn't even remember his name. We met at a bar; each arrived with our friends, but left together. Both of us drunk, we went to his place, enjoyed a dip in the Jacuzzi until my underwear and bra disappeared. Instead of the walk of shame from a bedroom, I did one from a Jacuzzi, but not that well. I fell out of it, spread-eagled on the ground laughing, my clothes scattered around me. It took me a while to stop the laughing fit and find my underwear and bra. He pulled them off every time I got them on. I slapped at his hand, stumbled back and grabbed a chair to break my fall. My arm kept my balance, but I broke my wrist in the process. It was sad and the guy didn't help the situation. He drove me to the hospital, dropped me off at the emergency room and took off. With my shirt on backwards, zipper still down, words slipped around my tongue as I tried to explain what happened.

A shift in temperature woke me from my reverie. I glanced over at Easton, who sat content. I had to let him know how I appreciated the ride, food, and his home. Instead, what nagged me was why.

My good intentions melted, and before thanking him, I swallowed the words. The next thing I knew, my mouth released an idiotic question. "Can I ask why you're being nice to me when you don't even know me?"

Without even a simple gaze in my direction, he said, "I was at the bar when you got arrested. Before your ex-boyfriend showed, I watched you get drunk while you talked to yourself and played rough with some guy. You were in your own zone, that is, until you attacked that woman. While the police handcuffed you, you lifted your head and stared straight ahead—at me."

I covered my face with my hand. "So you felt sorry for me."

He turned to me and said, "Not sorry. I felt for you, that's all."

"I can't even imagine how I appeared, nor do I want to. I've spent the past month trying to forget about my actions." I placed my head against the chair. "I owe you an apology for my behavior then and now. Words to express how I feel aren't one of my strong points. You've been a gentleman, kind, and I ..."

"You don't have to go on."

My head lifted and our eyes met as I said, "Yeah I do. You at least deserve to know how much I appreciate all you've done for me without asking for anything in return."

"We haven't gotten to that yet."

Did he insinuate an exchange? Maybe sex?

I nodded while I said, "Oh! Yeah, I guess I misunderstood."

Easton remained quiet. He let his words soak in and watched until I got beat up by my assumptions. Then he let out a laugh and said, "Not that, Brand. I'm not a pervert."

I'm sure he saw my body sigh as I let out the breath I held in. "Well that's good, I mean, that you're not a pervert."

"You aren't sure why I helped you, and you're unsure what I want in exchange."

"Yes. I'm very interested to find out what it is you want."

"A date."

That's it? A date? With me, whose anger turned her into a Wildebeest at the bar? Whose appearance had taken a backseat to sarcasm? The back of my right hand slid across my eyes to dry them. I breathed in deep through my nose to clear the congestion. I didn't know if I should run away or sleep with the guy for caring.

I blinked a few times to get rid of the rest of the tears. "A date. You did all of this for me so I'd go on a date with you? There's more, right?"

Easton hesitated, looked at me, and said, "My line of work is investigations. Undercover work. Discretion. I infiltrate lives, get in people's heads, and learn about them without their knowledge." He leaned his head a bit in my direction and then relaxed. "I'm involved in an undercover case. For right now, that's all I can tell you."

He got my attention enough to have me sitting on the edge of the chair. "What does your work have to do with our date?"

Easton shook his head. "I can't tell you that. All I can ask you for is a date."

I rose thinking it would help replay what he said. "I'm thoroughly confused. Why would you tell me about your job when you can't tell me about your job? What does it have to do with our date?"

He stood with me. "Will you go on a date with me?"

"Well, yes but—"

"Good."

He went into the house. I followed him inside and said, "I'm not—"

Easton made a 180-degree turn and said, "You don't need to get it. The answers will follow later. Just accept the date as it is, a date."

"Is it an actual romantic date, or am I part of your investigation?"

He poured his coffee out into the sink, shook his head, and ignored the question. Easton went to the refrigerator and took some food out. He chopped lettuce, tomatoes, and cucumbers, all the while evading my stare.

I stood on the other side of the kitchen island. "I'm sorry to ask so many questions. I just want to know if you really want this date or need it for your job. It's important to me to understand what this is all about. I've been spinning through life, so I don't know how I would handle deception or humiliation."

Easton stopped chopping the vegetables, fixed his eyes on me and said, "I have no plans to hurt you. Our date will really be a date. I'd like to know how well we get along."

"But can't you tell with me here? Isn't it enough to

know whether or not we get along?"

"You here is part of it. The date is another part."

I pointed at him. "See? You're confusing me, like this is part of a big plan to—"

He pulled me toward him, held the back of my neck with the other, and kissed me. It wasn't a sloppy kiss, but a cautious one. I fell into him and allowed the kiss. Enjoyed the kiss. Then it ended. Easton released me.

He slanted his head to the right and said, "I figured that's the only way I could shut you up."

And he was right. I think he sucked all the words out of me and hid them away. We avoided the date subject for the rest of the evening, and enjoyed the cool night air and the company. When it was time for bed, he turned off all the lights, stopped at his bedroom door and said, "Good night, Brand. See ya tomorrow."

I pressed my forehead against the doorframe. "Thanks for dinner. Good night." We waited a second before disappearing into our rooms.

(Eleven) An Elephant in the Room

~~~~~~

Easton had shut the car off for some time while he told me about how I went home with him the day we met. Our breaths fogged the windows. The car started with cold air blowing at full blast. He turned the fan down, and swiped his hand across the driver's side of the windshield. Easton sat exhausted from conversation. I sat in a pool of questions. *Secrets. A date.* None of it made sense. I couldn't piece this new information together with what I had learned so far, except for the Jacuzzi.

My words crackled. "I remember falling out of a Jacuzzi."

"You do?"

I continued, glad to get some kind of response. "Yeah. I was laying on my back in the grass laughing. I can't recall the guy, though. I also had a flash of myself against a wall in a grayish room."

There was a hesitation. The volume of his voice became monotone. "I guess that's great that you remember."

"So I did fall out of a Jacuzzi?"

Easton wiped the condensation off the rest of the windshield, and in a matter-of-fact manner said, "Not with me."

He was drained and didn't want any more discussion, but the 'why' still hung like a dead leaf, brittle and ignored. I couldn't keep quiet, so I asked him.

The rain started again and Easton concentrated on

driving. There was a long pause and then I repeated, "Why? I won't ask you anything else. You still haven't answered why you helped me. Why you wanted to know about me?"

All I heard inside the car were the outdoor noises. I thought he would leave it unanswered. He must have considered whether to bother to respond. "You reminded me a lot of myself. I had dark periods in my life. Periods when I was alone and lost. I've been on my own since I turned eighteen. There wasn't much love lost between my parents and me. My father struggled with anger, and my mom struggled with reality. They've been out of my life the day I walked out that door." Easton paused to reflect on that altering moment of his life. He cleared his throat and continued. "While I watched you at the bar, I could tell by the way you were slugging those beers down that you wanted to be numb. I've done the same more times than I'd like to admit, and wished I had someone there to pull me out. When the cops handcuffed you and you went along with them, I knew you had lost all hope. I found out what happened to you through my job, investigated, and made sure I'd be there when you got out."

"And—"

He lifted his hand and said, "Uh-uh. No more." I left it at that.

Easton returned to work a couple of days later, and then spent a week working out of town. He offered to take more time off, but what was the point. There always seemed to be an elephant in the room when we were together, and I could tell he was antsy to get back to his job. Easton fell silent. There were no more talks down memory lane. His refusal to answer questions continued. Another week passed before we had any conversation about what I liked or didn't like, where I had or hadn't been, or what I had done with my life until this point. It only took a day for us to find each other's presence uncomfortable. We didn't have to confront our situation the week he worked out of town. I didn't have to worry about upsetting him. He didn't have to get irritated with me. It was tough with no memory, but not understanding where the restlessness came from made me scream inside. Easton's moods and willingness to discuss our relationship fluctuated. Something was missing in our marriage, and I couldn't figure out the cause and effect. When he spoke of his parents, I lost him to a sad past, which punctured his soul. His reflection of youth and my questions seemed to have had an impact on him. Easton no longer felt the need to help me. Maybe he thought memories should remain in the past.

For a while, I pushed my questions and disappointments to the side. I had plenty of hours to make sure dinner was on the table and do my own investigation. Easton came home later and later each day. What dinner I made for us, wound up cold on the counter because he claimed to have eaten. Like the night before last, I'd open the garbage can, slide the food into it, and wash the dishes. He'd disappear into his room. By morning, I'd wake to an empty house.

Since he was disinterested in home, I decided to figure out my life and memories. There were piles of picture albums in the basement. I pulled them over to the couch and opened them. The captions helped me piece together what I could of the years. Of course, I searched for my baby album first. When I found it, I flipped through the pages my mother had fastened photos to and written on.

Much of what she had written confirmed that she had been a single mother, and I was her only child. An October baby, I was born weighing seven pounds twelve ounces with little hair. My mother had notated all the little things I had done from when I walked and talked to losing teeth and pooping on the potty. I sighed at the wonderful pictures she had taken of me and of her. She had the biggest smile in every one. The book ended with me at the age of two and a half years old. The pages of pictures and notations didn't trigger a memory, only a deep ache. I felt my memory loss was a betrayal to her.

I searched for the next book, which was easy to find because she had put dates on each one. It began where the baby book ended and went to the age of eight. Some of the pictures fell out of the plastic pockets, but I slid them back into place after I read what she had written. There were plenty of pictures of church functions and several pages of me making my First Holy Communion. I was gangly skinny. Not much had changed except for wrinkles and loose skin. It seemed my childhood had been a happy one. My mother had made it so, recording all the beautiful memories erased from my mind. I couldn't help but become emotional about the loss of my past, which included her. The one person who could calm nerves, heal a wound, feed a heartbreak, and relieve hardships was gone from my life. A bond broken forever. It didn't matter if I'd remember now, because the first recollection was the only one that held all the cuts and bruises of my mother's and my relationship. The tender years and fleeting moments of intimacy that can't be reconstructed.

When I finished a photo album, I moved on to the next until sleep rescued me from the fallen tears. I woke to Easton on the couch by my feet shuffling through the last book I had browsed. I rubbed my eyes, and glanced at the clock, 6:00 pm.

After he closed the album, he asked, "Have you been down here all day?"

I moved to the other side of the couch. "Yes. You've been busy the last several weeks, so I decided to go through these albums to make some sense of my life."

Easton sat back and yawned. "Sorry I haven't been around much. It's been busy at work."

"A lot more criminals?" The sarcasm went unnoticed.

"Huh. Kind of."

I stretched my legs out in front of me. "Can I ask you something?"

His head swiveled toward me, a roll of the eyes to mock another inquiry, and then said, "Can I stop you?"

I looked down into my lap and then back at him. "Are you mad at me? What did I do wrong?"

His arms dropped heavily to his sides, and he stood. "No. It's our situation. Things you know and don't know. Work."

I glanced at the stacks of photo albums around me. "I'm sorry I'm a burden. I knew you were aggravated with me, but your behavior is erratic. One minute you tell me about my life and kiss me, and the next you won't even talk to me, and leave the house before I even wake."

"The kiss was a mistake. I shouldn't have done it."

His words hit hard. I wanted him to leave the room. My struggle with amnesia was my main focus. I didn't want or need to get into it with him.

Easton came back over to the couch and said, "I'm not an asshole. You don't understand. Things with us were different. Are different."

"But I want to know how we met. When we fell in love. When we got married. I want to remember all of it.

"No you don't. Sometimes life isn't always what we think it is. There's heartache—"

"Don't lecture me about heartache. If you don't want to support me, fine, then don't, but please don't give me some sob story about heartache. From what I've gathered, I've been through a lot of it already."

He put his hands on his hips.

With one foot on a step, I said. "Don't! Don't treat me like I'm an idiot." My footsteps were heavy.

In my room, I pulled down a suitcase from the closet and put clothes into it. Easton knocked on the door and I told him to leave me alone. He ignored my wishes and opened the door to find me packing.

"What are you doing?"

I moved from dresser to suitcase to pile things inside. "There's no reason for me to stay."

Easton moved in front of me, but I moved around him to the dresser. He grabbed the things out of my hand and put them back into the drawer as he said, "Wait. Wait a minute. Let's talk about it."

"What's to talk about? You don't like talking. You don't want to be around me." My voice grew in volume with every word. "You've pretty much let me know that my amnesia bothers you!"

He took the items from the suitcase and put them back in the drawer. I shoveled them back into my arms, but he tried to take them from me. We struggled until it all fell on the floor. I bent down to pick them up, and Easton grabbed me by the arm. His fingers pinched my skin. Out of anger and frustration, I slapped him across the face. He stopped. My eyes filled with pain and fear. I was about to leave the room, but he gave me a bear hug.

He leaned down and whispered in my ear. "Don't hit me." Easton's breath warmed the side of my face. Even though he didn't hurt me, he loosened his arms and then turned me around to face him. I cowered when he lifted his hand to my face. He hesitated and then he leaned down pressing his lips against mine. This time, it was a gentle kiss, in slow motion. I didn't push away. I let him kiss me. Easton brushed his lips against mine, made them warm from the friction, and then moistened my lips with his tongue. It was loving. Intimate. Then it was over.

He said, "I would never deliberately hurt you."

I touched my fingers to my lips and responded. "Why did you use the word 'deliberately'? Does that mean you have hurt me?"

He swallowed hard and said, "We've both done our fair share of hurting."

"Why did you kiss me? Was it a mistake too? Another way to hurt me?"

His hand swept the hair off my forehead. I waited. Easton ignored my inquiries and told me about what had happened after the first night I stayed at his house once I had accepted the date.

(Twelve) Gettin' Fresh

~~~~~~

2001 - Dover, New Hampshire

In the morning, Easton was out on the patio. I poured myself a cup of coffee and joined him. He folded part of the newspaper, offered it to me then shuffled through the rest. I don't know how long we were absorbed in our reads before he decided to talk.

He put his paper down. "How about that date tonight?"

I clung to the mug and said, "Fine with me."

"The weather is supposed to be great today, 80s and sunshine, so why don't we go to dinner at a place called Gettin' Fresh. Afterward—"

My hand went up for him to stop as I let out a laugh and said, "You're kidding. That's the name of a restaurant?"

Easton's smile was like a good hug. "Yeah. Why?"

"It's funny. I'm guessing it's a fish place?"

"Yep." His smile collapsed. "You do like fish, right?"

"I do. One of my favorite meals. Is it a fancy place?" I shook my head. "If it is, I—"

"It isn't, but I have a few things you can pick from if you'd like."

"Okay, that's sick. Why would you have women's clothes?"

He let his shoulders relax, turned back to his paper and said, "In due time. In due time."

I slammed the paper down on the table, spilled some of my coffee, and was about to go into the house. He enclosed his hand around my right forearm with enough pressure to stop me, but not enough to hurt. "I know you're upset." "Damn right I am." I turned and twisted my arm free from his hand. "Everything's a secret. You expect me to go along with this whole charade without any information." I folded my arms in front of me.

"I'd like to tell you, but I can't right now. After we go on our date, I promise to let you know more."

After the date? What was all this? All of a sudden, I felt he had chosen me long ago. He must have known me from somewhere else other than the bar. He definitely had known about rehab. There's no way he all of sudden appeared the day I left. I was so stupid! Why didn't I figure that out earlier?

Because he's gorgeous and you were going nowhere with no money. What a way to recovery?

My body stiffened as I stared down at him. "How do you know me? And don't give me some bullshit excuse that you saw me at the bar. How is it that you arrived the day I left the center? That you knew I didn't have any money? That you—"

Easton stood straight, towered over me and said, "I told you. I saw you in the bar."

"Bullshit!"

He didn't raise his voice at all. "It's true. You looked lost."

"Lost enough for you to use me?" My voice rose. "You waited until I got out because you felt sorry for me and figured I was vulnerable enough to do whatever you wanted?"

Humiliation and anger smothered me. I smacked him across the face. He didn't expect it. Easton paused from shock, but he recovered fast. He grabbed my wrists to avoid the unexpected again, moved me against the doors and in a tight voice said, "First off, don't hit me. Second, I only know you from the bar. Third, I didn't feel sorry for you. I said, I felt for you, there's a difference. Fourth, I picked you for this because for some reason, I believe I can trust you. You're safe."

I waited for the heat in his eyes to cool down and the tightness in his voice to disappear. Easton let go of my wrists and I rubbed them to get the flow of blood again. Tears ran rampant, so I turned to open the door. His body crowded against my back. I froze, surprised by the erotic feelings frolicking around my fear. His breath warmed my ear as he said, "I have no plans to hurt you or let you get hurt. I fed you and you slept untouched. Yes, I did decide to pick you for the case. I knew you didn't have anyone. You were the perfect fit." He rotated me around to face him. "Brand. I know I'm expecting a lot from you. As we take each step, you'll learn more. For now, all I can say is that you trust me. Be patient."

He waited for me to talk. "Why should I? I don't know you? I have no idea what your ultimate motives are."

"You're right. But if I wanted to hurt you, you wouldn't be standing here talking to me right now."

A chill ran through my bones, so I covered my arms in front of me.

Easton took a step closer and whispered, "That wasn't a threat, Brand. I wanted to point out that you're safe with me. I'll take care of you. What do you have to lose?"

He was right. What more did I have to lose? I had already lost it all. I was sure my mom wouldn't have approved of me doing this, but she wasn't around to dissuade me. And Whiskey Dick had moved on with tall, skinny blonde. Easton seemed to be the only choice. This undercover work could be the next chapter. If something happened to me then it happened.

"Fine. I'll do what you want. And I'm sorry about the slap."

"Thanks." Easton sat down, but I headed for the shower. Fear. Sadness. Sexual tension. It all needed to go.

We arrived at the restaurant, and I felt self-conscious about my outfit. My arms are like pythons. Why did I pick that dress? Easton had a few summer dresses in the front closet. He didn't tell me whose dresses they were, and I didn't ask. It was best to keep some things secret. I didn't need to find out he was transgender and the dresses used to be his. I picked a form-fitting strapless dress. It was dark blue with white trim around the bust area and the hem. It just so happened that I fit into a pair of blue pumps with a sprinkle of white on the rounded toe also found in the closet. Aside from how it fit me, it was an affordable, classy outfit. After first meeting Easton, I made sure to wear some makeup, enough to hide my sins and enhance my best features— my eyes. I put my hair into a messy bun, some strands hung loose. When I came out of my room, Easton was standing by the fireplace. His face stretched from surprise, and then he let out a 'how do you do' whistle. Ha! He wasn't the only one who had secrets.

It had been a while since I had worn high heels, so at first my legs bowed while I tried to stand straight. My knees slightly buckled, and it wasn't until we reached our table that my legs finally found their strength. Easton pulled my seat out and I tugged at the top of my dress as I sat. He took the seat next to me. The restaurant gave the illusion of being underwater. There were rounded light beams around the room to give the impression of water reflections. It was one big room with all types of fish on the walls, and a huge fish tank with colorful fish in the middle of the main dining room. A tank full of lobsters ran along an entire wall.

The waitress dropped off some warm bread. Easton ordered a bottle of Chardonnay and shrimp cocktails for starters. Once the waitress left, he asked, "Is it all right that I ordered wine? I forgot that you—"

"Wine is good." Easton nodded and observed me without another word.

It was like being naked in Times Square, not that I was ever naked in Times Square. At least, I don't remember. Anyways, my eyes glanced around at others near us and then I turned back to him. His eyes were still on me. I began to wipe my cheeks with the tips of my fingers, and then I dabbed underneath my nose. It drove me nuts. "What? Do I have something on my face?"

"No." I put my hands in my lap. "Don't sweat it, Brand. I meant to tell you, you clean up well."

My dimples caved in as I stretched a toothless grin and let out a gentle laugh. "Thanks. I'm also appreciative to see you found the shower."

The wine arrived, and Easton poured us both a glass. He held his and I followed his lead. "Let's make a toast to this date and our adventures."

I lifted my glass. "To our adventures."

We clinked glasses and drank. I couldn't figure him out. His appearance didn't fit the stereotype. Easton, the secretiveness, made me come to life. The months that had led to this moment were filled with chaos and anguish, so the quest I was about to embark on gave me purpose.

I leaned toward him, and asked, "How's this date so far?"

He took a drink of his wine, moved a few inches from my face and said, "Like rowing over a lazy river."

Damn! Good looking, witty, and a poet.

Our shrimp cocktails arrived, and shortly after, the main course. We kept things light, mainly stuck to news topics and the occasional celebrity gossip. A stroll on the boardwalk followed our meal. The path trailed along the beach.

We came to a secluded place with a bench. Easton leaned on the wood railing and scanned the ocean. I moved next to him and did the same. My eyes closed. The sound of the waves drowned the butterflies I felt in my stomach. Where would this adventure take me? To his bed? I wouldn't mind that, although he was way, way out of my league.

He sighed and turned toward me. "This went pretty well. I think we'll be able to pull it off. If you follow my lead, go with the flow, this might actually work."

"I'm so glad I meet your standards."

"Who said anything about standards?"

"That's true. I mean, I am with you. "

Easton nudged my arm. "A smartass. I like that."

"Will it come in handy?"

"For what?"

"Our adventure. Investigation. Whatever you want to call it."

"It might. We could use it as a diversion."

I turned and rested my back against the rail. "All right. Don't you think it's time to let me in on what we're talking about even though I have no idea what we're talking about?"

He went down a pier with his hands buried far into his pockets. Of course, I followed until he stopped underneath a light then continued to walk to the end of the pier. I took in a deep breath. The ocean had its own smell—a fresh, sexy smell from its depths. It was how I felt when I was around Easton. He came next to me. All I could think about was kissing him after a romantic date. His body against mine while our hands explored. I turned toward him and he moved his face close to mine. We stared into each other's eyes before he kissed my forehead. Then he withdrew and pointed out into the waters. "Have you ever been on a boat?"

It took me a minute to recover from the loss of a real kiss. He had kissed my forehead. My forehead! Who does that? And then he asked some random question? I rolled my shoulders back to let him know his kiss-diss didn't bother me. I responded, "Yeah. A few times. Why?"

"Curious. The water's dark ink appearance at this time of night is intimidating. Who knows, we might be on a boat or yacht for the case. Can you handle dark waters?"

I started back for the car. Over my shoulder, I said, "I can handle anything."

(Thirteen) Disassembled

~~~~~~

When Easton finished talking about our first date, our investigative first date, he sat on the side of my bed and looked out onto the front of the yard. In full bloom, the tree shaded most of the sun. Little white flowers grew at the end of the stems, and some petals fell off and twirled to the ground. The air conditioner drowned out the outside noise, and I stood on the other side of the bed.

I was tired to rationalize and having solitude as a close companion. Without money, I couldn't go anywhere to break the monotony. I wanted things to move faster, before the distance widened.

"Our earlier relationship sounds entertaining," I said. Easton didn't return a response. "Sounds like we got along, but now I'm scared."

He nodded in agreement. "I don't know how to fix us."

"What are we supposed to fix?"

In the doorway, Easton said in a hoarse voice, "I don't know."

I fell on the bed and cried myself to sleep. My dreams added more questions and sadness than reality. In one dream, I rode on a train. My mother sat in the next car and Easton was outside the train. The doors closed, and he pressed his hands against the window. I pressed mine to his. He ran with the train, hands still flattened to the glass until he tripped and fell to the side. I watched him on the ground, mouth ajar, as he disappeared from sight. I heard my mother pounding on the door from the other car. I tried to open it, but it wouldn't budge. We both slapped our hands on the windows, staring at each other, and mouthed that we couldn't get it open. The cars disconnected and my mother banged harder as my train car moved farther away, and then, as if dipped in ink, thick blackness.

A loud noise woke me. I flung my legs off the bed and followed the sound. In the backyard, Easton was cutting down branches of a tree with a chainsaw. I moved to a chair and watched him disassemble the branches. That was me. Disassembled. My mind separated from the rest of my body. I couldn't call anyone to talk about how I felt because I didn't know anyone. Soon, the tears came but I didn't wipe them away. I let them ride down, fall, and then dry on my clothes. Easton saw me. He stopped the electric chainsaw for a moment. As if he thought it best to leave me alone, he broke our connection by yanking hard on the starter handle.

I didn't notice the woman until she stood right next to my chair. My hand shielded me from the sun. She yelled down at me. "Hi, Brand! How are you?" She extended a hand and I took it. Her head jerked toward the kitchen, so I went inside with her.

The door closed and she said, "I asked how you are?"

"I'm good." My head bobbed a few times until I asked, "I'm sorry, but you are?"

"Oh! Forgive me." She placed her hands on her chest for emphasis and continued. "I'm Jenny Carver. Your best friend."

I puffed out a large amount of air. Thank God, I'm not a pariah. "Are you the Jenny who sent flowers to the hospital?"

She giggled. "Guilty."

I smiled at her and signaled for us to sit at the table.

"Are you thirsty?"

"No, I'm fine. I wanted to come sooner, but I thought I'd give you time to get comfortable with being home. I'll admit, I also stayed away because I didn't know how to act around you. It was easier that way."

I had been home for a while. What kind of friend stays away that long, let alone a best friend? Instead of grilling her about why she didn't save me from my cruel loneliness, I figured I'd get to know her.

"Thanks for coming over. I had begun to think I didn't have any real friends."

She laughed, and then her face straightened out. "I bet this is hard for you. Has anything come back?"

I wiggled my hand from right to left a couple of times. "Some things feel familiar, but I can't quite figure out why. I went through some photo albums to help me understand the past." Quietness spread throughout the house. Easton took a break with the chainsaw.

I tried not to be obvious, but there was no way to avoid the fact of Jenny's attractiveness. She had large, brown eyes with thick, long eyelashes that fanned out when she blinked. She didn't wear much makeup other than mascara and the pink lipstick that brightened her face. Her long brown hair with red highlights fell in one length just past her shoulders. I realized I had on battered jeans shorts and a wrinkled shirt. Embarrassment singed my face when I remembered I didn't have any makeup on, my hair a mess from sleep.

The kitchen door opened and Easton came in. Jenny said hello. All she received back was a grunt. Easton filled a glass with water, chugged it and then put it on the counter.

He asked Jenny, "What do you want here?"

Uncomfortable with Easton's attitude, she adjusted

herself and fluffed her hair. "I thought I'd come and check on my friend, Brand." She smiled and covered my hand with hers.

"She's fine."

I froze from his behavior. Easton didn't hide his rudeness, and I couldn't believe he wanted everyone to know that we were fine. I thawed out enough to say, "Well, it hasn't gone as—

"You had planned, but the doctor said it will take some time," Easton said.

My face scrunched up. I didn't know what provoked such rudeness. "Yeah, I know, Easton, but I'd like to—"

"Remember a few things. I know. We'll get you there."

Jenny sensed the tension between us and patted my hand before she slid it back toward her. "I'll help you, Brand. We've been best friends for a long time. I can—"

Again Easton broke in and said, "I'm enough. She doesn't need a lot of people feeding her information about what she has done."

Jenny stood, as did I. "I better go. It was good to see you, Brand."

My hand gave her arm a gentle touch. "Oh don't go. It's so nice to have a visitor."

"She said she has to go, Brand. Besides, we'll be leaving soon."

I gave him a sideways glance. "What? Where?"

Jenny went to the door and I ran after her, turning a few times to see if Easton had followed. She gave me a hug, went out the door, and shouted back, "I'll call you soon."

The screen door slammed shut. "Please do. I'd love to get together."

When her car was out of sight, I stomped back into the kitchen to find Easton sitting at the table.

"What the hell is wrong with you? You don't want to talk to me, so why chase away someone who does?"

He waved my words away. "We don't need her help."

I pointed at myself and screamed, "Who is we? I need her help! I do!" My fist slammed on the table, as I continued. "I hate you! You know that. I can't believe I married someone like you." My body began to shake. I couldn't control it. He took a step closer. I backed away and said, "What? Do you think if you kiss me I'll forget about what an asshole you are?"

He came closer, and I stepped back again. This went on until my backside touched the kitchen wall. I scooted around the doorway and he came around to block me. I shoved him, but it was like pushing against a tree. I moved to the right and so did he.

My hands clamped onto my hips. "Oh, are we playing chess?"

I maneuvered to the left, and he mimicked me. "What the hell is wrong with you? You're really pissing me off."

He let his head drop. "It's not my intention."

"But?"

"But nothing. We have to figure out how to get your memory back and learn about you."

"Is that code for something?"

Easton took my hand, but I pulled it back. He said, "The date went well. After we left the beach, you were quiet until we got home. I told you a little about the case."

(Fourteen) The Cover

~~~~~~

When Easton and I returned home from our date, we changed clothes and met out on the patio. A bottle of wine chilled in a bucket and two glasses were on the table. Easton lit the fire in the fire pit and poured us each a glass of wine. The fire hadn't warmed the air yet, so I pulled my jacket tighter.

Easton asked, "Do you want a heavier coat? I have some—"

"No, I'm fine. Once it gets bigger it'll be warm enough." The smell and crackle of wood with a glass of wine happened to be a good way to end the day. I let the trickle of sweetness from the wine coat my throat and drown my words into a sedating pool. My eyes were heavy. I reflected on the things I had experienced the past six months. I missed my mom. I wished she were there with me to enjoy the moment. My nose felt pinched when tears pooled in my eyes. I opened them for the air to dry. Easton had his head on the back of the chair turned in my direction.

"Are you okay?"

I nodded without eye contact. He let my emotions settle like coffee grinds in a filter, dark and coarse. This really wasn't about my mother, even though I did miss her. I belonged nowhere. Displaced from home, I had severed all intimate connections in my life.

Before I got too carried away with my sorrows, Easton finally decided to let me in on a few things. "I need a good cover for the case I'm on. A convincing one so I could investigate from the inside. I need to be in a relationship, a serious relationship."

"For work? We need to ..." I quoted with my fingers for emphasis when I said, "'be a couple for a cover?' I thought this," I pointed from me to him back to me and continued, "is us getting to know each other. For real."

"It is, so it will feel real when the time comes for us to go undercover."

"I'm vulnerable, Easton. I can't pretend I feel for you, and possibly fall for you in the meantime, for the sake of your job."

"But I told you the date was part of it. I'm not trying to hurt you or lead you on. I want to be honest with you about how things will go. I saw you in the bar and in a sense, I understood you. I knew you fell on tough times. I knew your mother died and you didn't have anywhere to live. Maybe you would have gone to a friend's house, but I thought about my situation and figured we could both use each other."

I looked at him appalled. My mental pendulum swung heavy and hard, confused by feelings and loneliness. The passion inside me was out of control, which swung from one extreme to the next.

"Not 'use' use each other. You need a place to live until you figure out your life. I need a woman to go undercover with me to act as my girlfriend."

"And if I get killed in the process?"

"I'll have a nice burial for you?"

It hit me like a baseball in batting practice. I drew in a deep breath and redirected my attention to the darkness. "Very funny. And very rude. You expect me to risk my life for you?" He lowered his voice to soothe the situation. "I'll train you."

A puffed laugh came out as I stretched my neck from side to side. "Train me for what? How to kiss you? How to handcuff you?"

In a casual manner, he said, "That's a different preparation. I'll train you on how to use a gun."

"Seriously? There is no way I'll hold a gun let alone fire one. Do you really think I'm a hopeless person? Someone who should put her life on the line, because if I get killed there won't be anyone to mourn me?" I put my wine down and went to my bedroom. Why was it that I meant so little to him? To anyone? I became the loser Brand who could shrivel and die without it effecting anyone. I cuddled the pillow.

Easton came into the room. I heard him sigh and lean against the doorframe. "Brand, I'm sorry. I didn't mean to make you feel this way. I thought we'd help each other out, and I didn't think about how it would make you feel or the consequences. The reality is you can get hurt, but I ignored reality for the sake of the investigation. Of course, I'd do everything in my power to protect you, but that still doesn't mean it isn't dangerous."

What could I say? I was staying in his bedroom, in his house, ate dinner that he paid for and had nowhere else to go. Who knows, it could be fun to play a couple. The pendulum shifted. But my fragile emotions. He had no idea how great looking he was, or maybe he did? Either way, how could I *not* fall in love with him? We'd be a couple for God's sake! Kissing. Holding hands. Another shift of the pendulum. A past rubbed out! I had left rehab supposedly rehabilitated, yet my life didn't seem to have improved. Would I be worse off if I got hurt? And if I died, would that really be so bad? After rehab, I had no idea where I would go or what I was going to do. Opportunity showed itself. I could make it a game. Make a few rules for us. My life would have purpose, even if only for a little while.

I rolled onto my back to tell him I would do it.

"You will?"

"We will have to make a few rules about the relationship and I want to get paid. If I'm going to risk my life as your girlfriend, then I damn well better get a great compensation for it."

Easton nodded in agreement.

"I'm tired, Easton. Good night."

He wished me a good night and left the room. The more I thought about our case, the more I felt empowered. I needed to take control of the idea.

(Fifteen) An Affair

~~~~~~

By the time Easton finished about me accepting the case, my stiff body gripped the armrest with a tight facial expression. I couldn't believe he didn't consider the danger he would put me in. "Sounds like you haven't changed much. The way you treat me now sounds a lot like the way you treated me then. I must have been completely stupid or grief stricken."

"Hey, I would have done what I could to protect you. The last thing I wanted was for you to get hurt."

"What changed?"

He spread his arms and said, "Life. That's what changed."

"Well, I guess that answers all."

I went to put on some makeup and brush my hair. When I came downstairs, I saw Easton outside working on the tree again. Without a care, I took his car keys to go for a ride. I didn't have a clue where to, but I wanted to leave the house. The car had a GPS system, so it would get me home.

I came upon an area where they didn't allow traffic. Restaurants, bars, and shops lined the pedestrian area, so I found parking on one of the residential streets. People spilled out onto the sidewalks from filled restaurants and bars. A shop that sold bathroom accessories and soaps was a block down. The smells drifted outside where I remained when I saw the prices in the window.

Around the corner from the store was a hair salon. I went by the window, curved my hands around the sides of my face to block the sun, and saw two people talking while clumps of hair fell to the floor. The man who cut the hair saw me. I backed away from the window as he approached the door. A little bell rang above when he opened the door using one foot to hold it open. "What brings you here?"

"Huh?"

He opened and closed a pair of scissors as he asked, "Why are you here, Brand, besides looking horrible?"

I pointed to myself. "You know me?"

He rolled his eyes and hunched his shoulders. "Yes, Brand. Is this another game of yours?"

"Another game?" I waved my hands in front while I shook my head. "Not at all. I had a car accident and lost my memory."

His mouth and chin tensed into a 'yeah right' expression as he scrutinized me.

"Really. I can't remember anything."

He let out an exasperated breath then said, "How convenient. You get to forget all the awful things you've done."

"What awful things? I ..."

He indicated for me to come in by opening the door wider. The customer in the chair nodded and said, "Hi. You picked a great place to get your hair done. Mitchell is a Godsend."

Mitchell waved his hand to dismiss the compliment, and pointed at the chair next to the customer. "Have a seat."

I watched him work while he talked to the customer the entire time and gave me a few glances. Maybe he wanted to see if he could find some sign that I was lying. It didn't matter though, Easton drove me crazy the way he acted, and I wanted to find out from the guy how he knew me, and what exactly I had done. Then again, I was a psycho lush. Did I want to find out if there was a limit to my deficiencies?

The customer left. Mitchell turned the 'Open' sign to 'Closed' and sat next to me with his hands folded on his knee. "So Brand, you lost your memory. Sorry to hear that."

Through the mirror, I responded, "Yeah, it sounds like you are."

He lifted himself out of the chair and went to the cash register.

The place had granite shelves where stylists worked along with the shampoo bowls. Tall mirrors were at each stylist's station. It smelled of lemongrass. "Your name is Mitchell."

"All my life."

"And how do we know each other?"

He slammed the cash register door and said, "Come on. I'm not buying this memory loss. If you had been in a car accident, I would have known about it. Easton and I have been friends for years."

I continued to scope out the place. The recess lighting ran the length of the shop, which made the wood floor shine. "So you know me through Easton?"

"I talked to him last week, and Easton never told me you had been in an accident."

This Mitchell had money. "I don't know why he didn't."

"Oh wait, yeah, probably because we never bother to talk about you."

I went over to him. "I'm sorry, okay? I'm sorry you hate me. I'm sorry for whatever I did to you to hate me, but I don't remember."

"Then why did you come here if you don't remember?"

"A fluke! I found this area of shops and restaurants and saw the salon." I grabbed my hair and said, "As you so nicely put it, I look horrible. It would be nice to get a haircut."

He leaned in, and in a clipped voice said, "Watch it, Brand, I might cut it all off."

The frustration got to me and I couldn't hold in the tears. I fell into a chair close to the reception area and put my face in my hands. For a few minutes, Mitchell didn't move, only watched, probably with annoyance. Finally, he came and sat next to me and said, "What happened?"

I rubbed my eyes and sucked in the residual snot. "I don't remember exactly, except for a bright light, and an awful sound. Easton said I caused the accident by texting, but I don't even recall that. I woke to find Easton beside my bed. I haven't bothered to ask him about the accident because I've been too interested in my life." My face wilted. "How do you know Easton? What did I do, Mitchell, that was so bad? Please tell me. Easton won't talk to me about much. Only about my mother and how we first met. He's withdrawn. You're mad at me, and I have no idea why."

He slapped his hands on the tops of his thighs and said, "You had an affair."

It was a sucker punch to the stomach. Our breathing and his words hung in the air. Drifted until we both inhaled.

Mitchell rested his head on his hand. "I told you to take care of him, to be good to him. Instead, you broke his heart. You were the love of his life, and you broke his heart."

My lips trembled and a wave of emotion came over me. An affair? What the hell was wrong with me? Not only was I a psycho lush, but also an adulterer. A cheating psycho lush. I buried my face in my hands while my body trembled. At that moment, Mitchell realized I really had no recollections, because he placed a hand on my back and rubbed. He let me get it all out.

I finally said, "I can't believe I did that. I've already learned so much about myself that I don't like. Why would I cheat? Do you know whom I cheated with on Easton?"

Mitchell gestured he had no answers for me. He took my arm and led me to a hair salon chair. "Let's see what we can do with this," as he lifted my hair and let it flop to the sides of my face.

I squinted and asked, "You're not going to shave it off, are you?"

Mitchell smiled, and said, "Nah. But you are fabulously gorgeous in short hair."

I didn't know how to respond to his compliment.

"You really don't recall, do you?"

My fingers rubbed underneath my eyes. "Nope. And I probably should have kept it that way. I don't like myself right about now." My words came out gruff.

"And there are plenty of others who feel the same way." I flinched, and he followed with, "I don't mean you. We all have done things we're not proud of."

"But that's not what you meant. You meant that many people don't like me."

Mitchell closed his mouth, puffed out his cheeks and then released the air in slow motion. "Everyone liked you at first. I should clarify and say the few people who are in Easton's life. He keeps to himself, so there aren't a lot of people involved in his life."

His comment lifted me straighter in the chair. "This is what I want to know."

"What?"

"To learn about Easton. Our relationship. About me. Hopefully I wasn't all bad."

He mixed some color, placed the bowl on a tray and collected layers of hair. "No you weren't. I liked you when I met you. You had so much spunk, and at that time, I thought you two were an item. I didn't know about your undercover operation. Easton didn't talk about his cases while he worked them. Sometimes he'd discuss them afterward, if they were worth it."

"How did you meet Easton?"

"We went to high school together. Girl, I was in love with him and he knew it. Everyone did, and I suffered extreme humiliation because I'm gay. But Easton protected me. If he saw someone harassing me, he'd let them have it, and no one messed with Easton. After a while, people stopped and accepted it. I was forever grateful to him but mad as hell I couldn't have him." He cackled at his last comment while I smiled along with him.

"I wish I could remember our life together because he seems like a great guy. That is, if I could get him to talk."

"He is a great guy. Easton always took care of the underdogs, but he always kept his distance from people. Very few became a part of his life. Then you came along and changed him for the better. Easton became social. In your early years, you both made it a point to invite people over, especially me, and make people feel part of your life. The way he gazed at you … It was pure love. When you'd talk or were across the room, I'd catch Easton gaze with adoration. It's why no one could understand why you cheated on him."

I shrugged, and said, "Me neither." The room went quiet, all except the combing of hair and the crinkle of aluminium foil. I finally said, "Since Easton is the only one who could shed some light on the affair, could you tell me about how you and I met?"

"Sure. I heard about the case details later on."

I closed my eyes to listen to the slight song in Mitchell's voice when he spoke. He indulged me regarding the first day we met, and his voice made the story much better.

(Sixteen) Pistol-Whipped

~~~~~~

The preparations began. Over the next several days, we talked about guns, and our undercover relationship. I demanded guidelines. Easton knew of my vulnerability, so the relationship needed to be controlled.

At the kitchen table, we discussed our next steps. "Tomorrow we will go to a shooting range so you can get used to guns, see how others hold them, and learn to shoot. This will be the first of many."

I put my head on the table and said, "Can't I just be around your gun and see how you hold it?"

He ruffled my hair. "Are you flirting with me, Brand?"

I knocked his arm and chuckled. Easton listened to how I felt about things, one of them being my fear of guns. Before discussions started, I asked him about my compensation. He told me he had taken care of it. I would receive monthly compensation along with a lump sum at the end. I asked if I needed to sign papers. He brushed over the fact that he made me a confidential informant. Other than him, no one else knew I would be on the case, which made sense if I was a confidential informant. Even so, I was somewhat reluctant until he handed over the first month's payment. It would last long enough for me to figure out the next steps in life afterwards. We made small talk, which helped me avoid taking things too personal.

I sat back in my chair and let my smile fade. I wanted him to know the conversation just switched to serious. "We have to setup some guidelines for our undercover relationship." Easton frowned, and asked, "Guidelines? Does this mean sex is out of the question?"

"Come on, be serious. What are the living arrangements, house, condo?"

"We'll be set up in a townhouse in a small community area. The guy we're investigating lives there. He has a trophy wife, no children, and wears more gold than Flavor Flav."

My body slackened in my chair. "Trophy wife? So I'm up against some stiff competition."

Easton retrieved a folder from the other room. It contained information on our guy and his wife. Lucio Tumicelli had been on the police radar for almost his entire life. In his youth, he ran a small operation where he and his friends followed men home from bars, mugged them and took their money. They threatened to kill the men if they ever turned them in. At twenty, he ran out of luck when he tried to mug an undercover cop. He served a year for his first offense. After that, his dealings got more serious, and he became more cautious. The claims against Lucio had to do with tax evasion, money laundering, and drug trafficking. Even though he didn't control the drug business, Lucio knew and worked closely with the main kingpin. The police wanted the top person, and to find him or her, we needed Lucio and Anna.

Lucio's wife, Anna Marconi-Tumicelli, once a New Jersey beauty queen, had also been under surveillance since she married Lucio five years ago. A fifteen-year difference in age, Lucio's face had already started to betray him. Anna was petite, athletic with dark hair, and olive skin that drew attention to her light blue eyes. The kind of woman you never want to leave alone with your husband or boyfriend.

"These two are our main targets. Our townhouse will be directly across the street from theirs." He slid the file closer to me.

I browsed it. "I think I better start exercising." In an instant, I grew embarrassed of my appearance. The picture of Anna in the file resembled one taken at a model photo shoot. She did have the qualities of a beauty queen.

"It isn't a competition. Your job is to be my faithful girlfriend. Become friends with Anna and get her to trust you. The closer we get to both of them, the more information we can obtain."

"Are you really that clueless about women? Of course it's a competition. I have to get up to speed on presentation. Anna will not befriend someone she finds ugly, dull, or boring." I sat back and let out a heavy sigh because I needed a lot of work.

"If you'd like, I can take you to a friend of mine who will give you an entire makeover free of charge."

"So I *am* ugly, dull, and boring." My face burned.

"Shit! I didn't say that. I offered you help, if that's what you think you need." He put the file back.

Over my shoulder, I said, "I need. Call her, please."

"Who?" Easton came back into the room.

"Your makeover friend."

"Sexist. It's a guy." He folded his arms in front of him and then laughed.

That bit of news made me happy. Good to know he didn't have a close 'woman' friend in the beauty business. I didn't need to become jealous that early in the game.

Easton set me up with an appointment the next day with his friend, Mitchell Godfrey. Gorgeous, but gay as gay could be. I loved him and the magic he did with his hands and imagination. He had his work cut out for him. Mitchell squeezed and shaped me like a tube of toothpaste. Within a matter of hours, I not only improved my image, but *I* even wanted to date me. Mitchell cut my weeping willow hair into a short, layered, sassy hairstyle—short all around with longer layers on top, and gave life to my brown hair with golden highlights. He used a light bronze tone on my pale skin, champagne eye shadow to make my green eyes pop and thick, long eyelashes. Then he added a dash of mauve lip-gloss. To add to my already rockin' look, Mitchell took me to the shop next door to his salon, and had the owner help me with some outfits. I promised Mitchell I would pay him back, and he whispered, "No need. Easton took care of it. Just be good to him." The undercover relationship had worked even with his friend.

Easton was surprised. He couldn't keep his eyes off me or stop with the compliments. We went shoe shopping to match my new outfits. I felt like I won the lottery.

It was mid-week when we went to the shooting range. I had already held Easton's gun in my hand. The heavy, cold metal triggered thoughts of death. How many people had Easton killed with it? How would it feel to have a bullet shoot through my skin, tear into organs and muscles until it lodged against bone or exited the other side? I shivered at the thought.

Inside the range were ten rows of booths where the shooters stood and aimed at the target on the other side of the room. The target distance depended on the expertise of the shooter. We stopped behind a huge guy with a Frankenstein build, who happened to have gotten off three shots to the heart at thirty-three yards. An accumulation of saliva stuck in my throat.

Easton held out his hand and shook Frankenstein's. "Good to see you, Doyle. How have you been?"

He took his hand and nodded. "Can't complain."

Doyle's eyes outlined my entire body. He smiled and then his eyes bounced from my eyes to my ... well he didn't make it to my feet. Doyle wasn't too subtle. I folded my arms in front to block some of his view. He asked, "Who might this be?"

Easton placed his hand on my lower back, and introduced us. "Doyle, this is Brand. Brand, this is Doyle." To me, he said, "Doyle and I worked on a few cases together." Doyle held out his hand, which forced me to drop my arms. My hand got lost in his, and he didn't want to let it go. When Easton saw me trying to take my hand back, he said, "I think she's attached to hers, Doyle." When Doyle realized what Easton meant, he paused and then let it go. I shook it a few times to dry it out from his heat. "We're just here for some target practice."

Doyle took off his goggles and slid the chamber out of the gun, a lesson later learned. He pointed behind him with his thumb and said, "You can use this booth. I'm done."

They shook hands and wished each other well. Doyle turned to me, smiled and said, "Give me a call if you have any problems with this guy. I'll show you how to shoot a gun." Easton gave him a slight nudge, and turned toward the booth.

Occupied with the target, Easton said, "I think he likes

you."

"You think? Better that than getting pistol-whipped by him."

He handed me some goggles. "You never shoot here without protective eye gear." He put on a pair, indicated for me to do the same. Easton handled the gun as he explained its use. "Always point the gun away from you. Make sure the safety is on before and after you use it. Keep your finger off the trigger. The only time you put your finger on the trigger is when you aim and shoot." He turned the gun sideways and away from us. "The safety lever is on when it's down. On the left side is the release button for the magazine. Press and remove the magazine from the pistol. Pull back on the assembly so you can pull out the cartridge in the chamber. This is how to check to see if it's loaded, and if it is, then you unload the gun this way."

My armpits roasted and sweat droplets formed on my forehead and under my nose. The whole gun idea disturbed me. My right leg started to shake a little. I patted underneath my nose and glanced around to make sure we were alone. I spoke low. "Do I really need to carry a gun?"

Easton noticed my tension. He placed the gun on the counter so he could move behind me to massage my shoulders. "I know this is new to you. Guns are scary, especially around people who don't know how to use them. You might never need to use it. I hope I'm always there to protect you. But what if I'm not? What if I'm running after Lucio and Anna pulls a gun on you? I need to know, just like you need to know, that you can take care of yourself." My head rolled around from the massage, then he stopped to maneuver in front of me. "For both of our sakes, you need to learn how to handle and shoot it."

I rolled my shoulders, cracked what knuckles I could crack, and nodded. Easton held the gun to continue on how to load it. Press down on the magazine release button and remove the magazine. Load the magazine by sliding the cartridges with my thumb. Insert the magazine into the frame until it catches and secures in the frame with a click. The word *magazine* made my thoughts wander to Mitchell's salon, but my thoughts were broken when Easton handed me the gun and said, "Now you try to remove it." It took me a couple of attempts to get it out of the chamber. The hardest part was loading it.

"Good. You're a quick learner. We're ready to shoot now." Easton pressed a button on the right side of the booth and the target came toward us to about two feet away. He pointed to the middle of the target. "This is where you want to hit it." Easton pressed another button, and the target moved about ten yards away.

"Pick up the gun. Make sure the safety is on." Both my hands held the grip area. Easton told me to move all the way to the counter as he walked behind and brought his arms around both sides of me. He straightened my arms a little more, placed my right hand on the grip, pointer finger on the trigger, my left hand overlapped the right.

Seriously? I couldn't concentrate with his body courting mine. To lighten the mood, I asked, "Is that a candy bar in your pocket or are you—"

Easton put some distance between us, and said, "Concentrate."

I wiggled a little to loosen the gap along with the tension. I held the gun straight out in front of me.

He switched the safety off. "Okay, Brand, take your

first shot."

My hands relaxed a little on the grip as I pumped my finger on the trigger to get a feel for the resistance. As I held the icy heaviness of the gun, I began to think about how it could change a life forever. It's so quick, which brought an image of my mother to mind. Like the unexpected destruction caused by a gun, my mother did not expect to die that morning. One false move and she was gone. She went from life to death in seconds. I relaxed my arms, brushed my shoulder against my cheek to wipe away a tear, and then straightened my arms again. On the fourth pump of my finger, I brought it all the way back and the bullet shot out toward the target. It startled me. My held breath came out like a gust of wind, and a few more tears dropped as I put my arms on the counter.

I stared at the target. "I don't think I even hit it." I felt shaky all over.

Easton patted my shoulder. "Who cares? It was your first shot. I'm proud of you."

I turned to the target, closed my left eye to concentrate on the bull's eye, and pulled the trigger again. This time I saw the target move. I continued to shoot for a good hour. By the time we left, my arms were hot and stiff like an ironing board. It had been the first time of many, and even though I got better, the nausea and dislike of guns remained.

(Seventeen) Ta-da!

~~~~~~

Mitchell finished the story, placed his hands on my shoulders, and said, "Ta-da!"

I opened my eyes. My hair resembled the way he described it when we first met. The change brightened my mood. Finally, for the first time since I woke from the accident, I felt good about myself. For the moment, I pushed my flaws out of my mind.

Mitchell put his cheek next to mine and asked, "What do you think?"

Tears sprinkled the front of my face. "I love it." I put my hands over his. "Thank you. Really. I can't begin to tell you how much I appreciate this and not just the hair. You helped me understand Easton better. It's as if he locked himself off from the world. In the hospital and the first day home, Easton talked mostly about me and then he grew silent. But you let me see a little more of him."

He gave my shoulders a tender squeeze, sat down next to me, and said, "I'm glad. Besides, I kind of felt guilty because I was so mean to you."

My shoulders twitched before I said, "From what you told me, I deserved it."

"No you didn't. You were always friendly to me, so I should have kept my nose out of it. I guess I care too much about Easton. He didn't have many friends, by choice of course, and even when around others, he had this loneliness about him, an inability to fill an inner void. It's understandable with having his parents. Easton was on his own long before he physically left that house. But this is all just my assumption though, because Easton isn't one to let anyone get too close. That is, until you came along. I got mad when I heard about the affair, but your betrayal infuriated me more because there are so few he lets in."

I observed myself in the mirror, and then turned to Mitchell. "I'm truly sorry I hurt him. A good reason for me to get my memory back is to find out why I cheated on him. It sounds as if he was a great husband. I couldn't have been that callous to cheat for no reason."

He shook his head and said, "You weren't. But I can't help you out as to why you cheated. Once I found out, we didn't talk again, so you never confided in me as to why."

I put my hand on his arm. "Is that why you didn't know about my car accident? Or come by the hospital or house?"

Mitchell blew out a breath of air and ran his fingers through his hair. "Honestly, I don't know why Easton never told me. Maybe he didn't want to hear me put you down. I flapped my mouth when someone mentioned your name. Sometimes Easton would get pissed at me. Even after all that happened, he still loved you and didn't want to hear people insult you."

There was a knock on the door. We both turned to find Easton outside the shop. Perspiration misted his face with a tint of color. I muttered, "Uh, oh, he's pissed."

Mitchell asked why as he unlocked the door.

Easton pushed the door open. "What the fuck, Brand?" He stomped toward me. "I finished in the yard, searched the house for you, only to find my car gone. I appreciate it."

I bit my lower lip. "I'm sorry. I was upset so—"

"You took off with my car without telling me. What if I did that to you? Oh yeah, that's right, I can't because you don't have a car. You totaled it!"

Mitchell came by me and said, "She wanted—"

"Don't get involved, Mitchell! And with her, it's always about what she wants." In a dark tone, he said, "Give me the keys."

I shoved my shaky hand into my pocket and handed them over. Easton opened the door, so I asked, "Are you leaving me here?"

He turned so fast it caught me off guard. Easton's head tilted down, but his eyes stared at me. He clenched his jaw a few times, and then said, "What do you think?"

I took a step forward. "I don't know that's why I asked. Easton, I'm sorry. I shouldn't have taken your car especially since I didn't ask."

His body loosened as he said, "Let's go."

Before I followed him, I gave Mitchell an apologetic glance.

The drive home was brutal—the air heavy, my body tense. Easton's anger stifled any movement, and my heart raced with every traffic stop. It felt like how it would be if on trial for murder. The wait for a verdict. I turned toward my side window to avoid him. People rode bikes as they took advantage of the great weather. As busy and crowded as it had been outside the car, that's about how scared and lonely I felt inside. The few things I've learned about my past saddened me. Uncertain of the present and future, I didn't know what else I could do. Loss of memory had its limitations.

The car door shut, and I watched Easton disappear into the house. So preoccupied in thought, I didn't realize we were home. I stepped out onto the driveway. Some neighbors pulled weeds, cut grass, or planted flowers around their yards. A few noticed me, smiled, and then returned to their tasks. I dropped my head as I entered the house.

Easton was on his computer in the kitchen. I walked in, but he didn't budge. I offered another apology before I went outside on the patio, sat with my arms wrapped around my legs. My face dampened. Soon after, I heard the door open then a shadow fell over me. "I didn't mean to get so mad. When I couldn't find you, I panicked and thought you left for good. Then I saw my car gone, and the fear and anger mixed together."

My weakened voice garbled my words. I cleared my throat and repeated, "It's fine. I deserved it. I shouldn't have taken the car at all."

His shadow moved to the chair next to mine. We both drifted into the distance, not at anything in particular, but somewhere that allowed us the comfort of silence. We sat in our own thoughts, wondering what we should say, and what we shouldn't say. I was out of ideas.

Easton avoided eye contact when his pained words came out. "How can this be fixed?"

My right hand came around to wipe my tears and nose before I told him that I didn't know.

His words were weak as if all hope faded. "You can't remember, and I ... well, I'd rather forget some things."

I took a deep breath and said, "Like my affair?" His head twisted in my direction with wide eyes. "Mitchell told me."

He let out a whispered 'shit.' "He had no right. I wasn't even going to tell you."

"I know. But I begged him to tell me why the two of you were so mad at me. I need to know about me, you and us. We can't move forward without my memory. Or I should say I can't move forward."

Our words drifted around the yard. My left arm felt a soft touch. I took hold of Easton's hand. "I can't even begin to apologize. I can't believe I did that. It's very strange to ask for forgiveness for things I can't remember, but it seems I have a lot to apologize for." Easton remained silent. What did I expect him to say? "Easton?"

He leaned his head against the chair. "Yeah?"

"Please tell me more about the case. What did it entail? You said that's when we fell in love. I want to hear about what we did on the case. What made us fall in love?"

"There wasn't anything specific, it—"

"Just happened." We turned and smiled at one another. I gave his hand a soft squeeze and let it go. "Tell me about it."

He sighed and then complied. "We did a lot to prepare. It was important for us to know as much as possible about Lucio and Anna."

(Eighteen) Altered

~~~~~~

My wardrobe grew with an array of outfits. We spent weeks at the range, went over the files along with different strategies. Days and nights, we studied video footage of our neighbors, Anna and Lucio. She was punctual and a creature of habit. Every day at 7:00 am, she headed out for a jog. She returned home by 7:45 am, and then didn't leave the house until noon. Her petite body, giddy with money, went on a shopping spree for clothes, shoes or pampering until 2:00 pm when she met with her friend, Veronique. Veronique is a French woman with a bruised American accent, messy white hair, red lipstick that redefined her lips, and a small dog I could have used as a makeup brush. In other words, not in the same league as Anna.

Easton pointed at the video of Anna. "You should start getting into shape."

I sat on the couch next to him in mid-calf black stretch pants and a black shirt. Around Easton, I wore makeup and fixed my hair to appear messy. That was the sassiness in me. "I didn't realize I was out of shape. Besides, I'm not really a competitor."

"Now you can jog into competition. It'll be a good way to get to know Anna."

"Jog? I draw the line there. It's one of the worst workouts. Do you know what kind of toll it takes on your body?" Easton stared at the video. "Doesn't look like it has affected hers. As a matter of fact—" "Stop! I don't care to hear how her body is affecting yours."

Easton bumped his shoulder against me. "Come on.

While you jog, you can get some information from her."

I repositioned. "Why don't you go with her?"

He wrapped his arms around me. "Because I'm faithful to my sweet, adorable girlfriend, Claire Munroe."

I pushed him away. "I don't even get to pick my pretend name? I suppose you have a nice normal name."

"David Gibson."

I nudged against him and asked, "Wouldn't you like me to be a Marilyn?"

"No. But you can pick your other name."

My head swirled in his direction. "What other name? There's more to this than us as a couple to survey Lucio and Anna. Why didn't you tell me this before?"

"It was important for you to learn how to use a gun. Now that you're Annie Oakley and have learned about the case for weeks, I figured it's time for you to know the second part of our infiltration and surveillance. We'll move into our townhouse in a week so we need to be ready."

My body crumpled on the couch. "I'm horrible with names. Please tell me I don't have to play two people."

"We both will, except it won't be in real life. Lucio and Anna are not the main ringleaders. These two have to get the information back and forth to the top person some way—setup the drug arrivals and money. With the crackdown on terrorists, most organized crime groups are finding new ways to transfer information and money. And they are creative. My guess is Lucio and Anna do it through Alter Life." I jumped a bit to tuck my legs underneath me. "Alter Life? I like the place already."

"Good because we'll monitor them there too."

"Is it near the townhouse?"

"No. It's a virtual world." I shook my head and shrugged my shoulders. "It's on the internet. It's a virtual world where you create an avatar, a name, and do all kinds of things. It's another life—a dream life that many people would like to have but can't."

I pointed at him and said, "Now that's a life I want to sign up for."

He typed in the website, which brought us to the main page. The first thing I saw, once everything downloaded, was Easton's avatar, Callum Stone. In this virtual world, you choose a name and an avatar, which is an animated figure that represents real people as they explore the virtual world. Avatars walk and run, the same as human movements. I could even attach an animation to my avatar for facial expressions. Easton had already created his avatar. It was my turn to pick a name and a figure to represent me. I picked Candy Catwick. I wanted an avatar completely different from me: big boobs, dark hair, and purple eyes. The whole creation process was similar to a body part factory without the cost. Then I picked an outfit. Until this point, my life was normal, so I picked an outfit that would make Lady Gaga jealous— a purple corset with open slits on the sides and small silver spikes across the top and bottom, along with black fishnet stockings and black platform shoes with silver spikes on the toe part.

Easton pointed and laughed. "Really? That's what you want to wear?"

I flipped my head away from Easton. "You're just jealous."

"Of what?"

"That you can't wear a corset and fishnet stockings."

Easton took over the computer and said, "Oh yeah, like totally."

I listened to him clarify that being in the virtual world is referred to as *inworld*. So Easton and I were inworld as Candy and Callum. Easton explained how the virtual world worked. There were icons on the screen to search for places, find people, our avatar's friend list, and our avatar's inventory of clothes, body parts, animations, and so on. He typed in a place, such as Paris, and all the places in the virtual world that have to do with Paris emerged. Then he double-clicked one of the links to the place, the screen blacked out, and then all of a sudden a virtual Paris appeared on our screen as his avatar appeared there—teleported.

Easton sent me a teleport request, I accepted it, and teleported to the same place he was in Paris. I saw the Eiffel Tower and Notre Dame. Never visited Paris in real life, but the virtual world created Paris so I had the opportunity to see it. I typed in a local chat box that anyone in the vicinity could read, but he sent me a private message to stay out of public conversation.

This AL site was truly an altered life. What I might not be able to do in real life, due to money shortage, I could do in AL. Cities, countries, zoos, and universities had a presence in the virtual world. If I wanted to see what Princeton University looks like from a campus point of view, all I had to do was teleport there. Some avatars owned businesses, they bought land, houses, clothes, and went to so many different places with little to no cost. It was like living out a dream or a fairy tale. I sat back and let out a breath of air. "This is unbelievable. I wish I heard of this site earlier."

"Don't get too excited about it. We need to practice. We have to start calling each other by our undercover names to get used to them. I don't want us out to dinner over at the neighbor's and you say, 'Pass the wine,

Easton.'"

"I'd say, 'Please pass the wine, David.'"

"This is important. We have to refer to each other as David and Claire—the couple."

I dropped my head back. "Easton. David. We should let it come naturally."

"Really? Are we a loving couple? Do we adore each other? I don't want to take your hand and you snatch it back. As of right now, we are David and Claire, head over heels in love."

Easton bent over the back of the couch, kissed my cheek and went to the kitchen to get us a few beers. I was still on AL when he returned. He put the beers down, logged me off, and sat next to me. Easton raised his beer and said, "To our future. Whatever and wherever it will take David and Claire." We clinked beers. I took a sip of mine and watched the video play of Lucio and Anna. Easton moved the little wisps of hair that fell on my ear. The sensation tickled my nerves. He moved closer to me, his face a breath away from my ear, and he whispered, "I love the image you're sportin'."

I rose. "Wait! Easton—"

"No, no, dear Claire."

"Fine. David. We set boundaries. When we're in the townhouse, we don't have to be lovey-dovey. I have my own room and you have yours. It's only, and I stress 'only' when we're around other people that we act as if we can't stand to be apart. We don't need to rehearse hand holding, kissing, and perhaps a pat on the ass. We've both been there with other people."

He moved over and said, "I don't want neither of us to blow our cover."

My arms flapped about to get my point across. "And drinking beer and getting horny won't make our undercover stuff become real. This is awkward. I knew it would be, but—"

Easton put his beer down and stood. "This is why I think we need to get into the mindset of David Gibson and Claire Munroe, and *show* the world how much they care about each other. Then it won't seem so awkward and weird when we have to do it."

"I'm uncomfortable. Time for bed."

In my room, I grappled with the idea of make believe without letting it affect my feelings. How the hell was I going to manage that?

The next morning, Easton wore running shorts, a shirt to match, and shoes.

I asked, "What's with the outfit?"

He stretched out in the kitchen. "For jogging."

"You don't jog."

"I do now." He took his iPhone from the table, where a picture of Anna laid, put the earplugs in and left.

I was furious. He thought either it would aggravate me, or I would jog with him. If he wanted Anna, who was I to stand in his way? I made breakfast and went into the backyard with his laptop to get back onto AL. Easton came back and stretched next to me as I browsed around the virtual world.

With an annoyed expression, I asked, "Do you have to stretch out right here?"

He sprinkled me with the sweat from his hair. "Someone woke up on the wrong side of the bed?"

I tilted to the side, pushed him away, and turned back to the laptop. There was a desktop icon for AL so I double-clicked on it to log on. My avatar stood in the middle of some dance floor with disco lights flashing.

Seventies music played "Night Fever" by the Bee Gees. Someone had typed in chat for me to click on the blue ball to dance, and when I did, my avatar got her groove on. I had two left feet in real life.

Easton watched my avatar dance as he bent over the chair. He laughed and went into the house. It was as if he wanted to provoke me. Who practices love? It would come into play when needed.

My avatar went from one dance place to another. Some guy sent me a private text. He asked for my name, so I used my alias, Claire. Better that than my real name. We talked about what kind of music we liked and where we were from when Easton read the conversation. "Log out of there."

I ignored his order. "No. What's the big deal?"

Easton closed out of the virtual world. "Because this isn't a game. You're not there to meet people. We're undercover in real life and in the virtual world. If you don't want to practice being a couple, then you had better understand how to act in the virtual world. We need to find out who Lucio and Anna are in that world and where they hang out so we can connect with their boss and ultimately arrest him. I don't need you in AL so you can find yourself a guy."

My body went rigid. I made my way to the glass doors, and said, "Who do you think you are? It's not a big deal to talk to someone. Like he would figure out who I am."

He threw his arms out to the side. "How do you know? You want to spend time on that site, but you can't get used to your real life?"

"Go to hell. I've come a long way, done what you've asked of me, didn't ask questions or give you a hard time. You have no right to treat me as if I've committed a crime. I don't need this shit." I poured myself another cup of coffee, my jitter beans to add to my jitters. I leaned back against the kitchen cabinet and took a drink.

He walked in and said, "Okay. I overreacted." I kept quiet. "I'm sorry. I guess I'm nervous about this whole thing and you involved."

My head cranked to the side. "It's a little late to worry about my involvement."

"No it isn't. You can still back out. We haven't moved into the house. We're still Easton and Brand. You're right, you don't need this shit."

I gestured with my arms sweeping out to the side as if someone was safe at home base, and said "Forget it. I'm invested. We will do this and do it right. We're both nervous and it's getting the best of us. We'll continue to call each other Claire and David, keep it in our heads that we're a couple, and let things fall into place. If we force it now, it will never come easy for us. We have a week to take it slow, get into character, and become the wonderful couple, David and Claire."

Easton shifted his weight to the right. In an attempt to make light of the moment, he asked, "So sex is out of the question?"

Before I left the room, I said, "I don't know. Ask our hand."

(Nineteen) Loosening Amnesia

~~~~~~

2013 - Crystal Lane, Rhode Island

I couldn't believe my sex comment, gutsy and a smartass, all rolled into one. It surprised me how quick I had been with my tongue, whereas after the accident, my words always stalled. The past version of myself seemed unafraid from the version who woke in the hospital. Fear was the main emotion. I had feared never to regain my memory and feared that I would remember a moment I'd rather not know.

While he told me about the case, I started to have flashes of avatars and places in the virtual world. I connected with the story, which meant my amnesia was loosening. The stories of the past revealed an underlying easiness that existed between all our aliases, David and Claire, Candy and Callum. It was natural between the aliases, except now, we had come upon some turbulence. Even so, I trusted Easton after waking from the coma, just as I had trusted him when I got into his car after rehab.

I went inside to get a glass of water, and yelled out, "I have a tendency to trust you. Things always came naturally between us, am I right?"

"Yeah. From the start, we never tried to impress each other. The times of discomfort came when we had to hold back our true feelings for one another."

I came out, rested my hip on his chair and asked, "So you had feelings for me early on?"

Easton went over to the Jacuzzi to make sure the cover was secure. "Same as you. I always joked around about how hot I thought Anna was while I secretly thought of you."

I spoke with caution. "Except for now. You look at me with disgust."

Easton went to the patio doors and said, "I'll meet you down here in five minutes. You might want to change into a nicer outfit. Sweats won't cut it."

Even though he didn't respond to my comment, excitement carried me upstairs. I opened my closet door and put on white capris, a pink top, and white open-toe sandals with a decorative flower on the middle of my foot. I applied makeup and styled my hair with gel. I went downstairs a little too fast and lost my shoe on the second to the last step. Easton waited by the door as I slipped my foot into my sandal. His head dropped when he let out a small snort.

I stopped on the bottom stair and said, "What? I'm excited to get out of here."

We drove to a small airport. There was a flat-roofed, long building on an expanse of land with two airplanes on the side of it. The planes had two long wings toward the front. Four windows lined each side where the pilot and passengers sat. A lump formed in my throat.

An older man of about sixty came by us, saying, "Damn, I gotta lock these doors." He put his hand out, but instead, pulled Easton into a bear hug, and smacked him on the back a few times. "How you doin'?"

Easton released him and said, "Good." Directed at me, he said, "This is a good friend of mine, Gilberto."

Gilberto gave me a stern look and said, "Yeah, we've met before."

"Unfortunately Brand doesn't remember."I held out my hand. "Hello." Gilberto studied my hand as if covered in feces before taking it. He held my gaze, dropped my hand and then turned his attention to Easton.

My arms crossed in front of me. Judgment was heavy, and I didn't have the strength to confront it.

Gilberto signaled for us to follow him outside and asked Easton, "What brings you here?"

"I was wondering if we could get someone to fly us to Rhode Island."

Gilberto and I stopped and he asked, "Rhode Island?"

Easton gestured to me and said, "Yeah. I want to show Brand something. Does anyone need flight time?"

He ignored me when he spoke. "No, but I have the time. I'll get you there."

Gilberto checked the exterior and wheels of the plane, and then asked, "Any luggage?"

"No."

Gilberto's eyes caved in when he asked, "So you're returning today?"

Easton shrugged with another "no."

We were both confused by Easton's responses, but neither of us questioned him. Easton offered his hand as I climbed the ladder to get onto the plane and then followed behind. He sat in the seat next to Gilberto, and indicated for me to choose one of the four leather seats behind them. I sat behind Easton. We buckled our seatbelts and the two of them put on headsets. I couldn't wait to arrive so I didn't have to deal with anymore of Gilberto's sneers.

My mind shuffled through the darkness of memory to find anything about Rhode Island. Is that where the investigation took place? Did we go on our honeymoon there? I stared out the window at the different colored patches of terrain, trees, and buildings. All of a sudden, I remembered a yellow place. It was quiet with a forest nearby. I smiled and held onto the thought until I could ask Easton.

We arrived in Rhode Island, and they walked into a similar building while I stood outside. Easton dialed a cab company and gave our location.

Easton said to us, "They'll be here in ten minutes." All I could think was ten minutes seemed too long to be around Gilberto.

Gilberto pretended I wasn't there as he addressed Easton. "When will you want to come back?"

He glanced at me and then at Gilberto. "I haven't taken that into account yet."

"Since you don't have any luggage, I'd say you'll be back soon."

The two of them talked while I wandered outside to scope out the distance. A cab threw dirt around when it approached the building. I watched the dust settle. Easton and Gilberto came out, shook hands and we got into the cab. He gave an address to the driver.

Before I could forget again, I turned and blurted out, "Will we see a yellow house?"

"A yellow house?"

"Yes. I remembered a yellow house with a forest nearby."

He smiled. "That's right. Yeah, we lived in a yellow townhouse during our surveillance. It's where I had planned to take you, and then I thought we could probe your memory."

The cab stopped at a car rental place. It began to drizzle while we waited for the car. Easton said, "We finally finished our research on Anna and Lucio."

(Twenty) The Wallflower

~~~~~~

In the July heat, we unloaded our belongings at the townhouse and explored the place. Our yellow home for a while with white trim. Flowers and bushes ran the yard's boundary. The main floor had a living room, kitchen, and guest washroom. Upstairs were two bedrooms with a shared washroom. A door under the staircase led to a finished basement. From the inside, it looked more spacious than from the outside. Through the dining room's sliding glass door was a small patio with a built-in barbeque.

I took the smaller room to the left and began putting my things away. Easton came into the room. "You can't put your clothes in the drawers. If someone comes here and finds your stuff in this room, they'll get suspicious. Put all the clothes in the main bedroom."

We had practiced our relationship back home and things had come naturally. To get into character as David and Claire, we would hold hands while watching television on the couch, kissed when one of us left or went to bed, while at the same time I reminded myself it was a job, no love interest existed. Once we arrived at the townhouse though, we became cranky and tense.

At the start of our first week, I woke in enough time to see Anna leave the house for her jog. I wasn't at the point of kicking and screaming, but I put off exercising until we settled in. Anna had a natural beauty. Even without makeup, her petite body nicely tucked into her shorts and shirt. When she took off, I went into the kitchen for a cup of coffee, sat at the table and started the laptop we had bought for our inworld surveillance. I took the opportunity to roam around the virtual world of Alter Life (AL) to become acquainted with it and see what it had to offer.

AL had captured my interest, and I had been antsy to get back on. I slipped on my headphones and logged in. My avatar, Candy, appeared in the same place as the last time; a disco club with a disco ball's beamed lights over the dance floor. Several people told me in local chat to click on the blue ball to start dancing.

Instead, I did a search for karaoke, clicked on a link under one of the places and teleported there. The whole teleporting was cool. The screen faded to black and a message informed me I was going to the place I chose. An avatar sang at a microphone while several avatars watched. With the avatar's microphone activated, the person sang in real life. Wherever the person lived, I hoped no one could hear him. True to a real life karaoke bar, this guy sang off key. I couldn't help but laugh to myself while others applauded his failed efforts in local chat.

The coffee machine beeped to indicate the two hours of warming were over. I logged out of AL to check on our neighbors. As I was about to head upstairs for a shower, Easton happened to come down the stairs. He looked sexier than normal. He hadn't seen me yet, so I turned back toward the kitchen and slipped into the guest washroom. At his house, I went from bedroom to bathroom before coffee. Damnit! I had wasted too much time in the virtual world. Mornings were good to him. Mornings hated me. I looked like a cereal breath. My hair stuck up, dried saliva in the corners of my mouth, and (I blew into my hand) major bad breath. I turned on the faucet, put my hands underneath the water and splashed it on my face, concentrating on the crispy crust. Then I ran my wet hands through my hair to control the strands at attention. It didn't put me on the same level as Easton, but I believed it would help with the shell shock.

When I heard him pour his coffee, I tried to slip out, but he turned and winked. Before I could make a break for it with minimal exposure, he strode over to me and kissed me on the lips. I held my breath, hoping the stench didn't escape, and by his reaction, I held it in good. Then I made my way upstairs.

I finished with my shower then came back down to find Easton gone. It was mid-morning and I knew Anna would be home until noon. I made sure to dress appropriately for shopping with white capris, a pink top, and white open-toe sandals with a decorative flower in the middle of my foot. I ran gel through my hair to create layered chunks, and my makeup made my skin flawless. An opportunity to wipe out my earlier disaster.

I ventured out onto the back porch. The waist high fence outlined the yard. Not high enough to keep any nosy neighbors out of our business, especially the man next door, who made it a point to lower his sunglasses and scope me out from top to bottom. I smiled at him and then went back inside. There wouldn't be much time spent in the backyard. I heard voices in the front of the house, so I opened the door and saw Easton and Anna. She wore a short sleeve yellow blouse that tied at the waist to accentuate her stomach muscles. Tan, mid-thigh white shorts coddled her lifted, round ass, and she finished off with a pair of white high heel sandals that showed off her calf and thigh muscles. She had the sides of her dark hair pinned in the back with soft curls over her shoulders. Anna placed her hand on Easton's arm as she gave him a flirtatious smile.

Just before I could shut the door and go upstairs to change, Easton called my name and signaled me over. It felt like high school all over again. Taunts and giggles behind my back when I passed the popular girls with their shiny hair, thin, curvaceous bodies, and boyfriends I could only dream about. One boy in particular, Matt, had kept my attention all four years of high school while he dated the head cheerleader, Bonnie. He filled my dreams, and when I saw them together at school, I cried inside until I got home to let it out. When it came to presence, shape and style, Bonnie had it. I had felt like a wallflower, kind of like I felt at that moment when I saw Easton and Anna talking.

My hand gripped the doorknob to keep my legs from buckling. When I stiffened my body, I released the knob and joined them.

Easton kissed me and placed his hand on the center of my back. "Hey hon. This is our neighbor, Anna. Anna, this is my better half, Claire."

Anna removed her hand from Easton's arm, took a step to the side, and straightened her back. Her rigid demeanor let me know I intruded on their conversation. I held out my right hand and said, "Pleased to meet you."

She took my hand with a firm grip, and responded, "Nice to meet you, too." She clenched my hand harder, and then let it go. "I was just telling your husb ... I mean, boyfriend about the neighborhood. David tells me you jog."

I slid my arm around Easton's waist, and gave the best smile I could find in my bag of tricks. "I do. Unfortunately I've been out of practice for the past few weeks due to our move."

"Maybe I'll see you back out on the trail soon." Anna

looked at her watch and said, "I'm sorry. I didn't notice the time. Please forgive me for cutting this short, but I have some errands to run. I'll see you both tomorrow night. Take care."

When she left, I could still smell a faint whiff of her perfume. Easton watched her body sway and muscular legs disappear into the driver's seat of a BMW. He followed me into the house.

Once inside, I turned to face him, and asked, "I jog?"

Easton shrugged and said. "Yeah. I thought we decided you would become jogging partners with Anna. You know, get back on the trail soon."

I jabbed my finger into his chest. "You decided, Easton. I suggested you go with Miss Beauty Queen Anna."

He laughed, bent his head with a sly smile and said, "Tsk, tsk. If I didn't know better, I would think you're jealous."

I went into the kitchen to get some ice water. He came in, smacked my butt, and took a glass from the cabinet.

My eyes crinkled when I jumped away from him. "Knock it off. Boundaries, remember?"

He filled his glass with water, gulped it down, and just stood there.

I went into the other room where he joined me on the couch next to the chair.

Easton paused before saying, "You look good."

"Pfftt ... sure. Next to little miss sugar cube, I resemble a Powder Puff Girl."

He laughed. "No you don't. More like a sour grape."

I threw the chair's decorative pillow at him and waved a hand in front of my face. "Why don't you get rid of your rancid smell?"

"I should. I didn't know it would be this hot in Rhode

Island. My balls are sweating."

My head fell back as I said, "What is wrong with you?"

He pretended to be serious. "What? Don't you want to be the kind of couple that tells each other everything?"

"Not at all. I want to know as little about your stink and bodily fluids as possible. Oh, and by the way, what's happening tomorrow night?"

Before he ran upstairs, he said, "Our Anna invited us to dinner at an Italian restaurant in town. She said some of the other neighbors along with the Tumicellis meet there once a month." He gave a thumbs up. "We're off to a good start."

I yelled to him. "And today's plans?"

"Surveillance. We sit tight and watch their comings and goings."

Great. The wallflower had dressed for nothing.

(Twenty-One) Marinating Anger

~~~~~~

Easton said we watched Anna and Lucio come and go the whole day. He pulled in front of the townhouse. It brought me back to the present. The noiseless cul-de-sac had few cars on the street or in the driveways. I got out of the car and peered at the townhouse. A restlessness made my hair stand on end along with goose bumps the length of my arm. I saw visions in my mind of a restaurant. A bedroom. Easton and I on a bed. Why was I nervous? Did we have sex? I couldn't get the full picture and it made me anxious. Frustrated.

Easton started the car, went around the circle and drove a block away. My eyes bounced from townhouse to forest waiting for him to rejoin me. I thought about the restaurant and the people who had been there. I got a glimpse of a woman with dark shoulder length hair, petite and muscular. It could have been Anna. If so, I had understood why Easton had found her attractive. A flash of us in bed, fully clothed, but even in these flashes, I felt restless.

Easton arrived, pulled me toward the forest, and we found ourselves on a dirt path. Images of the past raced through my mind, so I stopped to catch a glimpse of a recollection.

I closed my eyes to get a full vision. With my eyes still closed, I said, "Anna. Was she petite and well-built with long brown hair?"

"Yes."

I opened my eyes to see how he would respond to my next comment. "Anna is beautiful."

He nodded and said, "Yes."

"One word responses won't help."

Easton stopped for a moment and said, "What do you want me to say? Yes she was beautiful with muscular legs and arms and a tight ass that I wanted to grab—"

"Fine! I get it."

We continued through the forest. Beneath the tall trees existed a peacefulness, which made me relax. Every now and then, a bird flapped above or a squirrel skirted around. Summer brought the foliage into full bloom. The stillness of the forest magnified the crunching of leaves and sticks beneath our feet. A stroll in the forest required better footwear than sandals. I tripped a few times on overgrown roots, but Easton prevented me from falling.

I broke the forest whispers. "Some of the images that have come to mind are of me nervous."

Without pause, Easton responded, "We were both nervous."

I stopped for a moment to ask, "I'm sure, but what made us, me, nervous? When I got out of the car, I felt edgy, not because of now. I saw us in a restaurant with the woman who you now confirmed as Anna. Then I saw us in a bed, clothed."

Easton paused before he continued to walk. "You were afraid you might give the wrong information or not know how to answer a question."

I drew near. "Wrong information? Why would I give the wrong information and to who?"

Easton had his hands in his pockets. "We had dinner with the neighbors. It was the first time we met with them and their friends. You feared you might blow our cover."

"Did I?"

Easton stopped, and for a brief moment, a faint light traveled over his face. I recognized it as a hint of admiration. "No. You actually did great." He dug the toe of his shoe into a hole. "I'm hungry. Let's eat."

I touched his arm and asked, "How about we go to the restaurant where we met the neighbors?"

"Exactly my thought."

From what I remembered, white Christmas lights brightened the restaurant's outdoor seating. Daytime stole the romanticism. We took a table by a ledge of flowers. The menu items and prices didn't match the ambience of the restaurant—the décor, too predictable, and the prices, too pretentious. The Italian restaurant didn't stand out from any other with its painted faux walls, and fake plants that hung in corners. I people watched as the patio filled before our lunch arrived. Several couples sat near us and a business lunch took place three tables over. I noticed one of the men looking over at us.

I leaned in toward Easton and whispered, "Three tables away are two gentlemen in suits. The one with dark hair keeps glancing over here. Do we know him? Did we ..." I watched Easton's face lose its color as he gripped the sides of the table. He held his breath, his body rigid. He reacted as if he were shot or stabbed. It frightened me.

He rose fast and said, "Let's go."

Confused by his behavior, yet not wanting to argue, we started to leave the outdoor patio when the man called after me and I turned. We inspected each other. There was a familiarity about him, but I couldn't figure out why. Easton saw our exchange, and he was about to approach the man. I placed my hand on his chest and jerked my head in the direction of the exit. Once outside,

Easton balled his hands into fists, pumped them a few times, and his face darkened. I stayed back a few steps in case he wanted to take his anger out on me.

We got into the car. When I thought we'd sit there for the rest of the afternoon, I heard his injured voice.

"That was the guy."

"What guy?"

He refused to look at me. "Aidan Hines. The guy you had an affair with."

My head moved in slow motion in the direction of the restaurant. I sucked in a quick breath, and held it as I thought about the man, recollections, and the current situation. I couldn't imagine Easton's hurt. Glimpses of the man popped in my head. He and I in bed, at the movies, and my face always expressed sadness. I let out the breath I held and wondered what next. What can I say about an affair I only have in pieces? Why did I seem sad? Did I love him?

Sorry didn't cut it. If anything, it would only aggravate the situation. Easton started the car and pulled out of the parking space. We drove for an hour before either of us spoke. The phrase, "The guy you had an affair with" demanded the time and space as it grew in strength, kneading the words.

E aston got us a suite at a hotel with a king size bed and floor to ceiling windows that overlooked a park. He went straight to the mini bar to pour himself a glass of whiskey while I sat in one of the chairs by the window. I didn't want to mention the man I had an affair with, so I decided to question him about our surveillance.

I cleared my throat and said, "What I've heard so far, it sounds like we had fun together on the investigation."

Not a word or sound escaped him. "Were you attracted to Anna?" More silence. I sighed in defeat. "Are we back to silence?" Nothing. I stood and said, "So this is it. This is how it ends? Why you won't help me? Because I slept with someone who I don't even remember sleeping with?"

Tears. They clouded my eyes and thoughts. They seem to be the only thing I could count on. Weakness. He doesn't care. Just when I decided to leave, he finally spoke. "It doesn't matter whether or not you remember the affair, because I still do. I didn't forget it. That's when our marriage troubles began."

With my back to him, I said, "And I can't erase that."

He swirled the ice cubes around and said, "No you can't. While you go down memory lane, I have to relive the good with the bad. I know! You have no recollection. Our situation is messed up."

"How is it that I had an affair with someone who lived in Rhode Island?"

Easton gulped down the rest of his drink. "He doesn't live here. Pure luck that he happens to be here when we are or he followed us. He lives in Dover, on the opposite side of town."

I looked him straight in the eye without thinking about the words. "Did we have a good sex life?"

Easton poured another drink. I waited, hoping he would swallow enough pain to tell me about it. A defeated 'yes' escaped his lips.

To think I strayed without a good reason, if there is such a thing, drove me to question him. Even about our sex life.

"How many times?"

"What?"

I came toward him. "Sex. How often did we have sex?

Two, three times a week?"

His face fell. "What the hell does it matter?"

"Because I want to know if we had an active sex life. Why did I cheat on you? What made me go elsewhere?"

He slammed the glass down on the bar. Easton's eyes seared into me, his voice even and full of angry words. "What made *you* go elsewhere? So it's my fault that *you* decided to wrap your legs around someone else? That's the most fucked up—"

I circled the couch, searched the walls, floor for an answer, and then Easton. "I didn't say it was your fault! What I want is to figure out why I would do it. The person I am now can't understand it."

Easton jiggled his glass as he pointed a finger at me, and said, "The person you are now doesn't understand a goddamn thing." He turned in the opposite direction, shrugged and then stretched out his arms with the ice cubes clinking against the glass. "Go ahead, try to figure out why you destroyed my trust in you and then let me know!"

I saw the slight shake of his hands—the anger marinating inside—the hurt was loud and clear. It brought clarity to me, and I knew Mitchell had been right. I was the love of his life.

"Maybe we should get back home so I could pack and stay somewhere else. Jenny's or—"

"No! Do me a favor and stay away from her."

"If that will make you happy."

Easton stopped all movement. "At this point, not much makes me happy. Just stay away from her. She isn't someone you can trust, especially with your memory."

"Okay. Well, maybe Mitchell will take me in."

"We're not dragging anyone into our problems. It's

no one else's business."

"Too bad!" It came out louder than I meant it to. "Why should I stay with some man who clearly doesn't want to be around me, doesn't want to help get my memory back, and hates me for things I did in the past that I don't know I did."

"Some man?"

"Yes, some man. I don't remember how we met, our wedding, our life together, so as far as I'm concerned, you're just some man."

He approached and grasped my arms, gave them a slight squeeze before he let them go. I rubbed my arms where his hands gripped. Easton put his back to me with his hands on his hips. "I was ... attracted to Anna. But it made me want you more. Anna is beautiful, yet she lacks many things that I liked about you."

"Liked?"

Easton turned toward me and said, "Quit playing semantics."

"I'm sorry. I don't know if you mean how I was in the past or how I still am."

"Well don't. There's a lot more information for you to collect and piece together before worrying about whether I'm using past or present tense."

"Fine. Then answer the question about our sex life?"

Easton's body tensed. It was as if he gathered his anger and pain to make a move. Without a word, he came at me in two strides, forcing me against the window, his body intimate with mine. His lips moved against mine while one hand slipped under my shirt as the other hand wandered without direction around my body. I squirmed and tried to move away from his lips, his body, but his weight and strength were too much. The coldness of the window instinctively forced my body into him. Easton thought I wanted this unsolicited action.

He finally released my lips and gave me a blank stare. With his fingers entangled in my hair, tightening so I couldn't move my head, his breathing intensified as he pushed me into the cold window. He whispered, "I'll show you our sex life." Wisps of hair blew off my face when he spoke. Easton's mouth slammed harder this time and with an agitated need. I quit fighting him. Instead, I began to whimper. I didn't think I had any tears left. My body shivered from his behavior. Easton eased up and then stopped. My hair gave way. He stretched his arms to put distance between us and then put his hands flat against the glass. He stared at me while tears soaked my cheeks. Our foreheads met. We remained that way for a while. Easton said, "I'm sorry. I didn't mean to scare you. I didn't mean to hurt you."

For the first time, I felt his emotions. A tear fell to the floor. It wasn't mine. I slid my hand to the side of his face. On tiptoe, I kissed his left cheek, rested my lips there, and with the other hand caressed the other side. Easton finally opened his eyes. He took my hand, curled his fingers in between, and with the other arm, drew me away from the window. Then he continued with the story about what happened at dinner with the neighbors. I rested my cheek against his to hear his faint voice. "Earlier you asked if you were nervous about the investigation. We had planned to meet Lucio, Anna, and the other neighbors for dinner. You worried about dinner and what might or might not be said to hurt the case. Once you met Anna, it heightened your nervousness."

(Twenty-Two) Getting to Know You

~~~~~~

2001 – Crystal Lane, Rhode Island

Yesterday's forced pleasantries with Anna only increased my insecurities and anxiety. I worried how dinner would go between the Tumicelli's and the other neighbors. A criminal couple. It didn't seem so bad in theory, but when the time came, it made me nauseous. Food didn't agree with me. We had studied these people, and now we became their neighbors. I would be in close proximity to them. Two people who have lived a life of crime. I stood in front of the closet with the belief that if I attracted attention with how I dressed, everything would be fine. My left leg bent to the side with my foot against my right ankle as my outstretched arms held onto the closet doors.

Easton came into the room, laid on the bed, put his hands behind his head and watched me. "What's in there?"

I inspected the closet. "Shh."

"Where did you go after breakfast? I thought you'd come back down to talk about tonight."

With my back still to him, I said, "My stomach hurts."

"You all right?"

I spun halfway around and grabbed onto the closet doors to face him. "No. Aren't you worried about what will happen tonight?"

He spoke to the ceiling. "What for? It's dinner."

"With criminals and other neighbors ..." My voice drifted low. "Who might also be criminals." I sighed.

"First impressions are important. Okay, I already met Anna, but now is the time to get her comfortable with me. What if I ruin it? What if I accidentally call you—"

"Don't say it."

On the right side of the bed, I fell onto my stomach and propped my head up with my hands under my chin. Easton slid into a seated position with his back against the headboard. For a brief period, we studied each other.

"We'll be fine, Brand. It's dinner with some friends. When you get nervous or don't know what to say, hold my hand and give it a slight squeeze. I'll try to take over the conversation."

"What if they want us to sit across from each other?"

He briefly touched my arm. "You're overthinking this whole dinner. Smile, be courteous, and let conversation flow."

I ran my fingers through my hair. "That's what I'm afraid of. What if they ask me a question I don't know how to answer?"

"Do you want to go over some things again?"

My legs bounced off the bed. "Could we? Just a few questions?"

He leaned his head against the headboard, closed his eyes and asked, "Where did we grow up?"

"You're from New Haven, Connecticut and I'm from Dover, New Hampshire."

"How did we meet?"

"We were at a bar in Boston separately with our friends. You sat next to me at the bar and I accidentally took a sip of your beer thinking it was mine."

He opened his eyes, smiled and said, "I still don't think it was an accident."

I rolled onto my back and giggled.

"How long ago did we meet?"

I stretched my legs in the air and touched my toes. "Five wonderful years ago."

He pulled on one of my toes. "Do we plan to marry?"

I laughed and put my feet flat on the bed. "We've talked about it, but it isn't a pressing matter."

"Do we want kids?"

I shook my head. "No. We're both only children and want to enjoy each other."

"How old are we?"

"Thirty-two, you being slightly older."

"What do we do for a living?"

One by one my legs bounced on the bed. "You are a computer consultant, and I used to be a social worker but can't find a job now."

Easton tapped on my head and asked, "And why did we make you a social worker?"

My head tilted back to see him. "Because Lucio was a foster child. It is a good way to connect with him."

"That one isn't a question they'll ask."

He lifted his right hand. I rolled onto my stomach and gave him a high-five. "Great. Our ages and childhood homes aren't far from the truth. You know the rest so keep it short. Try to ask more than answer. Keep in mind that we want to find out as much as we can and that applies to all the neighbors. Ask questions that you can answer if asked in return." He nodded his head. "We're good. You'll do fine."

Easton swung his legs off the bed to take a shower while I finally decided on an outfit.

The warm evening had a slight breeze. I heard Easton downstairs. "Come on Brand, we have to be there in ten minutes."

I went to the mirror one last time to check out my appearance. The outfit I had picked was to keep everyone's attention away from the possible calamity I might cause. My hand coasted down the banister as my bare legs moved in a pair of red-pointed high heel shoes. Three steps from the floor, I let my right leg dangle over the step before stepping all the way down so I could judge Easton's reaction. With his mouth ajar and his eyes big and bright, he took in my black pencil skirt with two V-stitched patterns, topped with a red sleeveless silk blouse that draped in front. I finally stepped down to the main level, repositioned my three loose silver bracelets on my left wrist, and the clasp of the silver teardrop necklace.

Easton stepped forward, took both my hands in his and spread them out to the side. "You look ..."

My hands fell to my side. I smiled and gave his black slacks, shoes and short-sleeve light brown shirt a once over. He smelled good.

"I look?"

"Like my Claire." I patted his chest and took my black purse. "Ready?"

The restaurant tried to combine the old with the new of Italy. A typical faux painting with the illusion of the Old World with painted colorful flower boxes. Fake plants hung in corners in the main area. There was an outdoor patio at the back of the restaurant. It had white garden pillars wrapped with ivy. The mini white Christmas lights shimmered off the glasses and silverware. The hostess escorted us to the patio where all the neighbors were waiting.

Easton took my hand and led the way. Anna leaned

over to Lucio, who in turn stood to introduce himself and to make room for us. We all said our names, shook hands, and rearranged the seating. Lucio sat at one end of the table with Anna to his left. I sat to his right with Easton next to me. Next to Easton sat a couple by the name of Leone and Lila Thorburn. Positioned at the other end of the table was our perverted next-door neighbor, Domenico Pierce, and to his right were Sophy Warwick and Clifton Mancini.

Anna smiled at me and said, "I'm glad the two of you could make it. I told the others how lucky we are to have a young, attractive couple in our little cul-de-sac." She went on to tell us about the others. Leone and Lila had been long-time friends of theirs. Mr. Pierce had become a recent widower. Sophy owned an upscale boutique. Clifton was unemployed and his partner, a lawyer, was currently working on a high-profile lawsuit in New York.

I tensed as Lucio turned his attention to me. "So Claire, Anna forgot to mention what a beautiful woman you are."

My leg started to shake. I leaned back in my seat and placed my hands on the top of my thighs. "Thank you."

Our drinks came and we all exchanged information about ourselves. I noticed Anna glanced over at Easton. I'm sure she was wishing I wasn't in the picture. I made a mental note, in case I disappeared, to leave a letter letting Easton know Anna did it.

Domenico pointed at me. "I saw you yesterday in your backyard. It will be nice to talk to someone while in the sun." I nodded and left it at that.

Both Lucio and Anna watched Easton and me as if they were gauging whether they could trust us or not. They acted cautious, unaware of who exactly we were and where we came from. When we made small talk with Sophy, Lucio leaned over whispering to Anna. Afterward he ordered another bottle of wine and rested his chin on his left hand all the while we were in eyesight. Easton placed a hand on my thigh and winked at me.

I turned to Lucio and asked, "Lucio. What type of profession are you in?" This got him out of his scrutinizing state.

He took a sip of his wine and then responded. "I'm an investment broker. But in today's economic times, I'm running out of companies to suggest to my clients to invest in." Everyone found it funny.

"Hmm … I might have to pick your brain on what we should invest in next."

He leaned back, swirled his wine and said, "Then let's get together some time to discuss your portfolio."

I glanced at Easton and then back at Lucio. "I'll give you a call. David and I are both clueless when it comes to investments." I placed my hand on Easton's forearm and smiled. "But David's good at so many other things."

Clifton asked, "David, I saw you jogging yesterday. Do you belong to a health club?"

"No. We moved in a few days ago." He took my hand in his and continued. "Claire and I worked out together in the mornings. Once we're settled, we hope to get back into our routine."

"What do you do?" Clifton took a sip of his drink. "If you don't mind me asking?"

"Not at all. I'm a computer consultant at a company called *Just the Specs, Please*. It's a small independent company that recently relocated here."

Anna wore a mischievous grin. "We could use you for our home computers that refuse to cooperate. Lucio and Claire can go over some investment options while you and I work on hard drives."

Everyone laughed at her pun, but it was no accident. That's exactly what she'd like to do with Easton. I glanced at him to catch his reaction. Easton's hand hugged mine, which rested on my leg.

There were conversations around the table, which left Lucio, Anna, Easton and me available. Lucio reached out for Anna's hand and grasped it. For a brief moment, they smiled at each other, but it was more of pride than endearment.

Still holding Anna's hand, Lucio asked, "What do you do for a living, Claire?"

"I'm a social worker. I mean, I was a social worker. Unfortunately I am unemployed right now because I couldn't find a job here when David got his transfer. I'm all right with time off to get situated." I smiled at Lucio and then Anna. "And get to know our new neighbors."

Easton said, "And I don't mind her at home either. Claire is a great cook. I can't complain about coming home to a beautiful woman and dinner on the table."

Lucio said to me. "Maybe you and Anna can swap some recipes. Anna makes a mean lasagna."

Anna kissed Lucio's hand. "My husband likes to flatter me. But I have to admit, it is great."

He pulled her closer to him. "My wife is modest. She's a great cook and baker. As you can tell, I'm the one who eats it all."

We ordered dinner and then I excused myself to use the ladies' room. Easton pulled out my chair, and we kissed before I left. On my way to the washroom, I heard Anna ask me to wait.

"It's so juvenile of me to follow, but I figured I should freshen up."

In the washroom, I went to the far stall and Anna

disappeared into another. We both exited the stalls at the same time and approached the sink. She applied her lipstick.

I spoke to the mirror and said, "That's a good shade on you."

She acted surprised at such an unexpected compliment and stopped halfway through applying her lipstick. "Thank you, Claire. I have to say you are exquisite tonight. David is a lucky man."

Yes he is and he's all mine.

"Thank you."

Anna slid the cap onto her lipstick when she said, "Since we both don't work and enjoy jogging, maybe we could start jogging in the mornings." She said it in a matter of fact way, which made me think she had her own agenda. When she put her lipstick in her purse, I caught a glimpse of a gun out of the corner of my eye.

I swallowed the fear that crept inside. "Yeah. It would be nice to have some company."

"I get out there at 7:00 am. Is that a problem?"

Nah. I enjoy jogging with my eyes still closed.

"Not at all. I love the quietness of the mornings, don't you?"

"Yes." With one arm on her hip, and the other dangling her purse, she continued, "And it will give us time to get to know one another." Anna didn't wear a smile. Her serious behavior emphasized her words. The image of her gun flashed in my head.

Anna acted different around Easton than me. This made my thoughts wander to the idea that she probably would like to know what kind of eggs he likes, and what type of grave she should dig for me. I'm sure she wanted to know about our relationship. It was obvious Lucio adored her, but I wouldn't put it past Anna to enjoy a little indulgence every now and then. Who really knew anyone though? Maybe Lucio dabbled in the extra-sexual activities by the way he examined me.

The rest of dinner went without incident. Everyone else talked about their upcoming week while we sat back and took it all in. By the time we got home, we were both exhausted, and the balls of my feet had deadened from their cramped, high quarters. We changed and met in the kitchen.

I rubbed my feet as Easton put decaf coffee, pens and paper on the table. He sat down, took my other foot onto his lap and massaged it. I didn't take it away.

"I'm proud of you. Not only did you charm everyone with your beauty, but you also made a connection with Lucio. Asking him for investment advice was classic! I couldn't have thought of a better excuse to get closer to them."

"Thank you, thank you, 'Twas nothing. His response opened the door for me. What about you? Mr. Techy. Anna sure wants your hard drive. I mean, wants you to work on their hard drives."

"She enjoyed that pun."

I had some coffee. "Yes she did. Was it uneventful when I went to the washroom?"

"Only Lucio's wandering eye. I believe he worships Anna, but still can't help the beauty of others. He watched you leave, and then his eyes fell on me. I bet he wanted to get my reaction. Lucio's a tough one. He doesn't trust either one of us, yet you're very good on the eyes."

"I can say the same about you with Anna. She was touchy, feely yesterday with you, and today, geez, she glanced over at you often. You don't think they cheat on each other, do you?"

"Maybe. Or maybe they're open with their marriage. They're not shy to express what's on their mind, like Anna's comments about us being an attractive couple. The way she flirted with me yesterday, and Lucio's interest in your appearance."

I took my foot off his lap so I could write notes about the group. Lila and Leone were in their own world. They had been friends with Lucio and Anna, but they were too much into themselves. Domenico Pierce, a lonely, perverted old man. He enjoyed women, touched them, and asked Sophy out to dinner. Way too young and smart, Sophy wouldn't waste her time with him. And then there was Clifton. A stay-at-home gay man with a tongue for gossip and an eye for fantasizing. Another one who took a liking to Easton.

It was late so we decided to finish our notes the next day. He put them in a safe and we went to bed.

(Twenty-Three) Sexual Weaponry

~~~~~~

2013 - Crystal Lane, Rhode Island

We still stood there, Easton's arm around me, my cheek pressed against his. When he finished about the dinner with the neighbors, I moved my head so I could see him. He didn't seem to be there with me. I lost him to nostalgia. With every step forward, we seemed to have taken several steps back. Easton had told me about what brought us together, but then later, regret stood between the present and future.

It was then that I noticed Easton went into the bedroom. I wanted to check to see if he was okay, yet I didn't want to intrude. He laid on his back on the bed with his eyes closed. Within a few minutes, his throat let out a gurgled sound, too weak for a snore. I folded my arms and leaned against the door. These recollections hurt him all over again. Here, I couldn't go on without a grasp of my past, and he couldn't go on grasping it.

I crossed the bedroom and went into the washroom. My makeup had smeared and blended into a likeness of a prostitute. I grabbed a folded towel on the sink, wet it, and scrubbed my face until it appeared red. All the while, I thought about how lost we had become.

My hand brushed against the wall to turn off the light. I stood near the bed with my arms crossed in front of me as he slept. Infidelity seemed outrageous, especially with what I had learned. Easton appeared to be the complete package, looks and personality. But we had become distant. My eyes skimmed over his body, rested on certain areas with perverted thoughts, and then moved to the next part. The times we kissed had scared the hell out of me, yet also aroused. For not knowing much about him, I couldn't believe the effect he had on me. I closed my eyes to think about some of our passionate moments. When his body drew heat to mine, I feared his anger but not his touch. His eyes sedated thoughts and movements, and his kisses melted my insides. The more we argued, the angrier we became, and the more I wanted him in a sexual way. I wanted his touch. I wanted to have dirty sex with him to feel his anger and tenderness. But he didn't want me.

I opened my eyes to find Easton awake. My one hand on my breast and the other rested near my inner thighs. My eyes widened as I bit my lower lip and left the bedroom. How embarrassing? I needed a drink. Maybe I first needed a blurry mind in order to clear it. Or maybe to get wasted and stop obsessing about the past. Psycho-slut-lush. I couldn't have lost all my unflattering traits. I threw ice into a glass, poured myself some whiskey, and gulped it down. My lips rested on the cold glass.

Easton came out of the room. I poured myself another and sucked it down before he spoke.

"Care to share?"

"Um ..."

He pointed to my glass and said, "Did you drink it all?"

My body relaxed as I grabbed another glass, filled it with ice and poured us both some more. He clinked his glass to mine and said, "Here's to thoughts and memories."

I put the glass to my mouth, peered over the top at him before tilting it toward me. The cold alcohol glided down my throat, tickled it then danced down to my limbs. He indicated he'd like another so I obliged. I could feel the liquor coerce my nerves, massage my muscles and ease into my body. Easton watched me watch him.

He put his glass down on the table and said, "Since we're here, we might as well take in the town."

I remembered my blemished face, similar to what confusion had done to my mind. "Like this? I have no makeup on and I'm—"

"So what?"

I agreed to venture out.

The air gave my senses a slight nudge. Neither of us had any other clothes, let alone a jacket, so I rubbed my arms to get the circulation flowing. Easton offered to buy me a jacket, but I declined. We strolled the streets, eyed the window displays and found ourselves in a darker part of town, yet not to the point of ghetto. The pedestrian activity reduced in size and the neon adult store signs drew us closer. The town's red light district. We waited in front of a store window that had an assortment of dirty goods until we both knew what the other wanted to do.

A bell rang above our heads when we opened the door. I don't know what possessed me to go in. Maybe the alcohol had already taken over my good judgment. Then again, the past version of me hadn't used too much sense either. The setup of the store had sections based on categories. On the right side hung countless whips and crops, and on the left hung nipple clamps and other types of sexual weaponry. I touched the top of a leather whip, ran my hand down to feel the tails slip through my fingers. Easton asked if I wanted it. I shook my head. We continued down the main aisle toward the back and found a room lined with leather vests, pants, corsets, handcuffs and restraint straps. Both of us found the multitude of pleasure clothes and toys interesting and amusing. I nudged Easton, pointed at a pair of men thongs. I couldn't picture any guy wearing a see-through thong let alone Easton. After our fair share of nudges, winks, giggles, and flirtatious smiles, we started to head to the front of the store. Easton took down the whip I had slipped my fingers through and bought it. From what I heard about my past, I wouldn't have been too surprised to find out that our marriage involved some bondage. Instead of ruining my erotic notions, I decided to keep my assumptions to myself.

Up and down the streets, we walked with our brown paper bag that hid the whip. The alcohol's effects began to disintegrate. We left the so-called 'red light district' and found an Irish pub several blocks away, not far from our hotel. Hungry and tired, we ordered beers and burgers. Easton put the bag on the table, neither of us able to ignore its presence. I thought about Easton using it on me. It represented excitement, something we apparently lost years ago. This purchase could be a sign of a better marriage to come.

Our eyes wandered around the room. About twenty feet away, a few guys were setting up music equipment in a small open area. The drinks and food kept us busy until a solo guitarist played rock songs, mixed with a few Irish classics. We ordered several more beers and listened. My thoughts didn't stray far from the whip, and I caught Easton touching the bag. The pleasure of alcohol returned.

The blaring music tried to provoke our numbness, but it couldn't. We were lost to the alcohol that slurred our thoughts. Each of us had an arm across the table, fingertips stroked the other's hand. The brown bag enticed us making our thoughts wander toward provocative matters. Agony strained our faces. As much as we wanted to be together, the past came around at the damndest times. The waiter brought us drinks we didn't order. When questioned, he pointed toward the bar as we saw Jenny Carver wave at us. Our arms slinked back to their rightful places, as we both tipped our glasses at each other and watched Jenny make her way over.

She sat next to me to explain she was in town visiting friends. Odd because we didn't see her with anyone. Easton sat back, a non-participant, while Jenny talked about our friendship. My concentration tumbled as if in a dryer watching Jenny's mouth move. At one point, she reached for the brown bag and asked what we bought. Easton snatched it and I said it was our leftovers. By the time Jenny ran out of subjects, my head almost fell on the table. Easton threw a few bucks down and left. Jenny let me slide out of the booth. I couldn't listen to her anymore, so I waved over my shoulder and joined Easton outside.

The cool night air opened my eyes enough to notice we swayed. I didn't ask Easton about Jenny because I didn't care. I wanted to know what happened next after the dinner with the neighbors.

"I don't know, Brand. I don't think you could handle more."

I stopped and asked, "Why? I mean, yes I can. I can handle it."

Easton put out his arm for me to slip mine in and said, "It got quite interesting. Sexually."

"Huh?"

He patted my hand that held onto his arm. "Not us. Lucio and Anna began to trust us. In fact, they wanted us to become their new buddies in more ways than one."

(Twenty-Four) Yes, Master!

~~~~~

Our dinner with the neighbors had been successful. Anna asked if I'd like to jog with her, and I accepted. The following week we started our routine. It proved to be difficult to dress for the bi-polar weather. One day it started out sunny and turned into thunderstorms halfway through, and the next day it started out cold and then felt like the sun would melt my clothes into my skin. Of course, Anna was always prepared. I hated jogging, but we'd take a few minute breaks to catch our breath and get to know each other. Anna made it easy to get to know her. She couldn't think of a better subject to talk about than herself.

Anna came from money. A daddy's girl given everything she asked for, and she was not embarrassed to admit it. When Lucio came along, she fell head over heels in love. He reminded her of her father, stern yet loving, so they married within a matter of a few months. Whatever Anna wanted Lucio made sure she got. Five years later, they were still strong. She described her wedding and asked when David and I planned to marry.

"No plans. It isn't a priority for us. We know we'll spend the rest of our lives together, so marriage would just be a formality."

Anna slowed down, stretched her neck and in a snippy tone said, "You better watch out, Claire. Some woman might swoop in and claim him for her own."

Like you!

I let out a small laugh. "If that happens then we weren't meant to be."

She stopped and squinted toward me. "How smart of you to think that way. And how naïve of you. Men stray. You better keep your eye on your man or someone else will."

I shrugged and said, "I guess."

Anna remained quiet the rest of the jog. Probably to figure out how to get me out of the picture. On occasion, she'd give me a sideward glance. We got to the townhouses and Anna jogged in place for a few seconds then crossed over by me to jog in place. She invited us to join them in the evening at a club they frequent.

It was obvious Anna and Lucio wanted to get to know us. They provided opportunities, so I told Anna we'd be there. I kept my outfit casual and sexy, aware of the competition from across the street. A pair of expensive jeans shorts, a black form fitting, off-the-shoulder blouse, and black high-heel sandals with several ankle straps. As usual, Easton wore a pair of black pants and a short-sleeved black silk shirt like a model.

We were to meet Lucio and Anna at a club called After Dusk. Easton and I parked a few blocks away and walked hand in hand. The weather cooperated. When we approached the club, we didn't expect to see a line a block long from the entrance. Easton took a chance and told the bouncer that Lucio and Anna Tumicelli had invited us. They unclasped the red velvet rope separating them from the crowd and pointed up the stairs to the VIP room.

The place darkened as we went down a hallway to the carpeted stairs that led to the room where the Tumicelli's knew how to entertain. When the door opened, a burst of laughter, conversations, and lights greeted us. People lingered around the room, gathered in groups, and all had some sort of drink in their hand. Dress code didn't matter as there were suits, evening dresses, and club attire. There were two bars on opposite sides of the room, and a buffet table filled with fancy vegetables and dips, bruschetta, quiches, to name a few, and desserts for the sweet tooth lovers. My eyes took in all the goodies before I spotted Anna. I made my way over where she gave me an old-fashioned European pretend kiss on each cheek, and then took Easton's hands in hers. She spoke directly to him, "I'm so glad you could come."

Her earlier words echoed in my head as I wondered if she literally meant she would keep her eye on Easton. Or I thought she might be testing me. Either way, her behavior rubbed me the wrong way.

Before I was able to respond, Lucio came over, offered me a *real* European kiss on each cheek and left his hand on the center of my back. A lingering wetness remained on my cheeks smelling of a mixture of beer, garlic, and cologne. "Again, you look beautiful, Claire. David had better keep a close eye on you. There are plenty of men here eager to have a young, gorgeous woman like you on their arm."

I placed my hand on his, giggled, and said, "Oh Lucio, you flatter me. Too bad I'm not as young as you think."

He brought me to a group of men seated in a circular booth. Over my shoulder, I saw Easton still with Anna. I offered a greeting to each man along with a handshake. They all wore suits, and as they rose to shake my hand, I noticed they had guns in a side holster underneath their suit jackets. In an instant, my face got warm, so I took a deep breath. Lucio asked if I was okay, and I told him I could use a glass of water. We went to the bar farthest away from Anna and Easton. He ordered me a water along with a glass of wine.

"If you don't mind, I'd like a scotch on the rocks."

Lucio's eyebrows rose, as he said, "A girl after my own heart." He waited until I drank my water and then said, "Tell me a little about yourself."

Oh shit! Oh shit! About me? Where was Easton?

I took my hand that held the cold water glass and patted my face.

His hundred-proof-alcohol breath puffed into my face. "Are you sure you're okay?"

My nerves got the best of me. "Yes. I'm sorry. I haven't eaten much since early this afternoon."

We made our way over to the buffet table. I took a plate and loaded it with foods I could identify. He laughed and said, "I guess you are hungry."

I put one food after another in my mouth. After several bites, Lucio advised me to slow down or I'd get sick. He excused himself for a moment and went to the door to say hello to someone. I chased the food down with my scotch.

Easton came over and stood next to me. "Hungry?"

My arm slipped into his as I pulled him toward the bar to get another drink. I told him about the group of guns at the table and Lucio's interest in me.

He kissed me on the cheek, and whispered in my ear, "Stop freaking out. Nothing will happen. We've gone over this a million times. Stick with simple answers and redirect."

I took a gulp of my scotch, stared in Lucio's direction. "Right. Simple."

He placed his hand on mine that held the scotch to get my attention. "Let's slow it down with the drinks. I know they're free, but—"

I patted his cheek. "Funny." I fluffed my hair, adjusted my shirt and then said, "Okay, I can do this."

Easton placed his hand on my butt and said, "Yes you

can." Startled, I turned to him, and he said, "Do you feel that?" I nodded. "Good. You're still with me. You're the love of my life. Don't forget it." He gave my butt a slight tap and went to the buffet table. I ordered a seltzer water with a lime and strode around.

Lucio joined me again, and asked, "So where were we, Claire?"

I saw a few chairs at a table and indicated for us to sit. "You wanted to know some more about me."

His hand rested on my knee. "Yes. Where did you grow up?"

"Dover, New Hampshire. And you?"

"I never really had a specific place to call home until now. I moved around a lot as a kid."

I bet!

"Oh? Was your mother or father in the military?"

He let out a gruff laugh and said, "No. My parents died when I was young. I'm an ex-foster child."

I placed my hand on his forearm and apologized.

"It's why I found it interesting that you are a social worker. I dealt with plenty of them. Overworked and underpaid. They couldn't match all the cases that came in. Too many kids fell through the cracks. It's a tough occupation, you know?"

I shook my head to emphasize my agreement. "It is a tough job. That's why I don't mind the time off."

Lucio's eyes drifted down my body and settled for a second on my bare legs before he met my eyes. "You know, Claire. In a way, you being a social worker and me an ex-foster child connects us. You remind me of one of my social workers. She had a gentle way about her, and your eyes resemble hers, deep and kind." By this time, his hand rubbed my bare knee and his thumb circled the bone. Lucio saw my shocked expression when I slipped his hand off.

I touched his arm, tried to make light of the situation. "You're right. It does bond us. Very few people understand the struggles of the foster care system. The employees and children suffer."

He placed his arm around the back of my chair, and asked, "Don't you feel alone sometimes? Like no one understands you?"

Our faces were close, and my words cracked when I said, "Yes. No matter how much David and I confide in each other, he just doesn't realize all that's involved in the responsibility of children." I wanted Lucio to trust me, which is why Easton made me a social worker. We knew of Lucio's torn childhood. The key strategy required trust. He needed to be comfortable with me. But I didn't want him to feel too comfortable. I leaned back in my chair to put some distance between us.

Anna ran over. I rose ready for her to take a swing at me. Instead, she took Lucio to the side and whispered in his ear. Easton came over, and I asked, "What happened?"

"I don't know, but maybe we should use the opportunity to get out of here."

As we were about to leave, a few large men came in and headed over to Lucio and Anna. We watched the muffled exchange, and then the Tumicellis left with the men out a back door. We could have stuck around and followed them, but instead, we went home to discuss our encounters.

Anna called the next day to apologize for their abrupt departure. In lieu of an explanation, we received a bouquet of flowers. Easton checked it to make sure there wasn't a bug in it.

W e had been jogging for a couple of weeks when Anna asked more questions—personal questions. I wasn't sure what she wanted to find out, and I didn't want my responses to be abrupt and harsh to risk abandoning our so-called friendship. If that happened, how would Easton and I get information about our crime-infested neighbors?

Through the forest, we opted for the manmade paths. We stopped twenty minutes into our jog, removed the water bottles strapped to our upper arms and drank. Anna sat on a rock with her left foot bent. The sun reflected off her sock, which caught my attention. I moved closer. Anna noticed my interest and removed a small pistol from a little holster underneath her sock. I took a step back, and swallowed hard. She had figured out how to get me out of the picture.

Anna turned the gun in different directions, and said, "For protection."

My hands were on my chest when I responded. "From me?"

"No." Then she considered it and waved the gun as a joke. "Do I need protection from you?"

"Only unless you don't like our jogging route."

Anna put the gun back in the holster, let out a laugh, and examined me before saying, "I like you, Claire. I can't say that about many women. It isn't often I feel easy around a woman, because they're so damn judgmental, but you're different. You're uncomplicated, a "go with the flow kind of woman". I like that. It makes for a simple friendship."

I shifted my weight and said, "Simple is good. Heck, I'd rather you like me than the alternative." My eyes shifted to her gun.

She registered my apprehension and said, "It's not

unheard of for a woman to carry a gun."

"Is it legal in Rhode Island?"

She tugged her body in the opposite direction as if I asked an odd question. "Yes, if you have a permit to carry." I glanced around. "A gun gives you a little edge. You're too trusting and could use one."

I crossed my arms in front. "Why is that?"

Anna came close to me, strapped my water bottle to my upper arm, pulled the Velcro tighter than needed and said, "It's unnatural for a woman to trust a man so much and assume if he strays it wasn't meant to be."

Anna replaced her bottle as I said, "You trust Lucio."

"Yes, but I'm not stupid to believe he wouldn't go off and find another woman if I gave him the opportunity."

I took offense to her comments. "I'm not giving David an opportunity."

Anna shrugged and said, "Okay."

"No. Don't 'okay' me. I love David, but I won't keep him on a leash to satisfy my own insecurities."

As I drank some water, Anna smiled with her eyes and said, "There's nothing wrong with leashes." She paused and then asked, "How is your sex life?"

The water went down the wrong pipe and I coughed. She patted my back. "Sorry. I should have waited until you were done."

I tried to figure out how to respond. One minute she insulted me, and the next, she asked a personal question. I had to chill. Stop being so defensive.

I took a deep breath and grinned. "Yeah. Waiting would've helped."

Anna let her guard down. She hunched her shoulders, and shifted her weight to one side. "Just curious. You seem so comfortable with your relationship, so I had to ask."

"We've been together for five years."

She swatted at a fly when she responded. "Really? You seem so into each other."

We started to walk instead of run. "David and I try not to take each other for granted." The conversation shifted to a whole new level. I couldn't tell if I replied as Brand or Claire.

We let the quietness fill the void in our conversation. Anna kicked a few rocks, sighed and continued. "This is nice. To confide in each other." I nodded and indicated whether we should jog again, but Anna continued to talk. "This is our time to share. Bond as you might call it." Again, I agreed without comment. Anna had something on her mind and wanted to see how far she could trust me. "Since we're opening up, I'm curious ..." Anna let the word stretch, waited for my reaction, which happened to be confusion. "How's your sex life?"

I let out a hearty laugh. "You really don't quit." Words coated my tongue, quenched my thirst to respond. In the end, I decided to stay close to the truth. "We explore different avenues. All couples need variety to keep the excitement in bed. Role-play is one way. Sex shops. Stuff like that."

She seemed satisfied. "Role-play is definitely a good time. What do you think about BDSM?"

I stopped in mid-step. My head swirled with thoughts of Easton and me. Anything having to do with Easton gave me a high.

Aside from handcuffs, I didn't have any BDSM experiences, but it piqued my interest. I could have said I wasn't interested, but I heard myself say, "We haven't tried it yet."

"Yet? So you might like to?"

"I'm always open to trying anything once."

Then the oddest thing happened. Anna touched my arm, as if to indicate a connection, and smiled.

On Saturday, we received an invitation for dinner at the Tumicelli's house, a casual dinner amongst friends. We both threw on a pair of jeans and a nice shirt, and brought over a bottle of wine. Cliché, I know, but we didn't have any condoms.

As it turned out, we were the only couple invited. We heard a ding and Anna, about to disappear into the kitchen, asked, "Could you help me, David?" He put down his drink, kissed me, and went with Anna. I wandered over to the fireplace that contained numerous pictures of Lucio and Anna on the mantle.

Lucio approached and stood closer than normal. "If I didn't know better, I'd think you're trying to make David jealous by being so beautiful."

I blushed. "Thank you. You look handsome yourself."

"Anna goes on and on about your outings, and I'm beginning to get a little jealous. Here I thought we had a connection, and now she gets most of the time with you."

I turned on dumb blonde mode. "I'm sorry. If you don't want us together—"

He fanned his hands in front to wipe away the thought. "No, no, you misunderstood. I love the fact that my Anna jogs with someone. I don't have to worry about her out there alone. I just wish I could join in on the fun."

I nodded. Nothing would happen to the gun toting Anna. It's everyone else that has to worry.

"Anna tells me you and David have been together the same amount of years as us."

Lucio reached out to move the hair that sprinkled my left ear, and let his finger caress the side of my face.

Easton walked in at that moment. Lucio clasped his hands behind his back. I knew David saw it but pretended he didn't.

Lucio sat on the couch. "Did my wife put you to work?"

"Glad I could help her out."

"I said to Claire that I wish I could go jogging with her and Anna. Unfortunately, I'm not in as good of shape as Anna." He patted his growing belly. "As you can tell, I enjoy the finer things in life. Exercise isn't one of them."

Anna came into the room with a tray full of shrimp. Her face flushed. She smiled at us and asked Lucio to help her carry out the rest of the appetizers. When they were gone, Easton turned to me amused. "What's with you and Lucio?"

"I don't know. Ever since the first time we met, he gets cozier with me."

"So is Anna."

I moved closer to him. "What did she do?"

Lucio and Anna came back into the room, placed some appetizers on the table and sat on opposite couches. Lucio invited me to sit next to him, so Easton joined Anna on the other couch. We glanced at one another until Anna placed her hand on Easton's leg and said, "Thank you so much for your assistance in the kitchen."

"No problem."

Lucio chimed in. "I told Claire how jealous I am about your time together. I wouldn't mind coming along."

"Sorry, Lucio, but it's our girl time. Right, Claire?"

I watched Anna's hand stroke Easton's leg and then my eyes met hers. "Right, Anna."

Lucio put his arm behind me on the back of the couch. Easton watched as Lucio shifted his weight to the side closest to me. "I told David how beautiful Claire is tonight. Don't you think, Anna?"

"She always looks beautiful." Her hand moved closer to Easton's crotch when she said, "Like David is always handsome." He placed his hand on top of hers and rested both on his knee, stopped her in an unaggressive way.

Lucio shifted back to normal but left his arm behind me. "We wanted to have you both over tonight because we want to discuss something with you."

Easton let go of Anna's hand and moved by the fireplace.

Lucio noticed our hesitation. "Have a seat, David. It's not a big deal. We want to talk to you about it. More like share it with you."

Easton returned to the couch about a foot away from Anna. "What is it?"

Anna cut in. "Why don't we enjoy a few drinks and dinner before we get too serious?" She gave a warm smile, went over to the bar and poured herself a glass of wine.

All kinds of thoughts swirled around in our heads. Anna and Lucio brought in the food, so we whispered to each other as to what we assumed they wanted. The way they warmed up to us, we wondered if they wanted to recruit us into their criminal acts. We hadn't prepared for it. All the preparation, research into their lives started to evaporate. I then had a vision of me with a gun in my hand, yelled for someone to put the loot in the bag. Did we act too vulnerable or too laidback? Did they think we could use the money since I was out of a job?

Anna's hand brought me back to the present. "Hello Claire. Are you with us?"

I laughed off her comment. "Yes. My mind wandered about if I had locked the door to our house." Easton nodded. "I figured so. I'm usually good at double-checking to make sure everything is in order. Now what did you say?"

Anna released a loud exhalation to let me know that she didn't appreciate my wandered thoughts. "As I was saying, Claire, our cook and servant have the night off. We wanted undivided attention." Her eyes linked to mine, and she didn't turn away until I gave a sign of agreement.

Lucio waved us over to the table to break the icy conversation. "Come on. Come on. Let's eat and not fight. This is supposed to be an evening with friends."

Anna nodded and said, "Friends do fight on occasion, right Claire?"

I sat in a chair Easton pulled out for me and said, "That is correct. We can't all be in agreement all the time."

The meal consisted of prime rib, double-baked potatoes, and asparagus with almond slivers. We started with a chopped salad, pine nuts and blue cheese followed by gazpacho soup. All the different flavors kept me occupied. Lucio and Anna told us about investments they had recently made, and now was the time to buy.

Lucio said, "Let me know whenever you want to go over your investment portfolio."

Easton put his fork down. "Definitely. We are in the process of collecting our paperwork, but yeah, we want to go over our options with you to find out the best strategy."

He nudged his hand in both our direction. "You two are not only attractive, but you're smart and open-minded."

A bit of prime rib rubbed hard against my esophagus. I thought, "Here we go." The best approach was to let

Easton talk.

Anna dabbed at her lips and said, "Lucio and I could use the two of you."

Our eyes traveled from one person to the next until they landed on each other. Easton responded, "For what?"

She folded her hands in front, rested her chin on top and said, "The circles Lucio and I associate with are unusual. We tend to drift with people of like minds. Open to opportunity. Open to ideas. The two of you fit into these circles. What we want to do is increase our circle. Recruit the elite into a wonderful world of advantages. When we find a couple, such as yourselves, eager to better their lives physically and financially, Lucio and I make offers. Suggest things that won't always come your way. We pass on our good fortune and knowledge to those we find worthy enough to handle such circumstances."

It was my turn to put down the silverware and pat my lips. I made myself as comfortable as possible and listened.

Lucio slid his plate to the side. "What Anna means is we associate with like-minded people. People who can be private, and will do for others in return for the same."

Easton rested against the table. "So what exactly are we talking about here?"

Anna and Lucio exchanged glances, and then Lucio responded, "What we're talking about is excitement. If we all use proper discretion, we can take some risks, which will ultimately change our lives."

"Does this entail danger?"

He laughed and said, "It can be."

In my head, I counted to defuse my tension. The hours spent at the shooting range prepared me for moments like this one. We are about to cross from undercover investigators to undercover criminals. I gripped the armrests and let out a long breath.

They all looked at me. Lucio asked, "What about you, Claire? Are you interested in adventure?"

Before I could respond, Easton said, "Claire and I are interested in these adventures. I can't guarantee we'll accept, but we're open to listening."

"It's all we ask and that you respect our privacy." Lucio swiped the chair back and stood. "To make this easier, we want to show you something. Whether you're interested or not, all we ask is this conversation and what you see remains with this group. Like we said, the people we associate with observe privacy, and we believe we can trust the two of you to comply."

We followed Anna and Lucio down a hallway. Easton grabbed my hand. We hadn't prepared to become accomplices in their criminal acts, but we couldn't discount their request. It was obvious we built their trust. Easton mouthed to me that we would be fine.

Lucio unlocked a door at the end of the hallway and pushed it open. My previous thoughts had been better than what I saw. I wasn't sure if I should laugh or run. A room for the sexually ambitious. Black leather pads covered the walls. In the middle of the room, stood a four-poster bed with a mirror above it and bondage straps connected to the four corners. A leather chair hung from the ceiling, all four sides attached by chains, and in another place hung a spreader bar with handcuffs clipped to it. In addition to these, there was a bench with handcuffs at one end and a dildo at the other. A cabinet to the right of the door contained all types of sex toys; whips, nipple clamps, vibrators, gag balls, and many others I didn't have a clue what to do with but could be assured the Tumicelli's would explain, if needed.

They waved us into their dungeon. Easton and I took a few steps in. They wanted us to join in their sexual desires. An undercover criminal sounded so much better.

Anna said to me, "When I mentioned BDSM, you said you were willing to try anything once."

Easton responded to me. "Really? Willing to try it?"

My face reddened, and I said, "Anna asked what I thought of BDSM, and I told her we hadn't tried it yet."

He started to laugh, and then observed all of us. "No, we haven't tried it yet. As a matter of fact, I didn't even know *we* were interested in it."

Lucio went over to Anna and kissed her cheek. "Well, if you are, so are we. Anna and I have had plenty of good times here. We've role-played, like Claire said you do." Again, I noted Easton's astonishment. "Anna is a slave and enjoys it. She wouldn't mind another Master. We liked the two of you from the start. Think about it, and no hard feelings if you decide you don't want to."

They let us absorb what we saw. The kinky room brought some sexual mood to the surface. While standing, I crossed my right leg over my left. "WOW! I mean, I'm flattered and all. Aren't you, David?"

Easton struggled with words. "Uh, yeah, flattered. Definitely something to think about."

Lucio loosened and said, "Take your time. Let us know if and when you're ready."

"Thanks ... that's uh ... great to know."

We smiled at them, turned and left the room. Since we had finished dinner, we excused ourselves and returned home.

Once we were inside, we both dropped onto the couch, stared straight ahead. It wasn't until I laughed that Easton directed his confused face toward me.

He lifted his body, and saw no humor in the situation. "Are you nuts? You're willing to try anything once?"

My hands flew to my mouth. "What? She caught me off-guard."

Easton paced. "And after you had this little discussion with Anna, you couldn't find the time to tell me about it?"

"I forgot." I couldn't tell Easton that I had fantasies about BDSM with him. "So what do we do now?"

His arms dropped to his sides, and said, "I guess them," and smiled.

I laughed at his response. "Stop! We have to get out of this situation."

He sat down. "We won't take them up on their offer."

My head fell back. "Thank God."

"Don't bring him into it. And the next time Anna catches you off-guard, remember to think 'no comment' and then reply with a, 'I'll have to talk to David about it.'"

(Twenty-Five) Brown Paper Bag

~~~~~~

2013 - Crystal Lane, Rhode Island

Someone yelled our names, so Easton stopped the story and we turned around. Jenny ran toward us with a brown paper bag. We gave each other a painful glance. Out of breath, she met us, but our attention drifted to the bag.

Jenny lifted it and said, "You forgot your ... leftovers. I just finished my drink when I noticed it on the seat."

She jiggled the bag and grinned before Easton grabbed it. I thanked her for bringing it to us.

Jenny brushed the hair off her face and said, "I didn't do it to be nosy, but I opened the bag to see if it contained something valuable."

Easton's arms dropped to his side. "Valuable? In a brown paper bag? No. You're not nosy."

I tried to control the situation and said, "Okay, Jenny, it's not a big deal. We appreciate that you went out of your way to return it."

Her face strained. "Since I did take a peek inside, does this mean you two made amends?"

Easton took the whip out of the bag and said, "You know what? I should beat you with this right now!"

Jenny breathed in when the tears began to build. I grabbed the whip, put it back in the bag and said, "Time will tell. Thanks."

She dabbed under her eyes, hugged me and said, "You're welcome." Jenny held me at arm's length and said, "I've tried to call, but I get your voice mail. I do want to get together for some great girl talk."

I agreed to meet her when I got back home. Easton

had already started toward the hotel. I thanked her, turned and went after him. When I got within a few feet of Easton, he mumbled to himself. For some reason, Jenny wasn't his favorite person. I remember he warned me to stay away from her. I fell behind his fast pace.

Finally, I grabbed his arm and said, "Easton, slow down. What's the big hurry?"

He turned in a circle, flapped his arms around. "Nothing. Everything."

"You're not a big fan of Jenny, are you?"

He threw his hands into the air, and said, "Oh, how can you tell?"

"All right. You can quit with the sarcasm. I don't understand what the big deal is with her. I thought she was my best friend."

"She's your best enemy."

I took short breaths to maintain Easton's speed. His indirect responses drove me nuts. I stopped and yelled, "You talk in circles. Come out and tell me what the problem is with her instead of acting like an asshole."

He came toward me and yelled, "Because she isn't worth my time!" Easton jabbed his finger in the air toward me. "If I tell you to stay away from someone, stay away from them."

I took a step back. "Oh sure, whatever you say." I threw the brown bag at him. "I don't give a shit what you tell me."

Easton stepped within inches of me and stiffened his jaw. "No, I guess you wouldn't. If you did, you never would have fucked someone else."

The words wrapped around us and tightened their grip. I couldn't believe he said that and with such venom. I stomped my way back to the hotel and I didn't notice him behind me until I was down the hall from our room.

My legs moved faster. I buzzed opened the door, slammed it and put the security chain on.

I heard him put his key card into the door. It buzzed, but the chain stopped him from entering. "Take the goddamn chain off, Brand!"

I backed away and said, "No. You'll hurt me."

Easton tucked his face between the door and the doorjamb. "I will if you don't open the damn door!"

I moved out of sight and said, "See!"

He shut the door and spoke to me through it. "If you don't take this chain off, I'll check out of the hotel and go home. You'll be stranded."

My fingers slid through my hair. A half-hour earlier, I had wanted him sexually. At that moment, I didn't want him by me. Controversy had a way of snapping our relationship like a twig. Easton frightened me with his temper, yet my desire to want him worried me more. I hesitated, removed the chain, and went across the room from the door. Easton pushed it open so hard, it slammed against the doorstopper.

I stood by the windows. "Can you be a little more dramatic?"

Easton smiled as he threw the brown bag on the chair.

His smile went right through me. "Your other self returned, the distant and mean one." My comment slapped the smirk off his face.

Easton used words to hit me. "You mean the two things you're good at."

"Oh! Is that another 'Brand did me wrong' comment."

My sarcasm made the situation worse. He grabbed the glass off the table and whipped it across the room. It shattered when it hit the wall and a piece nicked my right arm. I saw the blood and ran to get a towel. Before I could close the door, he came in.

Through the mirror, I yelled, "Get out!"

He ignored me. "Let me see it."

"I mean it. Get out!"

He placed me on the bathroom vanity. Easton saw some glass in my arm and took it out. He grabbed a towel, soaked it in cold water before pressing it against my arm.

Easton held the towel tight on my arm and said, "I'm sorry."

My anger weakened. He removed the towel to see if I needed stitches. The bleeding continued.

"I think we should take you to the hospital."

It was a busy night in the emergency room. Easton checked me in and we found a few seats in the back near the window. They informed us of a long wait. The room smelled of pain and fear. Some people held onto an assumed broken arm or leg with perspiration and moans. I turned away. I couldn't believe we were there. Hospitals made me uncomfortable after I spent a few weeks in one.

I felt his eyes on me. Easton put his hand on my leg. I ignored it. With my body spent from the events of the day and evening, my eyes closed to release some of the tension. Before I knew it, my head jerked me awake. I must have had just fallen asleep, because Easton put his arm behind me and told me to rest my head on it. I complied and fell asleep until the chaotic emergency room woke me. A bus had crashed into a building and paramedics were bringing a majority of the people to the hospital. It meant a longer time in the ER. I lifted the towel from my arm. As soon as I moved it, the blood flowed again.

Easton asked, "I can go down to the cafeteria for you. Or I can go down the street to one of the fast food places?"

"I'm not hungry."

"How about coffee?"

I shrugged.

He went to a vending machine to get us a coffee and settled back down.

I held it in my lap and said, "Since we will be here for quite a while, why don't you continue with the story? What happened after dinner at Lucio and Anna's house? Please tell me we didn't agree to share."

Easton laughed. "We told them we had to think about it. They were both eager to have us join in on the fun, but neither of us were interested."

I asked, "You weren't interested in the bondage scene?"

Easton touched the tip of my nose and said, "No. You were my interest." He let those words sink in before he started again.

(Twenty-Six) Some Other Bimbo

~~~~~~~

2001 - Crystal Lane, Rhode Island

I fought for sleep, but in the end images and thoughts of sex and the dungeon pulled me out of bed. My feet shuffled toward the washroom where I slammed the door after seeing myself in the mirror. Lack of sleep left bloodshot, puffy eyes, fitting with my hair that lifted and turned in all directions. A hairstyle for the mentally insane. The warm water ran hard as I drenched my hair to force it to lie down. I put several drops of Visine into my eyes covering the darkness of exhaustion the best I could.

Anna waved me over to the front of her house as she stretched her legs. Her prep routine was double time from what I did to prepare my body for a jog. She sat on the ground with her right leg bent, pulled her foot toward her with the other leg stretched to the side, and then she switched. After her ground stretching, she stood, pulled her arms back and then she bent one leg behind her, grabbed hold of her foot and counted to twenty before she switched legs. I joined her on the last leg stretch.

All smiles, Anna asked, "How'd you sleep? I'm sure Lucio and I surprised the both of you with our proposal."

I let out a slight humph to release the awkward moment. "We certainly weren't expecting that from the two of you."

"If we made the wrong assumption about you two, please say so. I'd hate to think we ruined your impression of us."

As criminals? What's to ruin?

"No, no. We're honored ..."

... you picked us as your slaves.

"... you trusted us enough to share. But after careful consideration, David and I think it's best not to join in."

Anna's face fell, but she hid her disappointment as she said, "Oh, okay. That's okay. We understand. But just so you know, I love Lucio. I don't mind Lucio with another woman, especially one I know and picked. It allows me to control the situation. I'd rather see him with you than him go behind my back with some other bimbo."

Some other bimbo? Bite me, bitch.

"I'm sure other bimbos would be as appreciative about it as I am."

Anna placed her hand on my forearm. "I didn't mean to insinuate that you're a bimbo. What I should have said was, 'It's better Lucio sleeps with you than go behind my back with some bimbo.'"

I smiled and said, "Much better."

We started our jog, but my leg started to cramp after a short time. I guess there is a reason to stretch. It gave us an opportunity to clear the air, so we stopped to drink some water.

Anna didn't appreciate the quietness as much as I did. She even talked when we jogged, which I couldn't understand how since I was out of breath most of the time. "Claire, may I ask you a personal question?"

"And what category does the question, 'How is your sex life' fit into?"

She sat down on a large rock and sighed. "I'm serious. I know I ask personal questions. I guess it's because I like you. I really like you!"

I let out a laugh. "You say it with such surprise. Like it's a bad thing."

Anna started to flex her feet, rubbed at her calf

muscle, and then stood to alternate flexing her butt cheeks. "I've always had a tough time with women. Many are jealous of me. Not that I'm the most gorgeous woman they've ever met, but I live a life they want. I'm married to a man who adores me, we're rich, I'm reasonably attractive, if not highly, and I'm in good shape. Don't you think women are judgmental?"

To ignore Anna's flexing ass, I pressed my heel into the ground, bent the other leg and shifted back to stretch my calf muscle. "Sure we are. One of our X chromosomes contains the mean gene."

Anna laughed and slapped my back. She repositioned her gun in her sock and asked, "Have you ever cheated on David?"

My eyes glanced over to the gun and I responded, "Never."

She stood, breasts stuck out and tightened muscles. "Have you ever considered an affair?"

I wasn't sure if this was her way of bullying me to give her Easton, so I turned the questions on her. "Why do you ask? Do you plan on cheating on Lucio?"

"Only if there was a swap. But there isn't, so no plans. Actually, it wouldn't be considered unfaithful because Lucio would know about it."

We walked before Anna asked another intrusive question. "Do you think David has ever cheated on you?"

I didn't look at her when I said, "I don't think so. But who really knows for sure." I then took her on and asked, "Do you think Lucio has cheated on you?"

She let out a strained laugh. "If I ever catch him, all of the bullets in my gun will be in him."

I didn't know how to respond to that comment, so the wind took it away while I drank water. We jogged back to our homes steering clear of additional conversation.

Easton sat in the kitchen on his computer, while I prepared for the day. After primping, I got comfortable downstairs with my feet on the table, and went through the virtual world as the hours ticked by. I needed to find a clue. Any clue as to who Anna and Lucio were and who they hung out with inworld. I grew frustrated and put the laptop to the side to rest. In my head, I replayed my conversation with Anna that morning. Her question, "Have you ever considered cheating on him?" flashed along with "I don't mind Lucio with another woman … allows me to control the situation." The clue was right in front of me.

I yelled to Easton in the kitchen. "Are you on AL?"

"No. The department sent me some files on Lucio."

Confident, I said, "It just dawned on me where we can find Lucio and Anna in the virtual world?"

He stopped and asked, "Where?"

"Any BDSM place. These two, or shall I say, Anna is very much interested to be someone else's slave. As a cover, and to have a little fun, my guess is that they're probably at BDSM places. I wouldn't doubt it if they acted out their sexual desires in AL."

Easton joined me with his laptop. "Very nice detective work, Brand." While we waited for our laptops to boot up, he said, "You seem to know a lot about BDSM. What does it actually mean?"

I scooted in my chair, and let the words drip in a casual way. "Bondage. Discipline / Dominance. Submissive / Sadism. Masochism."

Easton pretended to shiver with excitement. "Hmm … I'll have to research this some more."

"Now's your chance. Ms. Anna would love to have you as her Master. Before I told her we weren't interested, I think she had an orgasm fantasizing about it."

"So you told her we weren't interested?"

I leaned back. "Yeah. You're the one who told me to think 'no comment' and then respond with 'I have to talk to David'. Since I talked to you already, I decided to put her out of her anticipated misery."

"How did she take it?"

I shrugged and said, "Fine. I assured her they didn't ruin our impression of them."

"Ha! As criminals?"

I pointed my finger at him. "Oh my God! That's what I thought! Especially when she readjusted her gun."

Easton moved closer to me and asked, "She carries a gun when you two jog? You never told me that."

"I forgot. Besides, she's never threatened me with it."

He put his hand on my shoulder. "You tend to forget to tell me a lot. Be careful and don't turn your back on her. Even though they've never showed signs of violence, you can never be too careful around criminals."

I glanced at his hand on my shoulder and said, "I will."

He slipped his hand off. The room got a bit smaller from our serious thoughts, so he changed the subject. "Anna is a kinky one, isn't she?"

"As much as I'd love to tell you we should go for it, I'm not about to be whipped, clamped, tied, or have Lucio put anything in me."

Easton stopped for a moment. "So if it wasn't Lucio, you wouldn't mind it?"

"Stop with the 'what ifs.' We need to hang out more in AL to find out their names." I moved my computer next to Easton and said, 'Let's pop onto the site and go to a few BDSM places. Maybe we'll get lucky."

"Damn, I hope so."

"Not that way!"

"There's no harm in a little fun while we investigate."

I clicked on the AL icon, and watched as the virtual world pixels downloaded into a scene. I put in my avatar name, Candy Catwick, and password. My avatar appeared at the same place I was the last time I logged out. The Karaoke place. Some woman screamed a Whitney Houston song, but everyone cheered her on. Mute. I wish I had a mute button in real life.

Easton leaned over. "Where the hell are you?"

"At some Karaoke place. Do you want to see?"

"Hold on so you can teleport me there."

The people at the karaoke place had boring avatars and clothes. I, on the other hand, was as sweet as Candy, sexually. In the lower right corner of the screen, a visible bubble showed Callum (Easton) online and then the bubble faded. We were friends in AL, so I could see whether he was online.

I went to his profile, clicked on teleport, and he appeared in front of me, a floating blob until his avatar downloaded.

Callum sent me a private message. "So where to?"

Candy: Search for BDSM.

Callum: That turns me on.

Candy: You're easy.

Callum: I'm open to anything, sweetheart.

Candy: Great. Just find a place, Don Juan.

Callum Disappeared but sent me a message. "Oh, you'll love this one."

He sent me a teleport request and I accepted. I teleported into the craziest scene I had seen in a long time. Lucio and Anna's dungeon didn't come close to this virtual place—a sexual amusement park. Everyone was naked, and the discussions meshed with the activity. People propositioned each other and talked sexually to anyone who would respond. Loaded with pink and blue sex balls, a person only needed to click on it for the avatar to move with the motion of the programmed sex ball. The place had all kinds of positions and sexual acts with countless toys and tables. Everyone participated in some sexual activity. A large orgy of people used three-dimensional characters to fulfill their needs.

In public chat, someone by the name of Kilcutty told me to take off my clothes.

Callum: How sweet. Candy has a fan.

Candy: Funny. Did you know that if you right-click on someone's avatar, you could read their profile?

Callum: Nice. How did you know that?

Candy: I tried it. :D

We both received a message that the place had a "NO CLOTHES" rule.

There was a knock on our front door. We closed out of AL and shut down our computers. Lucio stood there with a gritty smile. He smacked Easton on the shoulder and said, "Come join me for a scotch and cigar. I know a great place. Private. We won't be disturbed while we enjoy good booze, smokes, and conversation."

I placed my hand on his lower back. "Sounds great."

Lucio tipped his head and said, "I figured since you and Anna have your time together, David and I can get to know each other, too."

"You're right." I addressed Easton. "Don't you think it's a nice invite?"

"Definitely, but don't you need to go to the store?"

I waved my hand in dismissal. "Oh I can do that another time. You go have fun with Lucio." I nudged Easton forward. Once he got into Lucio's car, I closed the door, leaned my back against it, and sighed.

(Twenty-Seven) The Wall

~~~~~~

It seemed another lifetime ago, as I listened about my experiences with Anna and AL. My arm no longer throbbed, and the ER room had a few stragglers left including us. I saw the ER doctor, who closed the wound with a few dissolvable stitches and covered it with a child's bandage. The only dressing that survived the rush of treatment was Dora the Explorer. We left in the early hours scouring the streets for fast food to eat in the hotel.

Once finished, I fell onto the bed. Easton came in shortly after and did the same.

I turned to him and asked, "Are you sleeping here?"

"Yeah. There's only one bed." I dampened the situation like a wet blanket in spite of my internal turmoil. All the sexual stirring inside along with the frustration and loneliness of his distance rushed in at once. Bits and pieces of us glided around my memory like a conveyer belt. Easton and I in his car. Me slapping him. Us out to dinner with Anna and Lucio. Then both of us in bed. Both of us in bed? When did that happen?

The thoughts disappeared when Easton asked, "Don't tell me you want me to sleep on the couch? This is a king size bed. I promise I won't touch you."

My body slinked under the covers, clothes on, and nodded an okay. The sheets covered me to the neck. I tried to avoid Easton as he undressed for bed, but he didn't make it easy. He took off his shirt and had his pants unbuttoned.

"You can use the washroom to change."

His upper body rocked back as he said, "Change into

what? Besides, I sleep naked but I'll spare you the excitement."

I turned my back to him with the sheet high. "You won't find any excitement from me."

Easton slid under the covers. My loss of memory went to battle against my libido. He moved closer to me until skin touched skin. All of his skin.

He said under his breath, "You can say that again."

I propped myself up on my elbows and asked, "What's that supposed to mean?" My face crinkled like paper as I asked, "Are you naked?"

He lifted the sheet and then let it drop. "Looks like it. Want to see?"

My mouth stretched to the size of a gasp as I turned away. This triggered Easton into a fit of hysteria. Tears rolled down his cheeks from his out of control response. I scooted away, my face sour from confusion. He wiped his eyes dry as the laughter subsided.

When he finished, he said, "This is crazy."

I sat with the covers still pulled high. "What's crazy?"

"The way we're acting. We've been together for a long time. It doesn't matter whether you remember because what you said before was true. Is true. With us, life is natural. From the very beginning, even when you came out of your coma. Sure you were scared, but you still trusted me just like you did when you got into my car."

"I know, but ..."

"But what? Neither of us will get any sleep if we obsess over the fact we're in bed together. It's a big bed, and I doubt we'll even come close to one another."

I agreed as I scooted down diverting my eyes elsewhere. It took a while, but I fell into a deep sleep. I had dreams of a cabin. Anna and Lucio. Other couples.

And then a gurgled noise in my ear. I woke startled to find Easton's head rested on top of mine while he snored into my ear. His left leg crossed over my legs and he hugged my waist. It didn't matter that we were close, but I knew I couldn't sleep. I maneuvered my legs from under his, lifted his arm so I could get off the bed. The only obstacle was his head on top of mine. I put his arm down and stuffed the pillow underneath his head. Two snorts and his eyes opened. Instead of letting me go, he smiled and pulled me closer. I thought he would drift back to sleep, but instead he said, "Did you sleep all right?"

I whispered yes and placed my hand on the one wrapped around me. Easton turned me on my back and placed his left arm over me. Unexpectedly, he pressed his lips to mine. His were warm. Mine were chapped. I thought about my bad breath. Easton didn't. His lips pressed a little harder, separated mine, and his tongue slipped inside. My body tensed, relaxed, and then tensed again. My mouth hungered for his in spite of my tension. Easton's hand moved to my breast. When my eyes flipped open, he was watching me. It intoxicated me. He intoxicated me. And then his lips left mine. He slid his hand over my breast with the innocence of a schoolboy. The breath I held seeped out and then the hand on my breast rested on top.

In a whisper, he said, "I miss us."

"I do, too. And I don't even remember what I miss."

Easton's head fell back as he let out a howl. He raised his head to the ceiling and said, "God, how did our situation get so messed up?"

I readjusted my body, pulled a question somewhere from the back of my mind and asked without thinking. "Why don't you like Jenny Carver?"

With a jerk of his head, his eyes blinked. "Where did that come from?"

"I don't know. All these thoughts and memories had floated around in my head. Traces of what you've told me have connected with moments I started to remember. Maybe I asked because Jenny's here."

Easton pulled himself to the headboard, ran a hand over his face and said, "I slept with her." My body switched to fifth gear as it shot straight up.

He hesitated before he said, "It happened after you cheated on me."

"What? This entire time I've felt so bad and guilty when I learned of my infidelity and *now* you're confessing to have done the same?"

He shook his head. "It wasn't the same."

I slapped my hands on the bed. "The hell it isn't. Cheating is cheating."

"There are degrees of it. Your degree occurred in my absence, which was often."

"That's not fair. You can try to separate your behavior from mine, but it's not any different."

Easton moved off the bed. "No. No it's not. I got drunk and let my hurt control the situation. I knew Jenny wanted me from the moment we met."

This prompted me to stand as I argued on my side of the bed. "You knew? Aren't you the arrogant one?"

He stopped and twirled his finger in an upward motion. "Arrogant my ass. It's the facts. Jenny will sleep with anyone. She slithered her way into your life, hit on me every chance she got, and then slept with me, knowing how much I loved ..." He muttered a few choice words when he ran his hands through his hair.

"How much you loved what?"

Easton dropped his arms. Our eyes connected and I

saw him immersed in pain. He whispered 'you,' and then breathed in deep to push out another 'you' with force.

I took each step with care until I stood a foot in front of him. My hands held the sides of his face. I gave him a soft kiss. One that told him I felt the same way. One that told him I felt his pain. We let the small space between us disappear as we wrapped into a tight hug. It was better than his smile. I felt his hands on my skin, his muscles tense and his breath on my shoulders. Then tears began to dampen my skin. Easton's body jerked with every drop. My right hand rubbed the back of his head while the other did the same on his back. He started to take down the wall he placed between us. I knew it wouldn't come down all at once. The deep hurt needed healing. We needed to find each other again.

The phone rang. Easton released me to answer it. He gave a few short responses, replaced the receiver and went into the washroom. When he came back into the room, he put on his jeans. I didn't know what I did or said for him to break the moment, so I followed him into the other room. Easton poured two glasses of whiskey and handed one to me. At first, I glanced at the glasses as if to say, "Isn't it a bit early?" but then we washed it down before there came a knock on the door. Easton opened it to Jenny with a smile on her face.

She said, "I'm sorry to pop in like this, but I wanted to apologize for last night. I shouldn't have been so damn nosy. It isn't any of my business."

Easton said, "You're damn right it isn't any of your business. And how did you know where to find us?"

Jenny spoke to me. "When I left you, I got in my car and drove down the street. Then I saw you enter this hotel."

He moved away from her, but I moved closer. I glared

at her face. Her betraying face with its fake eyelashes. Even though I didn't remember the past, I sure as hell felt in the present. It took me four large steps to get to Jenny. My hand pushed out to the side, and with all my might, I brought my hand across her face. She fell back and pressed her hands to her red, burning flesh. Easton's mouth dropped open.

Once Jenny recovered, she yelled, "What is wrong with you?"

I took a step forward, pointed my finger at her, and she stepped back. "You're what's wrong with me. Pretended to be my friend."

"Pretended?"

"Stop! I know about you and Easton."

Anger colored and contorted Jenny's face when she spoke to Easton. "Why would you tell her?"

I responded instead of Easton. "Why?"

"Yes. It happened a long time ago. I didn't want our friendship to end. I knew if you found out, we'd never be friends again."

I folded my arms in front of me. "You're damn right about that."

"So you want to throw away years of friendship for one mistake? Aren't you being hypocritical?"

I snapped and grabbed her by the hair, pulled her to the floor. Flashes of me beating on Blondie started to dictate my moves. My fingers entwined in her hair as the other hand formed a fist. I punched her in the face while my other hand gripped and pulled her hair. She scratched at my arm, ripped off the bandage. I felt the burn. Easton stepped in and pulled me off her. He held me close to him. We watched Jenny pat down her hair, and battle the humiliation.

When she touched her nose, she had blood on her

fingers. Her eyes narrowed as she said, "You bitch! You think you're better than me? Ha! I fucked your husband because you were a cold fish. He needed you" she sneered at me, "but you were too busy wrapping your legs around someone else."

I lunged at her. Easton held me back and said to Jenny, "Just get the hell out of here. We don't need you in our lives. "

She took a step forward, enough to stay out of arm's reach, and pointed at Easton. "And you. You had no problem when you wanted to screw around."

I kicked at her and said, "You're such a bitch! Get out of here!"

She turned to leave. Before she closed the door, she said to me, "A whip? That's all you got? I gave him more than you could imagine in your frigid little head." I screamed as she slammed the door. Easton let me go, and I kicked at the door.

After I released a few breaths, I said, "I guess assault is in my blood."

He smiled. "You surprise me. I wasn't expecting that."

I put the glass on the table. "Now I understand why you didn't want me to hang around her. Anymore confessions?"

Easton pursed his lips together, looked off for a moment and then said, "Nope. That about covers it."

"Good because if I keep this up, I better get used to prison."

He gave me a flirtatious smile and said, "At least you look good in orange."

I slid my glass toward him. He filled it as he began to fill me in about more of the case.

(Twenty-Eight) Cabin Kibosh

~~~~~~

2001 - Crystal Lane, Rhode Island

The smell of alcohol and smoke strangled the air, woke me from a restless sleep. Easton cackled up the stairs, stumbled and crawled, after a night out with Lucio. I opened my bedroom door and watched as he tripped on the top step and fell into the hallway. On his back, he rolled into a ball as he rocked from side to side in hysterics.

"What's so funny? Do you have any idea what time it is?" He pointed at me and continued. I guess Lucio knew how to have a good time.

My fists rested on my hips as I watched him move around, laughing and attempting to stand. He grabbed the doorknob and fell. As if I wasn't there, he crawled into his bedroom, rolled onto his back, flung his arms and legs out to the sides and the snoring began. It didn't seem right to leave him that way. I bent down, slid one arm behind him, pulled on his right arm. We shuffled over to the side of the bed, and he fell backwards onto it. I removed his shoes and lifted his legs onto the bed. When I was about to pull the sheet over, he covered my hand with his and mumbled, "He won't get you." He patted my hand and said, "No, he won't get you. You're mine." His hand fell to the side and then he started his nightly musical.

By the time Easton made it downstairs, I had finished my jog, dressed, and was waiting for whatever plans he set for the day. Over the top of my coffee cup, I could see his body tense when he came into the kitchen. There was no hello or greeting, only a grunt, a cabinet opened, and coffee poured. His body collapsed into the chair next to mine, his face close to his cup, his hands gripped it tight.

A pathetic scene. His hair defied gravity. His eyes veined by the curse of alcohol. I tried not to laugh at his slouch and coffee romance. He perfected self-pity, which made me lose it.

Easton's elbows rested on the table, hands rose to his ears, and he squinted at me. "What's so funny?"

I shook my head. "Have you seen yourself? It's not a pretty sight."

"Yeah, I'll remind you of that the next time you're sick."

"It's your own fault. No one told you to stay out to the early hours." He took a sip of his coffee, folded his arms on the table in front of him, resting his head on top.

"What's the plan for today?"

"Shit if I know. Right now, all I want to do is go back to bed."

"Okay. I can go into AL or shop—"

He lifted his head and smacked the table with his hand. "Shit!" Easton touched his head to hush the disruption. "I just remembered that Lucio invited us to a friend's cabin this weekend. There will be four other couples."

"You said yes?"

"It sounded good over the fifth scotch. After that the night got hazy."

My hand slammed down on the table.

He jumped and asked, "What's wrong?"

"It's too soon. I'm not in the mood for any more surprises."

Easton held his head. "I highly doubt the rest of them are into BDSM."

"No, but we don't know these couples. Who are they? How do they know Lucio and Anna? We're not prepared!"

"You never know what will happen on a case. They could drag on forever or go fast. I couldn't say no. And once you meet them your questions will be answered."

"You could have said no."

"True, but ..."

"But you're a drunk ass who doesn't think!" I rose so fast my chair fell backward, and I didn't bother with it. Why couldn't he have asked me? I followed his directions, yet he couldn't include me in on some decisions. There was more to it than the BDSM. Anna's intrusive behavior, Lucio wanted to get close and all the guns I had seen from their friends and Anna. Easton introduced me to danger, and it danced with my nerves. The distance in AL made me feel safe. A cabin with four couples I didn't know, gave danger the opportunity to hang around. I went to my bedroom to cool off.

Easton stood in my doorway, hands pressed against the doorjamb.

I asked, "What time are we supposed to leave?"

"Six tonight." His head swayed until it steadied when he looked at me. "I'm sorry. I know it's late notice."

"Do you realize you could have put us in danger?"

He straightened to his natural height and folded his arms in front of him. "Danger? The entire case is dangerous."

"We don't know these—"

"I've been an investigator for years. I don't need some

inexperienced woman telling me that I put us in danger. I'm in control. Sure, maybe I shouldn't have agreed on such late notice. Right now, Lucio and Anna have no plans to hurt us, at least not in a deadly way."

I ignored him and faced the window. He closed the door to his room.

Several hours passed before I decided to get ready. His door remained closed, but all my clothes were in there. I found him face up on the bed, in his boxers, and his Cock-a-saurus Rex stood at attention. He didn't even flinch. I tried to avoid it, but my eyes drifted in that direction. From what I could tell, the family jewels were semi-costly.

I opened the closet door, pulled my suitcase from the top shelf and threw it on the floor. He moved on the bed. I unzipped the suitcase, looked into the closet to pack. Behind me, I heard Easton get out of bed and go into the washroom. I had filled my suitcase on one side when he walked over rubbing his eyes. I kneeled by the suitcase when he approached, of course with his Cock-a-saurus Rex at eye level, but asleep.

Easton looked down at my suitcase. "It's a weekend, Brand."

"Shut up. I want to be prepared; hiking, dinners, sitting by the campfire."

Easton pulled his duffel bag from the closet, unzipped it and threw boxer briefs, socks, and T-shirts in it.

"I hope you'll have a few nice outfits in case we go out to dinner."

He mimicked what I said. "Yes, Brand, I think I'll have room for shirts and pants."

Jerk!

"If not, you could always take out a few boxer briefs, or did you pack enough in case you dirty them from excitement?"

"Funny. You could use an orgasm to get rid of your bitchiness."

"Is that an offer? Wait. No, how could you possibly find the time after all your masturbation sessions?"

He pushed my shoulder, and I fell to the left side. I pushed his shoulder. Unfortunately, it didn't do much except throw me back to the side. Easton scoffed.

We packed and brought the suitcase and duffel bag downstairs. I had on a vintage Coca-Cola T-shirt and jeans with black clogs. He came down in a Bruce Springsteen T-shirt and jeans with gym shoes. I had a water bottle in my purse. When I went into the kitchen for snacks, he took the water bottle out and drank it.

I grabbed it from him. "What is wrong with you?"

"I was thirsty. What's the big deal?"

"It's for the ride to the cabin." I retrieved a few more bottles.

He followed me and asked, "Where's mine?"

"Where the rest of the water bottles are."

He grabbed a few and then finished loading the car.

We left but I wasn't sure if one of us would arrive dead. We were irritable; me from the trip, he from being hung over. Easton drove most of the one-and-a–half-hours while I played around with the air conditioner and radio—two things we both couldn't agree on. Easton blasted the air.

"It's cold."

"Put on a sweater."

I changed the station to classical music and set the volume higher. Easton changed it to classic rock. I changed it back, increased the volume every time he changed it.

He couldn't take it anymore. "Enough!" He turned the radio off.

We were the last to arrive. They had wine, cheese, and fruit platters on the table. When we walked in, all movement came to a halt. Anna approached, took Easton by the arm, and moved us toward the rest of the group.

"Everyone, these are our new neighbors, David and Claire. They are such a delight to have around and refreshing to say the least. I had to invite them so you could all meet."

By the fireplace, Anna introduced us to Eric and Olivia Buckley. There was one Hispanic couple by the names of Ty and Maria Torres, another couple, Fulton and Noelle Collins, a little older than us, dripping with money and attitude, and then Lila and Leone Thorburn, who we met at the restaurant. After introductions, Anna and Lucio showed us around the house and approached a room at the end of the upstairs hallway.

Anna opened the door and said, "This is your room. All the rooms have their own washroom." She pointed to the dresser by the door. "I left a bottle of wine and crackers for the two of you in case you get hungry." She then placed her hand on a box of condoms and K-Y Jelly. "And I wasn't sure if you brought any of these so I thought I'd supply you with some. If you need more, there's a store not far away in town." She winked at us, ushered Lucio out, and put her hand on the door. "We'll leave you alone to get yourselves comfortable. When you're ready, meet us downstairs for some appetizers and drinks." Before she shut the door, she added, "Oh, just so you know, our room is right next to yours. Holler if you need anything," and then she left.

My eyes shot over to Easton. "Damn! I forgot that

we'd have to share a room."

He threw his duffle bag in the corner, hopped on the bed and laid down. "It's no big deal."

"Maybe not to you, but it is to me." I shook my head at the condoms and K-Y Jelly. "Really? Could they be any more obvious?"

For a moment, he lifted his head then dropped it back on the pillow. "I think that's the point."

"What should we do with this crap?"

Easton smiled. "Oh, I could think of a few."

My fists clenched harder. "You think this is hilarious, don't you?"

"I think your reaction is hilarious."

I lifted and moved around objects. I went into the bathroom, pulled the shower curtain to the side, went through the medicine cabinet, and searched in the corners.

Still on the bed with his hands behind his head, Easton asked, "What is wrong with you?"

I came close to him and whispered, "I'm checking for bugs or a spy camera." His howl made me angrier. I clenched my teeth. "It's not unlikely after what they have in their house."

Easton pulled me onto the bed, flipped his leg on top, and kissed me. I fought him, but he wouldn't let go. Or maybe I really didn't want him to stop, so I gave in. We laid there with our mouths keeping a fluid rhythm— natural and even. I finally pushed him away to stand.

"What? We need to get into character."

I applied lipstick, straightened my shirt and said, "I am. Here's me in character," and I joined the rest of the group.

Not long after, Easton came. I made sure to stand by Lila and Leone since I had met them already, and they didn't ask too many questions. We sipped our wines and ate appetizers. I caught a fast buzz from lack of food. My body tingled. It helped me deal with the current situation. Easton put his arm around me, kissed my cheek, and asked if I wanted a refill of wine. My head nodded with a crooked grin. He paused for a minute, noticed my glassy eyes, and then headed for more wine. Anna detained him there.

Eric Buckley came over by me. "Where's your drink? Can I get you one?"

I jerked my chin toward Easton and said, "Thanks for the offer, but David is getting me a refill."

Eric took a sip of his wine as I browsed the room for his wife, Olivia. I felt him watch me so I turned and gave a slight nod with a smile.

He returned it and said, "It's a nice cabin."

"It is."

"Our room is down here," Eric pointed, "Where is your room?"

"We're in the room at the end of the upstairs hallway."

"Nice."

It was a noticeable silence. Olivia approached Eric, and my shoulders drooped from relief a little too soon.

Olivia pushed her plate between us. "Would either of you like some crackers and cheese?"

"No thank you. Although I'd like that glass of wine my husband went to fill."

Olivia turned her head toward Easton. "He'll be there for a while. Anna is a talker."

"How long have you known Anna and Lucio?"

"A long time, well Anna, that is. I've been friends with her since college. I married Eric in my mid-twenties. Anna was still having a good old time. She wanted to try different flavors, if you know what I mean.

But her attitude changed when she met Lucio."

Eric cleared his throat. "She hasn't changed much." Olivia's face went rigid and she nudged his arm. He left us without a word.

Easton made it back with my refill. "Sorry about that. I started talking to Anna and—"

"Watch yourself with her," Olivia cut in. "Anna has an insatiable appetite for being the center of attention, to be adored by every man around her. She'll do what she can to get your attention." Olivia left before we could ask her what she meant.

Anna called everyone's attention. "Lucio and I made reservations at a restaurant tonight. For those who want, you can go to your room to get ready. We'll meet down here in an hour."

Easton and I were the first ones upstairs to take a break from the group.

(Twenty-Nine) Spoonful of Affection

~~~~~~

Easton and I hadn't moved from the couch as he tried to refresh my memory about the cabin with Anna and Lucio. The alcohol settled into me. My body didn't care about emotions or my recollections. For the moment, I didn't care that my memory took a hiatus. I was getting to know Easton in a different way. The investigation let me know him on a personal level along with his accounts of the past. I remember a wooden cabin. A fire burning.

Easton stared at the swirling ice in his glass. To hear about how our early relationship played out made me happy. Anger and laughter had come natural to us, and our banter had never gone overboard. We seemed frustrated and amused.

"It sounds like we had fun when we were undercover."

"Fun?"

I moved my glass in a circular motion. "Yeah, we got angry, poked fun, but it never got out of hand."

Easton sat back in thought, smiled, and then said, "There were times it got out of hand. Our hidden affection was like walking on a tight rope. We got put into situations that wiggled the rope."

I tucked my feet underneath me. "Fascinating. What kind of situations?" He brought the bottle of whiskey over, filled our glasses and then got comfortable. "Like when we returned from the restaurant. We had to sleep in the same bed."   I shrugged. "We shared a bed now, and it wasn't that big of a deal."

He gave me a downward glance. "The idea didn't thrill you, so you can imagine the combination of a sexually charged criminal couple along with their behavior. You were agitated."

The coldness of the glass cooled down the heat created by the alcohol. I took another sip and said, "I gotta hear this one."

Easton talked about the first night at the cabin when we had to sleep in the same bed.

2001 - Crystal Lane, Rhode Island

Dinner remained uneventful. We ended the night with a nightcap and then the couples migrated to their rooms. Once we were in our room, I grabbed some clothes to change into. When I came out of the washroom, Easton was on the bed with the K-Y Jelly.

He pushed his hair out of his eyes and said. "This smells pretty good."

I slapped his leg and said, "Boundaries. Did you forget them?"

All of a sudden, he noticed I didn't have any makeup on. I wore sweats and a T-shirt with my bra still on. With a cocky attitude, he said, "You want to turn me off, don't you?"

Another knock on the door. I opened it to Anna's scrutinized glare. "Is that what you brought to wear on a romantic weekend in the woods?

Easton hopped out of bed, put his arm around my shoulder and sulked. "I know. I had hoped we could make this weekend special. I mean, it is our anniversary."

I turned to him at the same time Anna did, asking, "It is?"

"Yeah. It's the anniversary of the first time we met."

Anna put her hands together. "How sweet of you to remember?" She said to me, "You better hold onto this one. He's a romantic. He's like a warm sun on a chilly morning."

I put my hand around his waist, pulled him tight, and smiled. "You got that right. Like a vulture circling its prey."

They both frowned.

"Joke."

Anna gave me another once over. "I think I have an extra. Hold on."

Before I could object, she disappeared into her room and returned with pink babydoll lingerie with lace cups and trim, sheer mesh, satin bows, and a G-string. I swallowed hard.

"Uh ... I wouldn't feel comfortable wearing that."

Anna asked, "Why?"

Easton followed. "Yeah, why?"

"Because it's not mine. I don't mean to sound rude or ungrateful, but I don't want to wear another woman's"

"No, Claire. I've never worn this, see?" She showed me the price tags, which were outrageous by the way. "You can keep it. Think of it as my gift to you on your 'first time you met' anniversary. Try it on. Let me see if it fits. You could just put the top over your bra if you want."

I took the lingerie from her, gave Easton a 'watch your back' glance and went into the washroom. When I came out, they were both on the bed facing me. I took her advice and put the top over my bra with my sweats still on. Anna got up, circled around me, touched the strap and took hold of the bottom mesh. She lifted and dropped it to see it float.

"Beautiful, Claire." She turned to Easton who stared at my breasts and stomach. "What do you think David?

"Uh, yeah, beautiful."

Anna put her hands together. "Yes!   Have fun tonight." She left as fast as she arrived.

The heat on my face and my pumped fists at my sides was an indication for Easton to back off. He didn't heed my warning. He traced the lace around my breasts. My right arm bent, went back and came full blast into his stomach. He keeled over. I changed into my T-shirt as he coughed on the other side of the door.

When I came out, Easton gave me a bear hug. His words bit hard. "What the hell was that for?"

Not to make matters worse, I didn't try to get away or fight him. "For being an asshole and making me feel uncomfortable. For your disrespect."

He coughed to the side then brought his lips close to my right ear. "Didn't I warn you not to ever hit me again?"

I turned my head toward his face, saw him out of the corner of my eye. I grinded my teeth as I spoke. "Or what? You'll kill me?"

He released me. I went to the other side of the bed, got under the covers, and turned my back to him. He switched off the lights. The bed dipped down on his side. I was scared. And sad. I didn't want to be there. Why did I agree to the investigation? My body shivered. Easton's arm hugged me. That was it—a spoonful of affection. My tension melted, and my dreams entertained me for the rest of the night.

(Thirty) Chasing Fairy tales

~~~~~~

It surprised me that Anna wanted to get us to sleep together when she wanted to get Easton into her bed. I remembered the punch in the stomach. After I did it, I crumpled inside knowing I shouldn't have hit him, and wondered how he would react.

I put my drink down and said, "I did punch you. I remember."

Easton tossed his arms and let them fall onto the couch. "Figures you'd remember that."

I shrugged. "Why did Anna want to make our night special?"

"Probably to get in your good graces so you'd change your mind."

"Did you ever want to be with her?"

Easton went over to the window and said, "There wasn't a time that I wanted to be with her. At times, I wanted to choke you, but I did not want to be physical with Anna." He turned toward me. "You and I. We were a team."

The longer I stayed with Easton, the more my desires intensified. And it wasn't the alcohol. I remembered meeting him on that sidewalk. He had looked delicious. I had chosen to get into his car without much consideration. It surprised me still how easily I had gone along without the curiosity that he could possibly be a serial killer. But I had gotten into the car with him then, and again, after my stay in the hospital. Easton spent a lot of time with me in the hospital. In the beginning, I received several doses of sedatives to calm me down. I was disoriented and scared. Easton held my hand on those days and let me know it would be all right. For that moment in time, I believed him. Although foreign to me, I listened to him talk about our life, and trusted that he told the truth. He was talking about our fairy tale. I held onto the stories. Chased the fairy tale so I could hook a memory.

Once I arrived home, and parts of my life started to reveal themselves, I stopped chasing it. How we met, a drunk drowning her sorrows due to hard times wasn't the only secret to this memory puzzle. I came into this relationship hurt, and in the end, I hurt the one man I ever really trusted.

But maybe the hurt of losing my mother never left; it lingered in the background. The frailty to love another with all my heart was too great a risk. Alcohol had a tendency to find one's inner pain, wake it up, and let the anguish feed. Even though alcohol took advantage of my loss, I couldn't help but turn to it for relaxation. Sometimes to dig deep for a few answers. Fuzzy in my head, distorted, and discolored, a haze of questions remained, but I couldn't decipher what was real or not. What I did remember about my mom was good. Not a bad memory of her ever came to surface.

My mother had lived for me, the center of her life, yet I never realized it until she died. I had a few vivid dreams of rocking to sleep in her arms. Other memories that seeped to the front was of her holding my hand as we went to church, but the recollections always ended with me at her grave. I'd talk to her as if she was next to me, and squeezed a bouquet of flowers in my hand.

Easton brought me back by asking, "What's wrong?"

I realized then that I had tears in my eyes. "Instead of a verbal response, I just shook my head and wiped them away.

He came and sat across from me. "Why are you crying? Is this about Jenny?"

I let out a frustrated laugh. "No. My mom. Now that you mention it, I should cry about Jenny. What happened to us? Didn't we have a chunky love, one filled with adventures and desires?"

"Chunky love?"

"Yes. Chunky as if we overindulged in one other. Chunky like we couldn't get enough of us. The stories you told in the hospital seemed like an enchanted fairy tale. That's how I saw it anyways. You were this knight, here to save me from my loss of memory, and you'd talk about the wonderful things we did. Places we went to, such as Niagara Falls, and the time we flew to Italy for a week. I couldn't remember any of it, yet the beauty and romanticism of the way you described it captured my attention. What happened to our chunky, erupted love? I cheated. You cheated. Did we run out of things to talk about?"

Easton rested his right ankle over his left knee. "I think we stopped listening."

"About how we felt?"

"And about what we wanted. We also stopped with the small things that mattered, such as a simple show of affection. That chunky love you referred to became thin. There were times, especially during the case, when we enjoyed being together. We might not have admitted our feelings at that point, but our relationship seemed easier. Once we married and settled into our daily lives, the desires started to fade. The adventures got farther apart."

"Did I get frustrated with home?"

He sighed and said, "Yeah. It wasn't easy for you. And with me gone for sometimes weeks on end, I guess you felt neglected."

"Sounds as if our case triggered the adventure and excitement, and when it was over, we became just another couple."

"Another boring couple. When we revealed how we felt to each other, things fell into place. We didn't take us for granted."

I poured another drink. It was insane to continue drinking when it didn't help my memory, but it occupied the in-betweens of conversation. Besides, it was the only thing to do.

He stood and said, "Forget that drink. Let's eat. I'm starved."

I left the glass on the table. "Fine with me."

We found the lodge we had ventured into with Anna and Lucio. It had a huge lounge area that featured live music, several restaurants, and a few spas. I picked a seafood restaurant. There were two main window walls, one of them planked over a lake. It was early enough for us to get a table by the window. The beauty of the forest mesmerized me. Bulky trees of all sizes padded the lake's perimeter, reflected off the lake, and every so often, a fish rippled the water or a bird coasted to another tree. I smiled.

Easton put his menu down and said, "That's exactly how you were when we were on the hike."

I sat back surprised. "A hike? I can't picture Lucio on a hike."

He leaned halfway over the table. "What did you say?"

My shoulders rolled in and I slumped into my chair. "Uh ... I can't picture—"

"You must remember Lucio. I know I've talked about him, but for you to say that must mean it triggered a memory. "

It didn't occur to me until he said so. My body lifted and I grinned. "I don't know how or when that happened. When you mentioned it, I got this picture of Lucio in my head, a little belly, bald and decorated in gold. I even remember his voice. I think. Wasn't it high for a man of his so-called importance?"

He smacked the table and people turned around to see what happened. Easton didn't pay any attention to their stares. "Yes! Definitely annoying. That creeped you out about him."

"His voice, huh? I would assume it was his life of crime."

Easton agreed. We placed our orders and watched the sun at ease. The orange glowed like a fireball dipping into the lake as the surrounding trees darkened. It made me think about what Easton said of how we enjoyed our surroundings. We went for the hike to this same lodge. I asked him to tell me what happened after we got into our fight.

(Thirty-One) Take a Hike

~~~~~~

2001 - Crystal Lane, Rhode Island

I woke to find us facing each other. Easton's chin rested on top of my head, his arm cuddled me. Tucked into the warmth and wonder of his body, I wanted to remain there forever. It felt good. Free. As much as I had to pee, it meant more to remain near his heart. I inched closer when he stirred and shifted his left leg over mine.

We remained that way until someone knocked on our door. Easton's eyes struggled to open. He removed his leg from me and answered the door. Anna stared at his boxer briefs. He angled his waist behind the door with his head in the opening.

He rubbed his eyes. Easton had a morning crackle when he asked, "What time is it?"

"It's 9:00 am. Everyone is at breakfast, so I thought I'd come and check on the two of you."

Easton's head propped against the door as he said, "We're sleeping. Thanks."

He was about to close the door, but she put her hand on it and said, "We have a hike planned for today. The group leaves at eleven."

"Good to know." He closed the door without saying good-bye and went into the washroom. Still under the covers, I turned on my back, put my hands behind my head and closed my eyes.

Easton climbed back into bed, laid on his back, and said, "A hike. Can't wait for that." His breath smelled minty, which reminded me to get in there. I hopped into the shower, shaved, got out and couldn't find the towels. There weren't any other than the hand towels. The washroom didn't have room for a cabinet. I opened the door about an inch. "Easton, are there any towels out there?"

The bed creaked again as he searched for them, which he found in the corner dresser drawer. He handed me both and told me to leave the other one in there for him. I brushed my hair back and wrapped the towel around me. Easton watched while I went through my suitcase in search of underwear, a bra, shorts, and a tank top.

I glanced over my shoulder, and with a bit of an attitude said, "Fixate elsewhere."

His playful smile made me lose the attitude. He turned his head as I slipped on my underwear and shorts, took the towel off, and put on my bra and tank top.

"Okay, I'm done."

I sat on my side of the bed with a handheld mirror to make myself more presentable. He crawled by me, peeked over my shoulder into the mirror and said, "I lied before. You look cute without makeup." He kissed my shoulder and went into the shower. I put the mirror down swimming in his words. If that was the way he apologized, I wouldn't have had any problem getting into fights.

We made it downstairs in enough time to grab something to eat. I brought a small backpack for bottled water. This time I included some for Easton. Anna explained that we had to go over to a lodge to meet up with a trail guide, who would take us on the walk. The distance to the lodge was around three city blocks away, so we could choose to walk or drive. Noelle and Fulton Collins were the only people who decided to drive. On the way to the lodge, some gathered in groups or wandered separately. Everyone kept quiet as we walked there. The forest kept our attention, the early sun warmed our faces.

Easton took the backpack from me before we started out. There was a comfortable quiet between us, caring gestures exchanged in the morning left us content. Ty and Maria Torres fell back so they could walk next to us. We briefly smiled at them.

Ty spoke. "We didn't get a chance to talk to either of you yesterday. In case you forgot, I'm Ty and this is my wife, Maria."

Easton and I both said our hellos, but didn't offer any information.

Ty continued his one-sided conversation. "We've recently met Lucio and Anna when we moved to Crystal Lane. They invited us on this trip to get to know their other friends."

We nodded when Ty said something we agreed with or to indicate we were listening, even though we drifted from conversation. The Torres's didn't fit in with the group. They were the only Hispanic couple, and they didn't connect with the others. After last night, Easton and I had crossed them off our investigate list.

Maria could tell we didn't want to talk. She took Ty's hand and said, "It was nice to meet the two of you," and they moved ahead of us.

When out of earshot, Easton asked, "Were we too rude?"

"Maybe. But we don't have to worry about them, and I want to enjoy the beauty and warmth." Easton took my hand.

The huge lodge featured live music, restaurants, lounge area, and a few spas. We gathered by the information desk, collected maps and brochures of other activities to do in the area. I handed a brochure to Easton and said, "Rafting sounds fun."

"Yeah. I'll ask the rest of the group later on to see if they're interested."

Noelle and Fulton were next to us. Fulton let out a long, leaking sigh and said, "Rafting is too much work." He turned to Easton, put out his hand and said, "I don't believe we had time to personally talk yesterday. The other couples took up our time. I'm Fulton and this is my lovely wife Noelle."

Easton took his hand, gripped it tighter than normal, and watched Fulton's eyes grow with panic. He eased up and said, "I'm David and this is my incredibly wonderful wife Claire, and we don't mind work."

Fulton's eyes narrowed and his right lip rose as he took his hand back, shook it out. They moved away and I turned to Easton. "You don't like them."

"He's a pompous asshole. I don't need to get to know them to figure that out."

I moved closer to him. "Don't forget, we don't want to make enemies out of these people."

"I'm not worried about those two. First, we won't learn too much from the Fulton's because the world revolves around them, and second, my gut tells me that the only taboo they've ever been involved in is marinating in their cologne and perfume."

A loud hoot escaped me. Easton cupped my face in his hands. He came closer until his lips wisped against mine and then covered them with a whimsical kiss, playful and deprived. We turned to find the Buckley's and Tumicelli's watching us. We nodded and turned to explore the lodge.

Anna called out, "Don't venture too far. We'll be leaving soon."

The guide stood in front of the group explaining what to expect. We would walk for a few hours and then stop for lunch at a restaurant that specialized in Southern cuisine. As the guide talked, Easton and I drank water and split a granola bar. The other couples had a tendency to check on us. We assumed public displays of affection irritated them, like a small pebble in their shoe.

The hike began with Easton and I holding hands. What was originally referred to as a hike turned out to be more of a nature walk. I had broken more of a sweat vacuuming. Maybe the word conjured up rugged thoughts that enticed Anna. We moved along mostly flat terrain that at times, veered away from the lake. Easton continued to carry the backpack.

Even though it turned out to be different from what I expected, I was in awe of the height of the trees and bursts of color from the sun. The forest Anna and I jogged through didn't have this kind of beauty. This forest had few dead trees lying across the forest bed. Our guide pointed out the trees in the forest amongst other foliage. It attracted different types of trees, thorny to soft—here, nature had a greedy eclectic décor. Evergreens fragranced the air. Oak trees towered high above, Red Maple trees changed to a beautiful red coloration in the fall, and the grayish bark of the Eastern White Pine added a nice contrast to the greens. Berry bushes emerged every few yards and small purple flowers carpeted the forest.

Before I knew it, we were at the restaurant for lunch. A few of the women, including me, went into the washroom to freshen ourselves. When I walked out of the stall, I found two sets of eyes on me.

I approached the sink and said, "Hello ladies."

Olivia and Anna acknowledged me. Anna asked,

"Claire, did you and David have a nice time last night?"

"We did. Then again, every night with David is nice." The faucet automatically shut off, and I grabbed a few paper towels and applied some lip-gloss. When I finished, I said, "You were all early risers today."

Anna responded, "I'm always early. You know that."

"That I do." I threw the paper towel away, opened the door and asked, "Are you ladies coming?"

The cast of characters was already seated, Easton and I at the far end near Lucio and Anna. Everyone ordered alcoholic beverages, but I stuck with lemon and water. Easton put his hand on my thigh as we listened to the others talk about the hike. It felt like we, Easton and Brand, were becoming this pretend couple. The natural touches. Glances. It didn't feel like make-believe anymore.

Fulton sat in the middle, across from the Torres's, and complained, "If I would have known the trail was going to be so bumpy, I'd have thought twice about it."

Ty nodded. "My shoe got caught in a few holes."

He had to make sure Ty knew their situation warranted more attention, so Fulton added, "Noelle stumbled a few times, caught herself on a tree trunk. She skinned her palm."

Eric Buckley shrugged. "Hiking isn't for everyone. Some people don't want to get dirty or come across bugs and/or reptiles."

Maria Torres asked Eric, "There are reptiles?"

Eric's eyebrows collapsed. "Of course there are. Where do you think frogs and snakes live?"

Ty patted his wife's arm. "You're fine, honey. They won't bother you as long as you don't bother them."

The conversation annoyed Anna by the way she held a straight face, stiff in her chair. Then she moved forward. "Like Eric said, hiking isn't for everyone, but I thought all of us could use some time away and meet new people."

Fulton sat back. "It hasn't been too bad. If I overlook the holes."

Maria didn't want to upset Anna. "I haven't run into any reptiles, so it's no big deal for me."

Anna turned to Easton and me and said, "You two are quiet today. Is everything okay?"

"Everything is fine. Thanks for the invite. As you mentioned, Claire and I are enjoying our time away."

Fulton leaned forward so he could see Easton. "What line of work are you in?"

"I'm a computer consultant."

"There's big money in technology for those who survived the dot com crash."

Easton folded his napkin on his lap. "Technology always changes. What do you do?"

He pulled on his shirt to remove the wrinkles and said with pride, "Self-made millionaire. Noelle and I worked hard to retire early and enjoy the good life."

Lucio refolded his napkin and placed it back on his lap. "Let's change the subject. We're here to get away from work."

Anna petted Lucio's arm and smiled. "Lucio's right. It's been such a beautiful day. We shouldn't ruin it with talk of work."

The rest of the lunch went by without a hitch. We returned to the cabin on foot where Easton and I retired to our room to discuss the different couples. It came down to one thing, Lucio and Anna's friends were bores. The only couple we put on our investigate list were Eric and Olivia Buckley. We hadn't quite figured out where they fit into the crime scheme, if they fit at all.

(Thirty-Two) Tango Dancing

~~~~~~

2013 - Crystal Lane, Rhode Island

The moon lit up the sky and casted a spotlight on our table. Its soft glow, tender to skin, made our dinner that much more romantic. I patted my lips with a napkin and placed it to the side. Discarded mussel shells piled high on a plate, and a second bottle of Chardonnay chilled in a bucket next to our table. We filled ourselves with seafood, bread, and wine. The alcohol massaged my muscles. Full and content, I settled back into my seat with thoughts of what Easton had told me about the hike.

He put his arms on the table enchanted by the moon. The mysterious moon stared back at him. Easton's skin appeared pale and beautiful. I wanted to be with him in so many improper ways, yet the past held us apart. I wanted my memory back along with our fairy tale.

Easton said, "I think this meal will keep me satisfied for a few hours."

I turned the stem of the wine glass between my fingers and then rested them on top of the base. "I think the alcohol I consumed today will keep me drunk for the rest of the week."

Easton glanced at my glass then back at the moon.

"Did anything happen when we went back to the room?" He sat back, took a sip of his wine and shook his head.

"Why did you antagonize me when Anna brought the lingerie? You knew I was nervous about being in the room with you."

He let out a soft laugh as he stared into the shimmering wine glass and shrugged. "Probably because we fought all the way there." Easton's dimples deepened. "And I wanted to see you in the lingerie."

I rotated the wine stem again, watched the wine swish against the inside of the glass. "Was Anna dangerous?"

He nodded several times. "Ah, change in subject."

I rubbed my ear with my shoulder. "Yes, but not because I'm embarrassed. It's something I've dreamt about and wondered if it was real."

"If what was real?"

"Ever since you told me about how Anna felt about you, I've had these so-called flashes about her. Many of the flashes show her glare right through me. We were at a barbeque in one of the flashbacks. She kept me in her sights all the time. I even had a flash of a conversation with one of Anna's friends, Olivia. In the flashback, Olivia warned me about Anna."

Easton swirled the wine around his glass, a few droplets ran down the side, and then he took a few sips. "Plenty happened at a barbeque they had the evening of the hike. We got some great information about Anna. She couldn't be trusted. Anna was one you didn't want to turn your back on."

I stopped turning my glass and asked, "Like what kind of information?"

"Let's get back to the hotel room. I'd rather not talk here. We can get comfortable, and I'll tell you all about the barbeque."

We returned to the hotel. I put on one of the bathrobes and made my way over to the wet bar. At the rate we had been drinking, the alcohol would cost more than the room. I positioned the collar higher, folded my left arm in front of me, and spun the ice cubes around the glass uninterested in the town out there. I heard Easton behind me, poured himself a drink, when I asked, "How long do you suppose we'll stay here?"

He put the bottle down and said, "I haven't thought that far."

"We should consider getting home tomorrow because we're low on clothes."

"I don't have a problem with what you have on."

I turned to see the smirk on his face. "I'm sure you don't." Then back at the white lights that littered miles of darkness, I said, "Seriously, it's probably best we return before I actually *do* turn into an alcoholic."

Easton moved behind me. I got weak when he narrowed the space between us, his warm breath on the back of my neck. I wanted him so much, but my emotional pendulum swung too hard at times. This happened to be one of them. I wasn't sure how to act. We were both lost when it came to our situation, and we both drank to forget all about it. He moved the collar of the bathrobe and replaced it with his lips. My nerves tightened, but his lips and tongue loosened my knots. I shifted my head enough to see him out of the corner of my eye. Easton paused. He placed his glass and mine on the small table near us. He took me in his arms and planted a much-needed kiss. For both of us. Easton coddled my head in his hand, the other arm held me tight, as if grasping to relive the past … and aiming to pave the way for the future.

Our movements weren't hurried. We hesitated and sought the other's approval with every touch. The moment broke when I started to let myself think. As I stood in front of the window, a lamp light shone on my naked body, the bathrobe gathered at my feet, my inhibitions squeezed in. I stopped Easton's lips. He complied, confused, while I slipped the robe back on. I pulled the belt tight and touched my lips. Easton didn't question me. Instead, he retrieved his drink and sat on the couch.

We seemed to have kept dancing the tango—swift turns. I didn't know how to explain how I felt to Easton. And he didn't ask. I went to the chair. For a time, the only sound in the room were ice cubes in a glass. As if he were the only one there, Easton talked about the barbeque.

(Thirty-Three) Gossip on the Barbie

~~~~~~

A large barbeque grill with steaks as well as chicken and shrimp shish kabobs blended and swirled around the air, the aromas pulled us out of the cabin. Anna and Lucio didn't hold back. Next to the grill stretched a long table with salads and side dishes. They had setup a bar area across from the grill stocked with water, soda, and a variety of wines, beers and hard liquor. In the middle were tables set for two draped in peach tablecloths. White lights hung to help brighten the place along with table candles. The ambiance and smells were so inviting that everyone mingled.

I made myself a drink behind the bar. Olivia came over and browsed the area as to make sure no one remained in earshot.

I loaded my glass with ice, filled a third of it with pear vodka and the rest, soda water. "Can I pour you a drink, Olivia?"

She watched what I made and said, "I think I'll try what you're making there."

I put her glass aside and grabbed a fresh one. She took a sip and her eyes popped with surprise. "Oh this is good. Have you ever bartended before?"

"No, but I have years' experience with alcohol."

We observed the others. Easton, Ty, and Maria Torres congregated together. Eric supervised the barbeque, and Lucio and Anna talked to Noelle and Fulton. We hadn't been too personable on the hike, so it was good that Easton talked to the Torres. Plus, the Fulton's kept Anna pre-occupied and unable to make a move on him.

But Olivia ... she had this unhappiness about her. I believed it stemmed from her marriage. I started conversation to confirm my belief. "So Olivia, do you have any children?"

She diverted her attention to Eric. "No. I was unable to get pregnant."

I put my glass down. "I'm sorry, Olivia. I didn't mean to pry."

Lost in thought, she shrugged and said, "It's all right. I've accepted it after all these years."

I took it slow to avoid the fact that I wanted information. "At least you're friends with Anna and could lean on her through difficult times."

Olivia's body turned entirely to me. She put her drink down before hissing her words. "Please. Let me tell you about our Anna. She doesn't do anything for anyone unless she can get something out of it."

I took a sip of my drink and kept quiet. It was best to let her talk.

"Sure, I turned to Anna when I found out I couldn't get pregnant, and she was there. In more ways than one." She took a break to suck down half her drink. Olivia checked to see if we were still alone. When satisfied, she continued, "Anna is a shark. She'll circle around when you're most vulnerable and do things to make it seem she went out of her way for you. By the time you realize it, she has already circled, bitten, and swallowed you whole." Olivia finished her drink and I poured her another.

When I handed it to her, I said, "I'm sorry to hear that Anna isn't a great friend. I appreciate the heads up. I'll watch my back." Again, Olivia didn't waste time with her drink. "May I ask what she did?"

She ran her tongue along her lips, licked off the excess drops. "You're beautiful, Claire. Confident. That combination upsets and threatens Anna. It's competition for her. If you turn to her for help, she'll find a way to break your confidence and get what she wants, all at the same time."

Olivia came around behind the bar, added to her drink and stayed next to me as she glared at Anna. "When Anna found out I couldn't get pregnant, she offered to be a surrogate. At first I protested because she didn't have any children of her own, and I thought it would make it too difficult for her to give up the baby. As time went on, I became more desperate so I accepted Anna's offer. After we told her about the insemination, it made her too uncomfortable to be under the microscope. She wanted to help, but it made her nervous. Instead of the insemination, I found out she slept with Eric. She claimed she did it for us. She thought the natural way might get her pregnant. That's how she convinced Eric." Olivia brought the glass to her mouth, let out a bitter laugh, and said, "At least that's what I told myself about Eric." Her drink disappeared. It was obvious she wanted to get drunk. Olivia started to pour herself another.

"Anyways, Anna never got pregnant. A few years later, I also found out that Eric and Anna had been together on many occasions. I confronted her about it. Anna turned it around and made me feel bad. She accused me of being ungrateful. She said she called Eric when she ovulated or had time to relax. I forgave her, but our relationship changed forever. Maybe deep down inside I knew Anna would turn on me at some point. I blame myself to have trusted her at my most vulnerable moment. Anna and I still talk, but I always have her at arm's length."

I couldn't respond. How could Anna do that to a friend when she really needed her? No wonder she couldn't wait to get her hands on David.

Anna came over. "Ladies. What are you two up to?"

Olivia didn't respond. Her glass was in the way. I stepped around the bar to stand next to Anna. "Olivia and I enjoyed a few drinks while we marveled how great this place is. You and Lucio outdid yourselves."

Anna rocked back on her heels and then forward with a smirk that hurt more than brightened the mood. "I'm glad you like it. We wanted everyone to enjoy themselves this weekend." She walked behind the bar next to Olivia, and slipped her arm through Olivia's arm. "Remember the old times, Liv? When we stayed awake through all hours of the night talking and smoking pot? It seemed so much easier back then, didn't it?" Olivia looked at her out of the corner of her eye and nodded.

Easton snuck in, hugged me and asked, "Who is bartending?" He kissed the side of my head and put his glass on the bar. Anna took it as Olivia swiped at her eyes. I winked at Olivia and smiled. It seemed to do the trick because she returned the smile.

Anna filled his glass with ice and asked, "What are you having, David?"

"I can't remember. Surprise me." Anna exaggerated by batting her eyes and poured a concoction of alcohol. Easton directed his question to me. "Did you see all the different foods on the grill?"

My forehead pressed against his. I nudged it before I said, "I did. And I don't know where to start."

Anna gave Easton his drink as she responded to me. "Try it all, please. We have enough food to feed everyone who is staying at that lodge we went to today."

"Sure, and then I'll have to jog twice as long as you to work it all off."

Easton said to Anna, "Before I forget, what are the plans for tomorrow? I was curious if you guys want to go rafting."

Anna went over to Easton, who had his right arm around me, and clasped her hands around his other that held his drink. "That would have been great if we had another day. We'll head home probably around lunchtime. But how about the four of us come back here another weekend?"

"Sounds good." Easton itched his nose to get Anna off his arm. She released her grip and Lucio invited everyone to eat. I saw Olivia's wounded eyes before she left the bar.

E aston and I sat at the table closest to the bar, not far from Olivia and Eric's table. We piled our plates with every item on the grill and took another plate to add the side dishes. I couldn't help but smile at all the delicious foods in front of me. Easton and I clinked glasses, washed down a mouthful of food, and charged at the side dishes. Halfway through the meal, I took a breather to glance over at the others. Anna glared right at me. Her unfriendly stare reminded me that she probably believed I had denied her of Easton. At that moment, I knew I had to watch out around Anna, and not because of her want for him but because she was a criminal. Her looks and lifestyle were deceiving. I didn't need her gun to *accidentally* fire while we jogged.

I turned back to Easton. Nothing had taken his attention away from his food. The sides of his mouth glistened with grease as he continued to saw the rest of the chicken off the bone. This case allowed me to see into his life, his mannerisms, and I started to feel like he belonged to me. Many times in my head, I grappled with the idea, even though I knew this was a means to an end. It was short-term, not long-term, which always made me feel like a pincushion, small pricks at my heart. Life after the investigation didn't really exist. I set my sights on work with Easton for shelter, food, and a purpose, and I had to ignore any other misconceptions. Easton didn't belong to anyone. For a few months, maybe longer, he had become my friend, imaginary lover and co-worker. Afterwards ... well I couldn't think that far ahead or it would affect our work.

Easton and I cleared our plates while the alcohol flowed. My body tingled from all the intoxicating fluids I had drained into it. A cleaning crew removed the dishes, packed the food, and left the group to music and conversation. A deejay played some romantic songs. Everyone filled their glasses, weary of the dance floor.

Except Anna. She headed toward us. Center of attention, indeed.

I hadn't noticed Easton leading me to an open area near the deejay because I was caught up in thoughts of Anna's claws dug into me. He put his left arm around my waist, took my hand in his right, and placed both in the nook between his chest and mine. We swayed together, Easton's mouth so close to my ear that I could feel the sizzle of his s's.

My eyes closed as he said, "Anna was coming, so I thought it best we get the first dance in before we mingled."

"Uh-huh."

I felt Easton pull back a bit and I opened my eyes to

find his stare. "What's wrong?"

My forehead puckered. "Zilch. Why?"

"Because you're kind of ... you're drunk, aren't you?"

I giggled and said, "A little."

"No more drinks for you."

Aggravated by his demand, I said, "Who will stop me?"

He pulled me to him. "Really? You're going to challenge me on this one?"

"If I can recall correctly, which I can because I'm not that drunk and I can still feel my legs, you were hungover on the way to the cabin after a late night with our friend, Lucio. Have you forgotten so quickly?" I pressed my finger into his chest and continued. "Maybe you're drunk—"

Easton covered my mouth with his, and we let the moment play out. We explored the sweetness and saltiness of our mouths and lips, our tongues did the tango, with pauses to reposition yet never lost contact. Recently, our personal touches and kisses had grown to a deeper level. It was if our souls just had a conversation. Our hearts an agreement. When we ended, the night air cooled our swollen lips. We stared at each other for a while.

Anna broke the spell by asking, "Look at you two. You act as if it was your first kiss."

Easton continued to gaze at me, smiled and said, "It's always like a first kiss with Claire."

His comment made Anna swallow her words. Out of the corner of my eye, I could see her roll her shoulders back, brush some strands of hair off her face, and clear her throat. "Anyways, I hope you have enjoyed yourselves. The others are over there," she pointed to the side, "and said what a wonderful time they had here.

They even want to come back."

When Easton and I didn't respond, she ignored the silence. "But we'll have to see about that since the four of us will probably be here soon to raft."

Easton and I breathed in deep, collected our manners, and turned our attention to Anna. In unison, we said, "We are."

We pointed at each other and laughed. This irritated Anna. She straightened and said, "I better get back to the others. They want to hear all about Lucio's and my vacation plans for this fall." She paused then disappeared into the group.

I pressed my cheek to Easton's chest, rocked and laughed because we knew damn well we pissed her off. After another dance, we shook off the romance that burned on our skin, the eroticism that frolicked between our legs, and joined the others with our fingers braided, palms moist.

With all the water I had drunk, the alcohol began to flush out of my system and left me tired and unsocial. I surveyed the sky, swayed, and then steadied myself. I never saw such blackness as I did that night. Stars scattered about as if someone had taken a pin and poked holes in black construction paper. It made me feel small.   My fingers released Easton's, and I excused myself from the others, who still had much more to talk about. I went to sleep, oblivious to when Easton came to the room or when he covered me like an electric blanket.

(Thirty-Four) Love Doesn't

~~~~~~

That evening, Easton finished telling me about the barbeque. I shuffled to the bedroom, and he slept on the couch. The back and forth of our sexual needs and wants were put on hold. A reminder for me to focus on my memories, not my libido.

Easton's personable friend, Gilberto, returned to fly us back to Dover the next day. They talked the entire flight, I believe, and forgot that I was in the back. The fun had ended. My plans upon returning home were to flush and irrigate my veins from all the alcohol I had consumed. Even though I had drunk a lot, Crystal Lane showed me that Easton and I could be human toward each other, and it revealed how much we still wanted one another. Next, I had to lasso my memory.

Home still carried the weight of a foreign place. I took a shower and ventured out onto the back porch where Easton sat.

Whiskey, wine, beer, they all became friends of mine over the past few days, and as much as they fogged my mind, they brought clarity to times in my life. Like Jenny. Infidelity.

Our infidelities were not about a trade-in. Our infidelities were about a loss of connection. A loss of importance. Based on our history, we had problems with expression, informed chats to let the other know how we felt. We donned another side of us.

Aware of the quietness, Easton readjusted in his chair and said, "I guess that trip was a bust."

I pulled on the hoodie strings of my sweatshirt and

responded, "Not necessarily. I did find out about you and Jenny, and more about the case."

His head rested against the back of the chair, used the sky for comfort. "I had hoped it would have jogged your memory."

I gave a crooked grin and said, "It might not have jogged my memory, but I now understand why I had to go to rehab all those years ago."

"Yeah, I think I should check into one soon."

"Instead of drinking our words, we probably should have written them down."

We both gave a dirty smile, which turned into a playful one. Easton and I were comfortable with not talking. It was the torment to communicate that wore us down. Unsure of the next steps, we simmered in our thoughts. The past few days had given us a renewed friendship. I traded in my memory for a second chance. Maybe the answer to my memories wasn't about discovering me, but discovering us.

Easton's eyes closed, and he spoke to no one in particular when he said, "I just wanted to write my anger off my soul."

And I closed my eyes, and responded with whatever popped into my head. "You haunted my thoughts throughout the day, and came to me in my dreams."

Easton's eyes shot open and studied me. "Love doesn't always make blind."

I looked over at him and finished the thought with, "Sometimes it opens the eyes."

His legs swung to the side, elbows rested on his knees, as he bent over and asked, "Where did you hear that?"

I imitated him and said, "From you. I …" My head circled around and rested on Easton. "I heard it from you. I remember it. Not in the context we spoke about it, but

I recall it."

"Brand! We said these lines to each other, 'Love doesn't always make blind. Sometimes it opens the eyes.' One would say the first part, and the other would say the second. It was for reassurance. After we fought or when a wedge came between us, we'd say this to each other."

I grabbed the bottom of my chair and dragged it sideways toward Easton, took his hands in mine and said, "Why did we stop?"

"Stop what?"

"Stop saying them."

My hands came back to me after his slid across mine and away. "I don't know."

We gazed downward as if the words were crumbs on the ground. Passion drove us to love, so I couldn't help but wonder what drove us to lose it. It started to bother me more than the loss of memory, unable to pinpoint the moment in time when we surrendered. I did remember. Points connected—layers started to unfold. Now the tables were turned, and I began to talk about our work.

I slid back in the chair, folded my hands over my stomach and said, "As the investigation moved on, I recall us somewhat closer, intimately."

Easton put his arms out and responded, "How could you *not* get closer to this," as he pointed to himself.

We let our smiles linger longer than usual and then our attention floated off into the yard. The days were long, but the sun withdrew leaving us in the shade with a cool breeze. Smoke from grills drifted around the neighborhood. Hamburgers, hot dogs, ribs, and more basted the air with the occasional scent of chlorine. These outdoor activities made me feel like part of the community while at the same time so alone. I noticed I lost Easton for the moment. He sipped his beer, rubbed his eyes, and moved his head around to the different noises.

I settled in, pulled my hands inside my sleeves to warm them and said, "The weekend ended without any raft adventure. I'll tell you what came next. Let me know if I got it right."

(Thirty-Five) As You Wish

~~~~~~

2001 - Crystal Lane, Rhode Island

All of us gathered our belongings, said our good-byes, and each car pulled out of the dirt driveway with strokes of dust behind floating in the air. Anger wasn't the cause of our quiet ride home. Easton sipped his coffee and listened to the news on the radio. I watched the massive trees whiz past us and remembered the stare Anna had given me last night. I should have spread my index and middle fingers into a V, pointed at my eyes and then at her, to indicate I was watching her. I would have needed courage to do that, but the situation sunk in more each day. We were dealing with people who had made crime an occupation. My stomach tossed the acid and liquids that accumulated from last night, and sourness crept up my esophagus, reached the back of my throat before I swallowed it down.

Our bags remained gathered by the door. Food was a priority and then notes. On the way, we bought cheeseburgers and fries. We wanted a greasy meal. Every so often, we stopped the food consumption long enough to release some words.

Easton wiped off the excess grease from his hands and asked, "So what happened last night? One minute you're there with us, and the next, you waved and left."

I shrugged at the question and responded, "I couldn't keep my eyes open. I had so much to drink and then the slowness of the night made me crash and burn. How long did you stay after I went to bed?"

"Long enough to figure out her virtual name."

I sat back hard in my chair. "No way! How?"

"We both know Anna will take any chance she can to talk to me. After you left, she didn't waste any time, just slid into your place."

I folded my arms. "Bitch."

He stopped eating and asked, "Is that jealousy I hear or an overall dislike for the woman?"

"Oh both. Totally. You're so mine." He laughed at my sarcasm. What he didn't know was that I disliked Anna and jealousy existed. "Back to the subject. How did you find out her name?"

"Alcohol is the perfect truth serum, so it was good you went to bed. Anna pulled me aside and whispered to me like, "If you and Claire were to change your minds, and you became my Master, what would you call me?"

I let out a howl. "What would you call her?"

Easton took a fry, put it by my mouth and I ate it. He said, "I spun the question around and asked her what she'd like me to call her."

"Debauchery Ho?"

He slammed his hand on the table; fell back in his chair with his head flipped back with laughter. Easton shook it away and said, "No. It's Sugar."

My arms fell along with my mouth. "Sugar? That's all she could come up with?"

His eyebrows lifted and he shimmied close to the table and asked, "Do you have a better one?"

"This isn't about me. This is about the Ho who goes by Sugar."

Easton folded his arms in front of him on the table. "Humor me. If you could pick a slave name, what would it be?"

"Humor, huh?" I let him stew in anticipation for a while. This path wasn't one I wanted to go down right now. Emotions taunted my nerves. I didn't want to massage sexual thoughts into the conversation, so I blurted, "Clee Torres."

Easton ignored the comment. "Okay, fine, we'll move on," and then he said, "for now."

"What? You don't want to be my Master Eric Shun?"

He pushed the greasy wax paper and bag. "Funny. Shall we get back to Anna?"

"Yes, please. Did you by chance get Sugar's last name?"

"Desmond."

"Great! It will help us find Lucio's. Let's get on our computers and enter Alter Life."

W e signed into the virtual world and our avatars were still at the BDSM place from the last time signed on. The local chat insisted we get naked or get out. I clicked on a link under Destinations and teleported out of there.

Callum: Hey! Where are you?

Candy: The crazies are on fire. I want to find a calm place to figure out what to do next.

Callum: I thought the next step was to get naked.

Candy: Think again. We need to first search for Anna's virtual name—

Callum: Fine, but teleport me to you. These people are vicious.

I sent a teleport and then he appeared in front of me.

Callum: You are a pro in this virtual world.

Candy: I took the time to learn, like right-clicking on someone's avatar to see their profile.

Callum: I just right-clicked on your avatar and it's blank. We should fill out our profiles.

Candy: Good idea. Before I do that, I'll click on the

search button, then people, and put in Anna's name, Sugar Desmond. We can get some ideas as to what to put under our profiles, and ...

Callum: And?

Candy: And you won't believe what I found under Anna's profile. It shows she's a slave to someone by the name of Bo Dugan. It could possibly be Lucio or someone else.

Callum: My guess is it's Lucio. Even though he will share his wife with others, he still wants to have the lead role.

Candy: Impressive profile. It shows her collared in May of this year.

Callum: What does that mean?

Candy: It means that she wears a collar around her neck, and Bo Dugan owns that collar. He's her Master, and she does what he says.

Callum: Shit I gotta get me one of those.

Candy: Collar or Master?

Callum: Collar. Then I can make you do what I say.

Candy: I'd have to want to wear a collar.

Callum: And you don't?

Candy: No! Now listen. She has in her profile that if another Master wants to be with her, he has to ask Bo Dugan. She's also open to being with women.

Callum: YES! This is a beautiful world.

Candy: Don't even think about it. There's no way I'll be with her here or in real life. Besides, she wants you too much.

Callum: What else does it say?

Candy: There's a place to put real life information, but hers is empty. I clicked on a group tab and it shows groups she has joined. I think we should join them.

Callum: How?

Candy: Click on the icon that says 'groups' and type in the name Beautiful Bitches.

He typed it in and the description was a woman's only group for beautiful slaves.

Callum: I'm not their type. Next group.

Candy: Masters and Slaves.

Callum: Okay it pulled up and I clicked 'Join.'

I checked Easton's profile and he added the group.

Candy: It's in your profile. Here's the next group. Sluts, Bondage, and More.

Callum: I like this job. Not only am I enjoying myself on someone else's dime, but I get to partake in some bondage.

I shook my head when I saw Easton bob his eyebrows with a cockeyed grin. I typed in private chat.

Candy: Easy there, boy. You're a bondage virgin. Maybe you should make sure you're not fully 'loaded' when you get in there.

I pointed to the washroom. He saw where I pointed and typed.

Callum: What's the point? You can do it for me right here.

My head shot up, eyes narrowed and typed into chat.

Candy: In your dreams, Romeo. You'll find enough people in here to release you from your load.

Callum: So does this mean we're not 'partners' in this world?

Candy: You mean sexually?

Callum: Yeah. We have to decide whether we're together inworld as we search and meet with 'Sugar and Bo' or if we need to find different partners.

I logged out of the virtual world and went into the kitchen.

Easton asked, "Hey! Why did you log off?"

"Because we have to talk."

He came into the kitchen. "Okay. What about?"

"About BDSM. Sex. Us?"

"It's a virtual world, Brand. None of it means anything."

"Of course it does. It may not be the real deal, but we will act it out, and that is a big deal. We set boundaries for a reason. I'm not—"

"You're not what? Having sex in a pretend world? Where no one knows us? Where the avatars are the ones having sex? Seriously?"

He was right. I sounded absurd, but I couldn't change how I felt. Easton was clueless. I might be in love, but I didn't want to call it that yet. My loneliness and loss had catapulted me into this situation. I had taken on a job that could possibly get me killed. I had gotten involved with a man I constantly thought about having sex with and a few even broke the law in some states. The notion of me as Easton's, whether here or in the virtual world, not only formed the excess moisture between my legs, but also made me scream inside, "take me long and hard." I couldn't help being horny and in love.

As I thought more about it, I had to be with Easton sexually in the virtual world. It was my job. My duty. I even thought it might release my anxiousness when I was around him. Squash some of the jealousy that rose when we were with Anna.

By the time I finished with all my thoughts, Easton made a sandwich. The man had an appetite in more ways than one.

"You're right."

He put his hand around his outer ear, leaned in and asked, "I'm sorry, what was that? Did you say I was right?"

In the living room, where our computers were, I said, "Don't push it smartass." I plopped down on the chair, arms stretched out on the armrests, and let my head drop. Easton came into the room with a piled-high sandwich on a plate.

"Did you not just eat?"

"I'm a growing boy. So anyway, what am I right about?"

"You're right that we have to decide what to do. It's a virtual world. Anna and Lucio are into BDSM, so in order for us to become friends with them, maybe even get them to back off in real life, we have to play their game—master and slave. So what color collar do you want?"

He put down his sandwich, chewed and let out a mouthful of air before saying, "What? I'm not wearing a damn collar. You have to be my slave for this to work."

"Why's that? They don't care who is the master or slave."

"Because I'm not good at taking orders."

I locked eyes with him and said, "Well I'm not submissive."

Easton put his plate down and moved toward my chair. I jumped to the other side of the table. He lunged at me and I let out a sissy scream. Easton just stopped still as a scarecrow until I let my guard down, then he grabbed hold of my arm, and wrestled me against the wall. His legs held mine apart to avoid an assault on the family jewels. I giggled and smiled at the way he tried to show off his strength, but then ...

I couldn't believe it. My eyes, lips, body let him

control the situation. Easton had me alongside the wall, his chest pinned me there while his hands held my wrists. His breath teased the wisps of hair that dangled around my face. Easton moved his head to the left side. I thought he was about to whisper in my ear. Instead, his lips pressed against my collarbone, his tongue traced its ascent to my shoulder and then so close, he turned to my cheek. Out of the corner of my eye, I could see him stare at me to watch my reaction. My breathing increased. I arched to push him away, but his weight wouldn't budge. His mouth wrapped around the side of my neck, tongue skated along skin, and then he slid his lips into a kiss, and sucked the wetness he created. My eyes closed to avoid his, but I smelled us. We smelled of sex. The scent of desire. His mouth and lips covered my neck again until I bent to the right, invited him for more. Easton's mouth trailed, his tongue outlined my lips and then he pressed his hard against mine. The want, the need to be with him made me whimper.

Then I felt the cool air dry my mouth, and my body was free from his grip. It took me a moment to realize my eyes remained closed. The rest of me still pressed against the wall. When I opened them, Easton stood a foot away, arms crossed, with a smeared grin on his face.

"And that, my partner, is what we call submissive." He returned to his sandwich and chewed, satisfaction clipped the corners of his mouth.

I, on the other hand, wasn't capable of playing it off as a joke. I straightened my shirt. Two steps at a time and I was in my room where I locked the door and found a pillow to handle the noise my body purged.

(Thirty-Six) Wrestling Match

~~~~~~

Easton had the biggest smile on his face when I finished. I wobbled my head still hazy with all the details.

"Did I get it right?"

He repositioned his body against the chair and said, "Yep. That's pretty much what happened."

"And you're still proud of yourself for tricking me into submission. I remember the surprise and embarrassment."

"Embarrassment? We both had to take care of our own tension."

It got quiet, except this time it was different. Our silence settled cold and wet like morning dew on grass. The last part of the story tarnished our minds regarding sexual needs. My mind faded into an abyss of fantasy. Naked bodies frantically ... It must have been a combination of his pride in making me submit and my thoughts, because it triggered something inside me. Whatever it was I couldn't control. I didn't want to control.

An out-of-body experience, yet I was fully aware of my actions. Confident. Exhilarated. I straddled Easton's lap, grabbed his shirt and pulled him to me. I saw the disbelief in his eyes before my mouth pressed hard against his mouth. Niceties need not apply. Hands and mouth touched, grabbed, and pulled in an attempt to get to him. I tore his shirt from his body. Easton tried to keep up, but I had the greater need. Hungrier. With what was left of his shirt, I pulled him up, kicked away the chair, and walked toward the glass doors. He stumbled backwards, caught his balance by hugging me. When he steadied himself, he turned us around to press me against the glass doors. Clothing ripped from our bodies. They laid strewn around us as if attacked by animals. We were the animals.

Fully naked, our bodies twisted into a wrestling match, limbs wrapped around limbs. Heavy gasps, our breaths made a haze around our frenzied bodies. Easton pinned my wrists against the glass doors. I nibbled and sucked on his lower lip to make it swell with the rest of his parts. My mouth traveled around his face, neck, and our whirlwind breathing intensified. For a moment, he released my wrists. I grabbed a long piece of Easton's shirt and tied it around his eyes. He let out moans, whimpered, while my hands and mouth explored his body. I felt the contours of his muscles, tasted his salty skin, and relished in his weakness. Easton suffered from the intensity of the convulsions I put him through but recovered.

The glass door slid open and we stumbled into the kitchen. Easton took off the makeshift blindfold and laid me across the kitchen table. He stretched my arms out to the sides, used the blindfold and kitchen towel to tie my wrists to the chairs. He climbed onto the table, opened my legs, and I felt the strength and steeliness I had fantasized about many times over. My feet knocked a few chairs over until they found his shoulders and curled over them. Easton wasted no time with his abrupt thrusts. The chair legs wobbled when I arched my back, hands balled into fists. The kitchen table screeched against the floor with his greedy need that forced unfamiliar noises from me.

As fast as we devoured our desires, we ended the spontaneous actions while our heat warmed the room. I remained tied to the chairs, struggled to quiet the wicked cravings that continued to rumble inside. Easton's skin stuck to mine. His chest rose and fell as he tried to catch his breath. The room dimmed. He released my wrists from their bindings.

I remained the way I finished. The ticking of the clock grew louder. Finally, Easton lifted his body enough to balance his weight on his forearms. Without a word, he scanned my face, hair, neck, shoulders, and eyes. His eyes glistened, and his thumb glided along my hairline in a back and forth motion. We watched each other. Our breathing stabilized. Our bodies chilled.

He lifted himself off, led me upstairs and grabbed the brown paper bag. There, Easton opened the door to our bedroom. The room we shared as husband and wife. The room I hadn't seen since the accident. Easton's hands danced on the back of my neck, and then combed through my hair. His other arm held me tight so I wouldn't fall as he walked me backwards, and tossed the bag on the bed. The back of my legs made contact with the silky fabric. Easton's eyes explored as if for the first time, unsure about what happened, and what was about to happen.

I placed my hands over his and brought them to the side. My body turned to the bed. I rubbed Easton's chest until I sat him on the edge. I straddled his lap. My lips touched his forehead. I kissed his face, brushed my lips from one area to the next, enjoyed the warmth. Easton's hands gripped my ass as he lifted our bodies onto the bed. We laid horizontal next to each other. Our subtle kisses set the tone. The rush was gone. We wanted the sweetness and cliché of the first time. To touch our bodies like braille. To take our time searching for the love that drifted away years ago. After we found the love, the tone changed to daring. I held the handle of the whip first.

Sunshine squeezed through the bedroom drapes. Easton's body fit around my silhouette, an arm under my pillow and the other hugged me. Our meshed legs were tailor-made for each other. I smelled soap and the aftermath of bodily fluids—a smell I'll never forget.

He kissed my head, rolled onto his back and rubbed his eyes. I rotated to my side and smiled.

Easton's eyes drifted over my face as he said, "Good morning."

I pulled the covers high, snuggled into the pillow, and responded, "Good morning."

He ran the back of his fingers along my jawline, and asked, "Are you okay?"

My hand caressed his cheek. "More than okay."

He kissed me on the lips and said, "I'll put on the coffee."

"Will you be back?"

"Yeah." Yesterday, things had moved fast, and then darkness had come upon us, so I didn't have an opportunity to see his body. It was beautiful. Flawless skin embraced muscles. He slipped boxer briefs on and left the room. On my back, I closed my eyes and thought about what I did yesterday. My face got warm. I drew the covers over my head, smiled to myself. It was wonderful.

The sunlight casted a soft glow in the room, signifying how I felt at that moment. Glowed. With the covers fitted tight over my breasts, my hands spread over them as I replayed the earlier events in my mind like recited lines from a favorite song. Actions and words flowed without hesitation. We reciprocated one another's feelings. The memories of our life connected. Some details were unclear, but I remembered the chronological order of events.

Easton walked into the room with two cups of coffee. The smell coerced me to pull myself up. He handed me a cup. With one hand on the sheets, I took the coffee with my other hand. Modesty snuck in. Easton slid under the covers. He grasped his cup with both hands. We focused on the window and drank.

He took my hand and asked, "Are you sure you're okay?"

I nodded and said, "Yeah, why do you ask?"

"Because you're clasping onto the sheet for dear life."

I laughed and relaxed my hand, but still left it on my chest. "I guess you could say I'm nervous."

He put down his coffee, did the same with mine and gathered me in his arms. "After what we did last night?"

Easton kissed me. At first, I didn't feel it, and then his soft, warm lips pressed harder. The tip of his tongue wiggled between my lips and ran along the length of my mouth until we opened to the wetness of our tongues. A methodic kiss, precise in movements, tender and ripe. I could have stayed in his arms all day.

Our bodies began to respond to the kiss. And then the doorbell rang.

Easton's right side of his upper lip lifted as he said, "GRRR!" He moved to the window. "It's Mitchell. Shit! Bad timing but it's my fault. He's left messages since we left town."

He turned to me and I said, "Alrighty then. I guess I'll get dressed."

I slid out of bed with the sheet in front of me. Before

I had the chance to wrap it around, Easton came over and pulled it down. In the morning light, I stood naked, self-conscious, I wanted to run and hide. I covered myself with my hands, but he pushed them away.

He put his hand under my chin, lifted to meet his eyes, and said, "Don't. I'm your husband." He kissed my cheek and shoulder before the doorbell rang again. "Shit." We stared at each other, and then he caught me off-guard. "I love you."

Mitchell had gotten anxious because he kept ringing the doorbell. Easton left before I could digest the words, "I love you." Touched. Emotional like a child's hands folded in prayer. Like catching fireflies and watching them glow in your hand. An "I love you" moment broken before reciprocated. I went into the washroom to shower. Last night shifted our lives. It felt like a new coat of paint for our marriage and future.

Easton only had a pair of shorts on when I came down. He was sitting outside with Mitchell eating bagels. They turned when they heard me.

With a bagel stuffed in one cheek, Mitchell mumbled, "I brought bagels."

I said, "Sounds good. Do you guys want me to put on another pot of coffee?" In unison, they said "yes."

While I prepared the coffee, Easton came in, hugged me and was about to run upstairs before I caught his arm and stopped him. "I just wanted to say that I love you too."

He grinned and said, "I know," and ran upstairs. I walked out and sat in a chair sheltered from the sun. I couldn't wipe the happiness from my face.

Mitchell said, "Happiness suits you."

I moved my hands around my face as if posing, and responded, "You did it."

He waved his hand to dismiss my comment. "Please, Brand. You're naturally beautiful." I didn't know how to respond. "Sorry to just drop by. I've tried to get a hold of Easton for days."

"No need to apologize. You're welcome here any time."

He took my hands in his and said, "You two are good."

I blushed. "I think so."

We made small talk until Easton joined us after he had showered and dressed. Mitchell and I watched him with admiration and pleasure.

Mitchell broke our trances when he addressed Easton. "I haven't asked you why you never told me about Brand's accident and loss of memory."

Easton addressed us both. "I was concentrating on Brand. Besides, I knew the way you felt about her, and I didn't want to get in a fight over any comments you might have made at the time."

"How do you know I'd make comments?"

Easton's nostrils flared. "Seriously? I don't really want to talk about this in front of Brand—"

"It's okay. I already know Mitchell didn't care for me."

Mitchell squeezed my cheek, and said, "I do now. Just look how happy you are." He said to Easton, "And you. It's been years since I've seen you smile this much."

Easton tried to cover his mouth and then shook his head to admit defeat.

I sat in the chair and said, "It's a new start for us. My memory has somehow crept back, and Easton and I ..." My words traveled off with my thoughts.

Mitchell whistled and pointed at us. "You two did it again, didn't you?"

We asked, "Did what?"

His eyes drifted from mine to Easton's and then to the sky. He clasped his hands together, and said, "Fell in love. You fell in love again. Do you have any idea how lucky you are when it comes to love? How many people do you know have fallen in love twice with the same person? There are people who have never fallen in love."

Our faces flushed when we glanced at each other. Mitchell hugged us both and went into the house.

Easton fiddled with his chair. He showed me the broken armrest. I covered my mouth.

Mitchell came back out and asked, "So what have you two been up to?"

Our laughter drowned out Mitchell's attempt at finding out what was so funny. Easton finally said we had relived the case we were on together.

Mitchell asked, "What about it?"

"I'm trying to help Brand with her memory."

"Where did you leave off?"

Easton winked at me and then said to Mitchell, "We left off at when we returned from the cabin."

Mitchell settled into his chair, took a sip of coffee and said, "Do you mind if I listen in? I promise that I won't have a clue about what you say."

Easton asked, "Do you mind, Brand?"

"It's okay, as long as it's not graphic."

"I didn't suggest that it would *not* be graphic."

Mitchell and I gave him a 'give me a break' look.

He sighed and said, "Fine. I won't get too—"

I said, "Did we get together during or after?"

"Toward the end. That's when we finally gave into our emotions, and the rest is history."

I snorted at the idea of history. History is the timeline of a person's life. My timeline had disappeared for a while, and now it seemed somewhat jagged in need of clarification. I wanted to make sure I remembered it correctly so I wouldn't create my own history.

"I can't remember exactly how the case ended."

"Once we told each other how we felt, I wanted you back at my house while I finished the case myself. I had planned to tell Lucio and Anna that there was a death in your family so you wouldn't be around for a while."

"What do you mean by 'wanted' and 'had planned to tell'?"

He shook his head. "Because you're so damn stubborn. You wanted to stay even if it meant you could get hurt."

I sat forward. "Oh, but it was all right that I got hurt before admission?"

Mitchell watched the verbal ping-pong match. "She got you there."

"Quiet." Easton took in a deep breath and let it out. "No. And yes. I really believed that you wouldn't get hurt. I had read the case file before I even approached you about it, and Lucio and Anna weren't so quick for the kill. Don't get me wrong, they were dangerous, but not to the extent of being reckless. I figured I would know when it got heated, and I could keep you safe."

I snuggled into the chair, "So let's hear it."

Easton ran his hands down his face, wiped away the leftover water from the shower, and told us about the end of the case.

(Thirty-Seven) Jack-O'-Lantern

~~~~~

2001 - Crystal Lane, Rhode Island

That day and the rest of the week, Easton and I stayed away from any kind of subject that incited sex. Although proud of his submission achievement, we both started to realize our friendship took a turn toward desire and we couldn't risk the distraction.

Anna and I continued our routine. She wasn't as talkative as in the past. Even though jogging dried my throat and I dedicated most of my breathing to it, I tried to ask her questions to get her to talk but she wouldn't bite. Even the simplest of questions, such as "Did you have a nice day yesterday?" came with a one-word response. Tension existed, although Easton and I weren't the cause. Her demeanor toward me was more like indifference than anger.

When I'd get back from my jog, we would spend most of our time in Alter Life, discussing Anna and Lucio and not much else. The hours put in staking them out in the virtual world paid off. It turned out that Bo Dugan, the avatar that collared Anna, was Lucio. Their avatars periodically came online, and we'd see them at particular places. By the end of the week, we knew where they frequented in AL, and followed them inworld. They both logged onto AL when they were home, but there wasn't a pattern in time.

Easton and I went to a Locks, Cocks, and Two Smoking Carols. Two women by the name of Carol had created the inworld place, along with their male slaves. I found out a few things about people in the virtual world. One was that some of them spent time with their spouses. They used the virtual world to add spice to their marriage.

I searched for Sugar Desmond (Anna) online. The time on my laptop showed 8:00 am. Apparently, Anna liked to spend some of her time online while Lucio was at work.

Candy: Anna's online.

Callum: Really? Can you see where she's at?

Candy: If you search for her, you can right-click on her avatar and then click on map. It shows the coordinates and the name of the place, which is Bondage Farm.

Callum: Please tell me it's not a place they do it with animals.

Candy: Ew! I hope not. Bestiality is completely off-limits.

Callum: How do you know all this shit? Being collared? BDSM? Are you into bondage?

Candy: Let's just say I've acquired a little experience throughout my life.

Callum: Now I feel so unexciting. I wonder what women really think of me in the bedroom.

Candy: I think it's best you continue to think you're a stallion.

Callum: I never said I was a stallion.

Candy: *rolls eyes*

Callum: Hey! I've been known to make a few women purr, and I always satisfy their needs.

Candy: Is that what they told you?

Callum: Uh ... Yeah ... And I could tell ...

Candy: What's with the ellipses? Did you drift off into

thought wondering if you really did fulfill their needs?

Callum: No! I know I did.

Candy: Whatever. Let's find Anna, or shall I say Sugar.

Callum: Don't say whatever. I hate that. It's like you have no other response so you say whatever.

Candy: Whatever.

Easton shook his head at me.

Callum: Where did you go?

Candy: I'm at the Bondage Farm.

Callum: Teleport me.

I sent him a teleport, and he appeared in front of me. Damn, I wish I had a teleport in real life. I'd teleport to the Bahamas.

Callum: Let me move to the other side of the place so it doesn't seem like we followed them again.

Interested in what the other avatars did there, I read the profiles. Many were from Europe with little to no information about their real lives. I stood near Sugar Desmond. She talked to some guy by the name of Jack-O'-Lantern. Cute name. I checked out his profile and it stated his inworld experiences consisted of sexual pleasure, and he wanted a submissive. He'd been on Alter Life for the same amount of time as Sugar.

Callum: I checked out Bo Dugan's (Lucio) profile and it showed he was online. I'll find out where he is and then head on over.

Candy: Don't bother. He just appeared by Sugar.

Callum: Jack-O'-Lantern doesn't seem to be leaving.

Candy: Like us, they must be in private chat because local chat is dormant.

Callum: Maybe one of us should type in local chat. See if we get some response.

I heard Easton's keyboard going and then saw what

he typed in local chat. "Anyone want to have some fun."

Candy: Very subtle.

Callum: Give me a break. This is all new to me. Hop right in there Bondage Queen.

I zoomed out to see where Sugar and Bo were but they were gone. I typed in private chat, "Shit! Sugar and Bo are gone."

Callum: I noticed. Their profiles show they're off-line. They weren't on for very long.

Candy: And Jack-O'-Lantern either. For someone there for sexual pleasure, he didn't get much of it. So what next?

Callum: We follow Anna and Lucio in real life.

Candy: What?

We closed out of Alter Life, shut down our computers, changed and waited. I paced the room while Easton sat on the couch to watch his cell phone.

I tugged on my lip and asked, "What are you doing?"

"Waiting for them to get in their car and take off."

"With your phone?"

Easton placed the phone on his lap, observed me before saying, "At the cabin, I put a tracking device under the car. I have an app on my phone that will track them." He took me by the shoulders. "We'll be fine. This is another stake out, but away from the townhouse."

I swiped his hands off my shoulders. "You don't know that. We could wind up running and then have to use our guns. "

To lighten the situation Easton said, "Well you're more than ready to run."

My eyes narrowed as I walked around him. "Not funny."

"You're right. This is serious, but we're prepared. You're prepared." He placed his hands on my shoulders, took them away and asked, "Where's your gun?" I lifted the bottom of my jeans to show him where I put it. "Good." He glanced at his phone and shoved it into his pocket. "We're on."

Anna and Lucio were out of sight before we opened the door and followed. Easton drove and it seemed to take forever. He pulled the car to the side of the road, and we watched Anna and Lucio get out of theirs with the ocean fifty feet away. My mind drifted to scary thoughts about cement shoes, chains and a large body of water. I had seen too many gangster movies and they raised my anxiety.

Easton gestured to my face with a tissue. I wiped the sweat and swiped my hands along my legs to rid them of the clamminess then I opened the passenger side door to vomit. Several frustrated noises came from him, sighs and colorful words under his breath, which didn't help me. When I finished, I wiped my mouth and closed the door.

"Don't do that again."

My face froze from shock. "Do what? Get sick? Sorry, but I have no control over it."

"Don't open the door. You could have blown our cover."

I shifted against the door, faced him and responded, "So you would have rather me thrown up in the car?"

"Yeah. There are bags in the back and glove compartment. It's always important not to raise attention. Do exactly as I say."

I faced forward to do what he said. He had the experience, not me. Anna and Lucio walked along the water, both glanced down at their watches. They were there to meet someone. Easton had tiny binoculars, and when he saw a BMW arrive, he handed them over to me. A man got out, walked over to them, gave Anna a kiss, and shook Lucio's hand. The man pointed toward a small building about a hundred feet or so from where they stood. We waited until they entered before we got out of the car. Easton gestured for me to stay behind him. He slipped his gun out of his holster and took the lead. I left mine strapped to my ankle. Easton tested a back door, opened it enough to check for anyone there, and slid in.

That part of the building had little light so we stayed still until our eyes adjusted to the darkness. We heard muffled talking. With his left hand, Easton took hold of mine, lead the way with his gun. A shot of light burst into the room from an opened door. The voices moved closer to us. Behind was a wood crate. Easton directed me to get in, and he laid on top of me.

He put his hand over my mouth and whispered in my ear, "Do not move or make any sound. Nod if you understand." I complied.

My eyeballs rolled to the side as the three stood a few feet away. To take my mind off it, I listened to their conversation.

The man spoke. "So why the hell are we here? That's what Alter Life is for, to trade information and instructions. This is risky, so this better be damn good.

Lucio said, "I think we need to take it easy in Alter Life. My gut tells me we're being followed there."

The man laughed, and then grew silent. "Maybe you're getting too old. You called me down here to tell me this shit!"

"Show some respect. I've done this before you could count. I know when something isn't right, and at the moment, something isn't right."

"Watch it, Lucio. Don't forget who is in charge here."

Anna tried to soften the situation. "Lucio just wants us to know how he feels. That's all, Michael."

Michael responded, "Anna, I don't give a fuck how Lucio or you feel. The shipment arrives soon, and I expect you all to be in the virtual world for detailed instructions. Don't you dare call me to meet again, do you hear me?"

There was a pause before Lucio and Anna agreed. Light shone into the crate when they left and then darkness. We waited a few minutes, listened for their shoes and voices. When they disappeared, Easton lifted the lid of the crate, and helped me out.

He felt my hands shake. "Let's go home."

(Thirty-Eight) Fall In Love Twice

~~~~~~

Mitchell and I pondered what we just heard and Easton went into the house for a glass of water. When he came out, we both razzed him about not finishing the story. SW

Easton raised his hands in surrender. "Give me a break. I got thirsty."

Mitchell slid his body forward in his chair and asked, "So was that Michael guy the Jack-O'-Lantern they met in the virtual world?"

Easton responded, "I thought you said you wouldn't understand what I say."

"I don't, but the story is exciting. Hard to believe the two of you involved in such a case."

I wanted to know, so I asked Mitchell's question again. Easton sat down and said, "Yes. Jack-O'-Lantern was Michael, the kingpin."

"I can't believe we were so close to such a person."

Mitchell nudged me and said, "Or that you knew so much about BDSM or being collared."

His comment burned my face. I let it silence me because I couldn't believe it either. From what I remembered from childhood and adolescence, I wasn't an odd one, only an adolescent who wanted people to hear her. My twenties are a blur, not because I can't remember, but because my memories concentrate on my mother. All she did for me, how I depended on her, and then one day, torn from me. It left me cold and flippant about life. The boyfriends, the attitude, were all filed under 'unimportant' memories in my head. At thirty, my mother's death emptied my life, because she was the one who reminded me that I had a full one.

Mitchell's hand on my arm brought me back to the moment. "Honey, are you okay?"

The wetness of tears gave it away. "I will be."

Easton tried to make light of the situation when he asked, "Are you upset I never collared you?"

I took my flip-flop off, threw it at him and laughed.

He dodged the flip-flop. "What? I'm curious."

"And I'm curious about the investigation. I thought I stuck around until the end."

Easton held up his hand. "I never said that. I said you're stubborn and I wanted you to head home. Fear won over your stubbornness. I finally got my way."

Mitchell asked, "Do you have any Margaritas? I think I'll need one for the rest of the story."

We both laughed at Mitchell.

Easton said, "We have beer or wine."

"On such a hot day, a margarita would be best. Can you guys wait with the story until I get some? I really want to hear the rest."

Easton asked, "Don't you have—"

I cut in. "That's fine, Mitchell. We can wait. I wouldn't mind one myself."

He threw his keys in the air, caught them, and said, "Be back soon."

Once Mitchell left, Easton got serious. "Are you really okay?"

I smiled and said, "Yeah. I'm fine. I find myself thinking about my mom."

Easton didn't know what to say, and I wanted the matter to disintegrate. The backyard resembled a storybook. The grass so lush, green, thick blades stood at attention. The wooden perimeter fences were decorated with trees and bushes. A stone-built wall circled a small pond in the back that housed gold fish and frogs. Flowers of all colors grew around the patio, submerged our nostrils in a unique aromatic blend.

I closed my eyes, smelled the air, and let a carefree smile stretch across my face. My body flinched when Easton's lips touched against mine. I intertwined my fingers around his neck, brought him closer, and continued the interrupted morning kiss. He bent down, held his weight on the armrests, moved his mouth along my lips, on the side of my face, neck, and back to my lips.

We allowed a moment of rest. I released my hands from behind his neck and rubbed my nose against his. "I love you. I'm so glad we got this second chance."

"Me too. The way things were, we probably would have divorced soon."

Easton lifted me, sat down on my chair and put me on his lap. I laid my arm across his shoulders to rest my head against his, and said, "Mitchell is right. We are lucky to have fallen in love twice. It's as if this memory journey has flattened the bumps in our marriage."

His cell phone vibrated on the table. We both saw Mitchell's name. Easton hit a button and Mitchell's voice boomed. "You two have nothing there, so I bought some munchies, hamburgers, and all the trimmings. Just callin' to let you get prepared."

Easton told Mitchell that it all sounded great. He ended the call. We stayed that way until Mitchell arrived with several bags. I went to help him unload and put the items away while Easton got out the blender for him. Mitchell filled it with ice and ingredients and then asked if we wanted one.

I looked at the filled blender when I said, "I don't

know. I'd hate to take any from you."

Mitchell didn't get the sarcasm. "Oh sweetheart. I brought this for all of us."

Easton grabbed a beer out of the refrigerator and said, "I'll pass."

I threw one more ice cube in the blender. "Okay, you talked me into it."

Easton said to me, "I thought you stopped drinking."

"Did I say that?" I glanced at the clock and said, "I probably shouldn't have one. It's only quarter to twelve."

"As the saying goes, 'It's five o'clock somewhere'," and he walked out onto the patio.

Mitchell hip checked me and said, "I really am glad it's back to the way it used to be when you two first got together."

I hugged him. "I am too. I don't want you as an enemy."

He kissed my cheek, and from outside, we heard Easton say, "Stop flirting with my wife."

I joined Easton. "So will we hear the rest of the story?"

"Sure. There isn't much left. But don't you remember it now?"

"It's still a little foggy. Besides, I love to hear you talk."

Mitchell handed me my margarita and took his place. "Where did I leave off?"

Mitchell took a sip of his drink, rolled his eyes with pleasure and said, "Where you two got out of the crate and headed home?"

"Yeah. Brand was pretty shaken up. I didn't want to jeopardize the case, so we returned to the townhouse."

(Thirty-Nine) Promise Me

~~~~~~

2001 - Crystal Lane, Rhode Island

We returned to the townhouse, and I went straight to my bedroom. I was embarrassed and frightened how spooked I got in a crate as I listened to a conversation. My reaction could have jeopardized our case. With my face buried in the pillow, I didn't hear Easton knock on the door or enter the room. On the side of the bed, he rubbed my back. I pushed my face into the pillow, swiveled my body until I was lying face up. I wiped my eyes to avoid Easton.

"Brand. I didn't mean to upset you when you got sick."

I turned my head away from him and said, "You were right." Congestion gurgled my words, so I sucked in the mucus, and said, "Plus I freaked in the crate. I could get us killed."

His hand glided along my arm as he talked. "It happens to the best of agents."

I finally faced him and asked, "Did it happen to you?"

He diverted his eyes, shrugged a shoulder and said, "No, but I've been with other agents who lost it." Easton wiped the wisps of hair off my face. "Besides, you're not an agent. You didn't go through school or trained for this so it's no surprise that it affected you this way."

The tears spilled to the point that I couldn't control them anymore. I rolled on my side with my back toward him. "I know this is your way to make me feel better, but … I'm upset and scared. I'll get over it."

There was a pause before he shifted on the bed next to me. On his side with his arm bent, he held his head. I sniffed, coughed and wiped.

"I ... I think it's best you go back to my house. You can continue the investigation through AL."

"Why? You don't think I can finish the case?" I put my hands in my lap.

"Look how this has effected you? And we only watched them. I'd hate for you to get hurt because you froze, or—"

"I did have a negative response to the situation, but you have to admit it was the first time we were put in danger's way."

Easton rose and went to the window. "Which is why you should return before any real danger occurs."

My arms and legs pushed off the bed and I stood next to him. "No. No. We made a deal. I play your devoted girlfriend while we find out about these criminals. I need the money."

His head turned to the side, as he said. "You'll still get paid. I'll arrange for you to return to the house."

Easton turned to leave, but I stood in front of him. "I said I was sorry. I said it won't happen again. Why won't you let me work the case?"

"Because it's—"

"Knock it off. We both knew of the danger, and yes, my reaction was bad but I can do this, Easton."

"Forget it. I don't need you for this part of the case. A cab will come for you tomorrow and take you to an airport where you'll return to Dover. From the house, you can work it in the virtual world." He went downstairs and I followed.

"Wait. I can't leave. I've earned Anna's trust. Without me here, you'll have to step in and I don't feel comfortable with that."

His arms crossed his chest. "Why don't you feel

comfortable with it?"

I challenged him. "What's the real reason you want me gone?"

We both confronted each other, but failed to express how we really felt. Easton grabbed a few wine glasses, poured us each a glass, and said, "To your last day."

I took the glass, threw it in his face and returned to my room. When my suitcase was half packed, he approached void of anger or revenge. He wore defeat; shoulders curled forward, bowed neck and silence to hide his vulnerability. I ignored him as annoyance curdled in my stomach. Then I saw his shoulders straighten, neck lift, and in two strides he was in front of me. He took my face in his hands, stared into my eyes and drifted down to my lips. Easton touched them with his, took time to sense the heat, and our lips danced together. A hummingbird's heartbeat. The kiss was different from any in the past because he let the moment sink in. He didn't rush it. His hands examined me until one rested on my butt and the other on my upper back.

Easton gathered me close, our hips rubbed into each other. I let him undress me. I let his mouth and hands explore me. His movements and thirst answered why he wanted me to leave. And I didn't argue as I answered his questions with my movements. Our bodies fell into a cadence of give and take, slow and fast, and when he entered me, we both felt the overflow of energy we had kept to ourselves. His lips licked and planted themselves on various parts of my skin. My hands grabbed at him while my legs wrapped around his waist. The wetness from our bodies mixed, a desired scent created which encouraged our libidos.

When we finished, curled together, our lips saved words for another time. We knew it was time for me to leave. As much as it hurt to be apart, we felt better that I wouldn't need to use my gun. Sleep came upon us, and the day turned into night, then turned into gratification.

In the morning, we both moved about the townhouse relaxed and happy. It was good to become us again— Easton and Brand. I packed, and Easton called a cab. We stood in the kitchen, wrapped in each other's arms with the occasional facial touch and kiss. It was best to say our good-byes then so the neighbors wouldn't have an opportunity to question me.

Easton rested his lips on my head and whispered, "I'm going to miss you."

My arms wrapped around him tighter, as I whispered, "Me too." I held his face. "Promise me you'll be careful."

He hugged me tighter and said, "I will."

"Promise me."

He let out a gentle laugh. "I promise. Don't forget to make yourself at home. I had the IP rerouted and blocked, so there is no way they can track you through AL. You'll be safe there."

I talked to his chest to hide the tears. "Don't let Anna get too cozy with you."

Easton pulled me away enough to see me and said, "I'm taken. Besides, she doesn't come close to the beautiful and fabulous you."

My head shifted to the side. "You need glasses."

He perused my face and then rested on my eyes.

Emotions overwhelmed me. "That's the nicest thing anyone has ever said to me."

Easton held me to his chest. "Aw. Don't cry. It's the truth. I haven't known love until I met you."

The cab arrived. Easton put my suitcases in the trunk, kissed me and waved good-bye as it backed out and disappeared from the cul-de-sac.

When I arrived at Easton's house, the place was foreign to me. I tried to make myself at home, but time trespassed through my thoughts of the last time with Easton. A day went by and already I became antsy. Thoughts of him haunted my dreams, and in the day, my mind drifted back to our naked bodies. The fear of a broken heart dissolved. Easton wanted me, and a smile glued to my face. I couldn't wait to talk to him, so we met in AL.

I logged into the virtual world, searched for romantic places, and teleported to a place called Kismet Castle. A bubble popped up at the bottom when Easton signed in. I sent him a teleport invite, and he appeared in front of me, pixels connected to form his avatar, Callum. He sent me a private chat message.

Callum: Hey beautiful.

Candy: Hey handsome.

Callum: Do you come here often?

Candy: *smiles*

Callum: I miss you.

Candy: Same here. This house feels so empty without you. Have I missed any excitement?

Callum: Other than Lucio and Anna concerned about you, no.

Candy: What did you say?

Callum: I told them that someone died in your family, and you'd be gone for a while to take care of personal matters.

Candy: Did Anna want to throw a party?

Callum: *laughs hard* You're funny. She smiled, but nothing other than that. Do you want to stay here or should we head to the Bondage Farm where we saw them last?

Candy: I checked and they're all online. Let's head over there.

We teleported to the Bondage Farm. Lucio, Anna and Jack-O'-Lantern used their avatars to have sex. They had a threesome, but local chat remained empty. It was a diversion. We moved closer to them and found a few sex balls to activate for our avatars. It didn't come close to real life sex, but I could see people experimenting in the virtual world before an attempt in reality.

We were in a private conversation when Callum said, "They made contact."

Candy: No way!

Callum: Yep, but not in a good way. Lucio sent me a private message. He asked if we followed them in here. I said that I wouldn't waste my time. This was our favorite place.

In local chat, Jack-O'-Lantern typed: I think you two should move away from us.

Callum: Why? Will we contract a STD from your avatars?

Jack-O'Lantern: You'll contract pain if you don't.

Callum: Is this your place?

Jack-O'Lantern: I've seen the two of you a few times without any conversation in local chat. Plus, you seem to come around us instead of others.

He stopped his avatar from gyrating, walked over to Callum and typed: I won't tell you again. Get the hell out.

Candy: Come on Callum. Let's go.

Callum: No! Who do these people think they are to

tell us to leave? I can report you to the site administrator.

Jack O'Lantern: You'll regret it.

Callum: And how will I regret it?

Jack-O'Lantern: You'll find out when I'm on your front porch.

Easton glanced at his taskbar, clicked on a program, and noticed the program that hid his IP had shut off. He didn't know how long the program had disconnected. They could track him. He sent me a private message. "Log off now."

Candy: Why?

Callum: Just do it now! They can track me.

I got out of the virtual world, looked out the windows, and locked all doors. Time became my enemy since I didn't know what was happening with Easton. The day went by without any contact. Finally, I fell asleep in the early hours of the night. Another day passed with no contact, and I didn't know if he left me any messages in AL. I hadn't eaten. My mind played out horrific scenes of Easton tortured. Another evening passed, and I fell asleep with dried tears.

The next morning, I turned on the news and the newscasters reported on a large drug bust that went down in Rhode Island. They arrested a known drug dealer by the name of Michael Turlough, who controlled the operation of drugs from the Mississippi eastward.

I stood in front of the television, shook the remote, and said aloud, "Come on. Show him. Where are you, Easton?"

The news reporter continued with the story with no mention of Easton. I threw the remote down and cried. Several hours later, the front door opened. It roused me from my trance, and I just stood there frozen. With his left arm in a sling, face swollen, black and blue, Easton stepped into the foyer and smiled. I wrapped my arms around him as he winced.

I moved. "I'm sorry." My hands glided over his face.

He lowered the suitcase, put his hand over mine, and said, "It's okay."

"What happened? Why didn't you call me? What are your injuries?"

Easton walked into the room, favoring his left side, and eased himself onto the couch. I sat next to him. He put his right arm around me.

With tears in my eyes, I covered my mouth and asked, "What did they do to you?"

He patted my arm. "It's not that bad. Just a few broken ribs, left arm, and the rest are bruises."

"Can I get you an Ice pack? Aspirin?"

"If needed, I have some pain killers in my suitcase."

I shifted toward him, tucked my legs under me, and asked, "So after I signed off, what happened?"

"It went fast. I shut down, called for backup, and before I could leave, a few guys were in the front and back of the house. They got a hold of me and brought me to the area where Lucio, Anna and Jack-O'-Lantern had met before. All of them were there, along with the shipment. Lucio threw the first punch, and when I went for him, another guy punched me in the stomach. They dragged me to another room that had no windows. A fluorescent light hung from a wire in the corner. It smelled of gasoline. Handcuffed to a chair, Anna walked in alone. She circled the chair, stood in front, and slapped both sides of my face. She expressed her disappointment as she grabbed me by the hair and yanked my head back. Then she pressed her lips hard against mine, but I tightened mine, and when she loosened my hair, I turned away."

"That bitch! I should have stayed just so I could punch her out. Or better yet, hit her with my gun."

He laughed, winced, and slanted to the left until the pain subsided. "Anyways, she left and then the big guns came in. Lucio made accusations to rattle me. I kept quiet. Jack-O'-Lantern introduced himself as Michael Turlough. I'm glad you weren't there because this guy is dangerous. He dripped poison when he talked, and he didn't give a damn about anyone. Michael told the other men to make sure I suffered, and before he left, he pulled out my thumbnail on my left hand."

He had it bandaged, so I couldn't see it. My heart ached to see him battered and I couldn't help him.

Easton said, "I'm fine, Brand."

"Have you seen yourself?"

"It's not as bad as it looks." He bumped me with his shoulder. "This is what happens when we get the bad guys." He exposed his teeth with an enthusiastic smile. "Thank God Lucio and Anna drove. The tracking device was on their car, so squad found me just in time before the cement shoes went on."

I jumped with a quick intake of air.

"Kidding. You talk in your sleep."

I cooked, gave him his painkillers, and let sleep heal his wounds. He remained at home until the ribs and arm healed.

(Forty) Snapshot Lies

~~~~~

Mitchell and I sighed from exhaustion. It seemed so surreal that I couldn't imagine being a part of it.

Mitchell asked, "What ever happened to Lucio and Anna?"

Easton bobbed his finger at me and said, "My woman and I got them."

My face flushed with a big grin.

He continued. "Michael and Lucio were tried in a court of law in front of a twelve-person jury. Anna entered into a plea bargain, pleaded guilty to drug trafficking. She claimed she knew nothing about money laundering or tax evasion. Since the authorities needed her to testify, they gave her three years in return for her testimony against both Michael and Lucio. She agreed without argument. I guess her loyalty to Lucio only went so far. She filed for divorce a few months after Lucio's trial ended."

I asked, "So she's out of jail?"

"Yes, but don't worry. Anna is probably back out there in search of another Lucio to take care of her. She has no time for revenge. She wasted three years of her beauty in jail, so she had to make up for lost time. The last I heard of her whereabouts, she moved to the West Coast. Maybe she thought Hollywood could make a film about her life."

Mitchell cut in and said, "Or BDSM porn."

We all got a laugh out of that one, and then I asked about Michael and Lucio.

Easton said, "Still in jail. Michael Turlough received

the maximum consecutive sentence of ten years for drug trafficking, forty years for money laundering, and five years for tax evasion. Even though Lucio wasn't the top guy for the drug trafficking, he had his hands dirty for too many years. He also received a consecutive sentence of five years for drug trafficking followed with three years supervision after prison, thirty years for money laundering and five years for tax evasion. The judge knocked off fifteen years of his sentence for cooperation with the whereabouts of his money."

For the rest of the day, we talked about the past and Mitchell's salon. And we laughed. That day, no one could steal our friendship and happiness. It all came natural, like I never was wicked Brand or lost my memory. The three of us poked fun at one another. Only close friends could toss around sarcasm and love as if they were one of the same. Drunk into the night, Mitchell called a cab. The mood and alcohol made us both more desirable.

L ife went on. Easton and I found our daily practices, and made it a point to show the other our love. Months into my second chance at love, I woke before Easton, looked out the window to find rain had glued leaves to the house and ground. A lazy day to cuddle. I felt so alive and calm as if my car accident happened years ago. The humidity from outside drifted into the house, so I made my way downstairs to boost the air conditioner and make coffee.

The coffee brewed while I stared out the window at the dreary weather—how different it was to how I felt inside. Once it finished, I poured a cup and went downstairs to go through the photo albums.

Since the first time I went through the albums, I had piled them in a corner until I could put them in chronological order. I sipped my coffee as I flipped through the pages, smiled at the memories I had with my mother and Easton. I picked an album on top of a pile farthest from the couch. It was our wedding album. We had a small ceremony with close friends. I didn't have any family left that I knew about, and Easton had family he didn't want to attend. In a small Catholic church, we exchanged vows and had the reception at Gilberto's home, Mr. Personality, who lived on five acres of land. Everyone changed into casual clothes after the ceremony. Easton and I glowed. It was difficult to believe when I saw how happy we were in the pictures that we had strayed from our marriage. We waited so long to find one another, both of us alone in the world.

I went through each picture as if I had never seen them, which in a sense, I hadn't. When I finished an album, I put it next to me and reached for another in the middle of the pile. It was of Easton in his twenties. He had longer hair pulled back into a ponytail. Most of the pictures were of him in some sort of rock T-shirt and jeans with construction boots. I flipped the page and found a newspaper article.

DUI in Fairy Moss Brook, New Hampshire Car Crash

A 50-year-old woman died early Wednesday morning in a head-on collision with an SUV on Route 21. Kalie Rye was driving northbound on Langston Road when an SUV, driving eastbound on Capers Blvd, ran a red light and collided with her vehicle. The passenger in the SUV was taken to the hospital with minor injuries. The 30-year old driver, Carey O'Keefe, was arrested and charged with driving under the influence and vehicular manslaughter.

My hand pressed against my chest as dread thickened the air. I swallowed to keep down the vomit. Upset to find the newspaper clipping, I went through the pages of the album, unable to find anything else about the crash. Why did Easton have this in a photo album? I started to panic as questions zoomed around my head. My hands continued their search, repeated in reverse order until I felt soft, wet lips on my neck. I jumped and turned around.

Easton withdrew. "Whoa! I didn't mean to scare you."

I couldn't control the intensity of my scorched insides.

"Brand, what's wrong?"

I finally said, "This." I turned to the newspaper and whipped it at him. "Why? Why do you have that in an album?"

He didn't watch it fall to the ground. He didn't need to. He knew exactly what I threw. "Brand. I can explain."

"Explain!"

Easton took in a deep breath, blew it out and looked at me. "Carey O'Keefe was a friend of mine."

"Wha ... huh?" I threw my arms out and my mouth remained opened.

"I was in the car with him."

My body split, the insides drained to my feet, the outer shell became stone solid. For a moment, I thought I lost my hearing as sound seized. Time took a pause, and with each puff of air, it started to pick up speed.

He took a step forward and I took a step back. "I'm sorry, Brand. I should have told you."

"Told me! Did you ever tell me?"

Easton shifted his head. "No. I didn't want to hurt you."

With every sentence, my voice rose in volume and I moved closer to him. "But you did. You hid it from me. You didn't just happen to meet me at the bar that night. You already knew me." I took the album and hurled it at him.

He blocked it with his arm, and spoke in a calm voice. "You're right, I did know you before then."

I screamed at the top of my lungs. My arms stretched downward, neck strained upward, my pain released like a machine gun. Easton let me. He didn't interfere until the screams transformed into moans.

The dullness prompted Easton to speak. "Carey and I were at a party the night of the accident. I shouldn't have let him drive, but I couldn't drive either. When I found out your mom died, I made it a point to know all about you. At the time, you had a boyfriend, Mason, so I kept an eye on you to make sure you were okay."

I glared at him. "Because of guilt?"

He shook his head. "Even though I wasn't the driver, I was a passenger in a car that killed someone."

A foot away from him, I clenched my hands into fists. "You fucking pitied me?"

"No! My conscience bothered me, but I never pitied you. I felt for you."

"Did you marry me out of guilt?" My fists slammed down on his chest, and then they flew all around, to make contact with whatever body part of his I could find. Easton let me hit him and scream in his face. He accepted blame. Finally exhausted, I slid down to the floor, and put my face in my hands. Easton didn't try to help me. He just left the room.

I laid on the floor until the lights were out. All my energy went into grieving and releasing my pain out on Easton. For the first time, I struggled with the idea that my marriage was a lie. I regained my memory only to find out that the photo albums meant nothing. They didn't hold our happiness. They were snapshot lies. I lifted my upper body with my arms, but the rest lay limp on the ground. It represented my heart. Again, my head dropped thinking about how the day began. How quickly happiness can sour and spoil.

When I no longer heard the footsteps above, I found the energy to drag myself upstairs to the room I had slept in. With no sign of Easton, I hopped into the shower to wash the pain, and get ready to leave. I wasn't sure where to go, but I had planned to look around the house for some money for a hotel room.

In my robe, I threw my clothes into suitcases found in the closet, which prompted more tears. I left most of the clothes in the drawers and took only those I had worn over the past months. I carried my suitcases downstairs and placed them by the door. I scrimmaged through the kitchen. In a small top drawer, I found a credit card with my name, Brand Bennet. A daunting laugh escaped as I shoved it into my pocket along with the car keys that sat on the counter.

Just as I was about to leave, Easton walked in the door. He saw the suitcases and then asked. "You're leaving?"

I reached for the doorknob. "Very perceptive of you."

Easton put his hand on top of mine. "Shouldn't we talk about it?"

"Talk about it?" I took my hand back and laughed. "That's all we've done was talk about our life. Our fucking fake life."

He reached for me, but I moved. "It wasn't and isn't fake, Brand."

My dagger eyes focused on his as I said, "Really?

Which part is the 'happily ever after' part?"

His hands moved in a stop position in front of him. "Please, don't do this to us."

"You did this to us." I jabbed my finger at him. "You found me and lied. I woke happy this morning, thought how wonderful our second chance was and that I got my memory back. But the pathetic thing about it is I didn't have a first chance. I'm sorry my recollections came back so I could reminisce about how shitty my life is and how I married a murderer."

"Hold on! I didn't kill your mother. Carey was driving."

"And you let him!"

Easton spoke in a neutral voice. "You mean to tell me you haven't done stupid shit in your life? Things that didn't make sense, or risked your life? I risked my life when I got into that car, but I was too drunk to care."

I pouted my lips and said, "Oh, poor Easton. Wait! Is that even your name?"

"Knock it off, Brand."

"Why is that question so absurd? You're a compulsive liar. I wouldn't put it past you to change your name. You're a fucking coward." I pushed open the door with my suitcases in hand.

(Forty-One) Lovesick Fool

~~~~~~

Mitchell's shoulder was the only one I could cry on, so I stayed with him until I could get my future in order. A week went by before I returned to the house for my laptop. I made sure to go in the daytime while Easton worked. He didn't cancel my credit card, and probably knew Mitchell had taken me in. As for my anger, it had subsided, replaced with hurt. Self-pity never had a problem keeping me company. While Mitchell cut hair, I went to the library to get out of the house and be able to connect to their Wi-Fi. I searched about divorce, and recovered memory after amnesia. Several reports and articles spoke about the observation of patients as they browsed old photos, and if they existed, read journals or diaries. I didn't have any diaries. I used my mother as my diary. Since she was gone, the idea of writing in a journal about my adolescence, loss, marriage, and amnesia didn't sound so bad. Maybe even therapeutic.

On occasion at the library, I saw Easton behind a bookshelf as I researched and documented my life. When I'd look up, he'd pretend to read a book or he would slip behind a bookcase. He spent an hour or so there, and then would disappear. I couldn't understand why he bothered when he could just ask Mitchell about me.

Sometimes I'd bring lunch over to the shop for Mitchell. Other times, when he had late hours, I ate dinner at one of those cheap restaurants that have an exorbitant amount of choices, and much of it tasting the same. Again, I'd find Easton in the parking lot, but he kept his distance. For an investigator, he failed at subtlety, yet I didn't want him to push himself on me. I knew in time we would have to talk, but I wanted it to be on my terms. When my visits to the library proved to be successful, I was still on an emotional sabbatical.

Friday came and Easton had left me alone for a good two weeks. I found my usual chair at the back of the library to read my emails. An email sent last night, sat in my Inbox with the subject line, *An Apology to My Wife*. Curiosity made me click on the link, which took me to a Facebook page. The name of the page was *An Apology to My Wife*. The page consisted of a sole video, and I could tell by the frozen picture of a man on a patio that it was Easton. I clicked play, and this is what he said.

> When I first saw you, I thought to myself that I have never witnessed perfection until that moment. Even though you believe otherwise, you stole my heart from the start and not because of pity or guilt. I was with you to make my life better, and that you did. Every moment with you is a feast for my soul.

> I know you wanted a fulfilled marriage—a forever one. You expected me, your husband, never to fail you. To protect you and keep you safe. I'm sorry I couldn't prevent the car accident. It hurts that I couldn't do anything about it, and I cried while you struggled with turmoil. So many times I wanted to take you in my arms and tell you it would be okay, but I couldn't. You needed to find *you* first.

> Love is hard to find. In my pursuit of making a wrong a right, I had no idea that I'd find love

in the process. All I wanted to do was make myself feel a little less guilty. Then you stood before me with attitude, beauty and intelligence, and I changed my pursuit toward you.

Besides a few bumps in the road, we've had a fufilled marriage, and one I hope will last forever. I know you don't believe me after the past few months of learning about our relationship, but it's true. We've had some great times, more so than the troubles. And although our troubles seem big, our love and happiness is much bigger. There's nothing more beautiful than waking up next to you. To see your face the first thing in the morning. Since I met you, I've known what luck is, and it still takes my breath away to know you said yes to the infamous question, "Will you marry me?"

I'm sorry that we fight, but many of those fights are about the love I feel for you. Like I've told you before, never argue with a lovesick fool. That's what I am, a lovesick fool.

All that you've learned about what we did and what we didn't do is true. The one thing I didn't tell you, the one thing I'm sorry about not saying is that you've given me life. Before you, I drifted like tumbleweed, and now my life with you is stable.

I know I made a mess of it. I kept secrets from you, which only made you mistrust me. But think about it. If I stayed with you for the reasons you think I did, do you think I would have invested twelve years of my life? My world is bigger and beautiful with you in it. I'm not about to lose you without a fight.

I'm sorry for not being a better husband. You deserve better, but I'm not giving up on us yet. I'll do what it takes until you trust me again. I'll become the husband you've always wanted. I'll never lie or keep secrets from you again. If you give me a chance, a third chance, I'll make my wrongs many, many rights.

Love you forever, Easton

By the time I finished, I couldn't wipe the tears away fast enough. The Facebook page went viral and people left comments by the second. Those around me lurked behind bookshelves to figure out what was wrong. I couldn't sit there anymore. I had to find Easton.

I shut down my computer and turned around.

Easton stood there and asked, "Where are you going?"

I used my shoulder as a handkerchief to brush away the tears. "To find you."

"I'm right here. I'll always be right here." He took me in his arms, placed his cheek against the side of my head and in slow motion, rocked us. My limbs turned to putty.

Epilogue

~~~~~~

Over the course of a month, Easton and I talked about my mother's accident amongst other things. Because he wasn't directly involved, I forgave him for his hidden secret. He told me that after the accident, he didn't talk to his friend, Carey, who received a three-year sentence in prison. Easton worked even harder in law enforcement. A natural at it, he transferred over to undercover operations.

I couldn't help but wonder if I was really part of the investigation, and it turned out that his boss never knew of my involvement. Easton told them he had an informant, a confidential informant. That's how he got the money to pay me. His employer never found out that I was on the case.

As for our marriage, we had already forgiven the infidelities. We needed to work on communication. Easton and I laid some ground rules. When the everyday life starts to feel like Groundhog Day, we make a few changes from the ordinary. We can't risk losing each other again—we are all we got. Our so-called fogged up fairy tale turned out not so fogged up, although it could use a polish. Easton even transferred to cold cases, so he can be around more.

We renewed our vows, and I'm about to publish this book. A few close friends we cherished joined us in the mountains where we rented a cabin for the reception and weekend party. Easton and I exchanged vows, but made our own. Our vows were, "I promise not to keep secrets. I will listen, hang around when you are feeling bad, and never pick up strangers. I will love you each day of my life, and will always remember that love doesn't always make blind. Sometimes it opens the eyes."

I joked with Easton while we sat at the reception and watched everyone mingle and dance to the DJ's choices. "I love you more than a cup of coffee in the morning."

Easton retorted. "I love you more than a vulture loves its prey." I bumped him with my shoulder and he slipped his arm around mine. "You know what?"

"What?" I waited for his response.

"I'm glad we're going to grow old together. But no matter how old we get, you'll always remain young and beautiful to me." His thumb swiped the tear away when he bent down to kiss me.

Acknowledgments

A book can only exist with readers and supporters. They both mean so much to me. What's important to each of us isn't necessarily important to others, but my fans made it so. Each voice and review makes a difference.

To my proofreader, Jeri Walker-Bickett (JeriWB.com), who worked months with me to mold my novel. Her notes, suggestions and questions churned out new and improved revisions. I thank you for your words of encouragement. To my beta readers, Carol McKeone and Jim Crocker, who graciously took the time to provide me with their thoughts.

Thanks to Ana Cruz, http://www.anacruz-arts.com/, my book cover art designer. It was a joy to work with you, and I look forward to future collaborations.

Huge thanks to my cheerleaders and coach, who continue to encourage me and cheer me on. Thanks to my sister, Vivian Anderson, who always has my back. To the Baer Family, especially Michelle Lostroscio, who takes that extra step for others. I'd like to thank my aunt, Judy Matula, and Edward Matula, for their kindness and generosity. To Jacquee Broderick, for always making me feel like a bestselling author. To Joe Sularz, who has been with me from the beginning. To Jim and Adrienne Strasser, for shouting out my name and promoting my work. No words can express my appreciation for your support. Thanks to Mary Lambros-Vazquez, for an inspiring road trip.

To my dear mother, Alma Baer. You taught me love and strength. In life, you made me who I am today, and in death, you get to see our accomplishments.

To my coach, partner, and love, Martin Haschka. Without your input and encouragement, my words would never see paper. You're the spark in my writing and in my world. What you said is true. "Love doesn't always make blind. Sometimes it opens the eyes." My eyes opened to an incredible love. Du bist ein Schatz.

Made in the USA
Charleston, SC
11 November 2016